DUST & ASHES

JACK WIMBERLEY

For my mom, who will always want the best for me, even if we disagree on what that may be.

I love you

Dust & Ashes: A Playlist

Andromeda - Weyes Blood
Vanish Into You - Lady Gaga
Every Road I Know - Solya
Ocean of Tears - Caroline Polachek
Gemini Moon - Renee Rapp
Lucky - Dora Jar
beautiful boy - Esha Tewari
While You Were Sleeping - Laufey
Just Keep Driving - Keni Titus
23:42 - Rachel Chinouriri
gimme all ur luv - Hemlocke Springs
Old Habits Die Hard - Allie X
Kissing Someone Else - Caroline Kingsbury
The Cage - Kevin Atwater
Fall in Love - Caroline Kingsbury
The Little Mess You Made - The Favors
Psychosweet - Luna Day
Skin - August Ponthier
Who? - Rina Sawayama
Call It What You Want - Taylor Swift
Cosmic Love - Florence + The Machine
Heavenly Bodies - MARIS
VV - Yeule

1

LUNION

I can barely recall how life was before the humans arrived, but I can vividly remember my best friend, Maula, chasing me around a tall, luminescent tree on our school playground. I can see our old house in the back of my mind and recall how small it stood compared to those around it, just as I can still hear my mother being sworn in as our new regional senator.

Shortly after moving into a high-end district apartment following her appointment, they came. With their pale aircraft and rifles, they unloaded onto our quaint planet.

I remember their shocked faces when they saw our developed neighborhoods, schools, government buildings, and malls. When that realization dawned, their generals sent their troops and weapons back aboard their ships, walked into our capital, and began negotiations.

They made it clear they were to set up a small outpost here, a checkpoint for their military, a short stop on the way to the rest of the universe. But this proved false and, as the years went on, more and more humans landed on our planet. To be fair, the humans are still very few, but we have felt their impact.

A planet we referred to as Nalia was now Earth-2102, an industrial trade port for the original Earth. The 2102 in the name marked the year we were discovered, and the year I turned 10.

For my family, it wasn't all bad. With my mom being a government official, we stayed in the region's urban center, Lelarea, and generally benefited from the booming human businesses.

Maula, however, did not see the same assimilation I did. She still lives on the same impoverished street we grew up on. I miss it. The sound of the bugs at night, the light buzz of our neighbor's bikes parking in the last hours of the night. Most of all, I miss her. We still hang out as much as possible, but in the noisy, distant capital city, it's much harder to see her.

The most confusing part of our situation was how the humans often discounted our competence. I understood that we were new to them, but we were alike in almost every way. Our species had both evolved on a comparable timeline, even developing a similar language that eased negotiations at the humans' first arrival. We had the same—or better—technologies, resources, and even operations. If you wanted a rhinoplasty, Lelarea's doctors were the best we had to offer.

The only sometimes-noticeable difference was our skin. Not the color, as we had the same vast array as humans, but the molecular makeup. Unlike our Terran counterparts, our bodies housed luciferins, allowing us to glow slightly in darker settings.

Scientists believed this was a direct effect of sharing a sun with Earth, but not orbiting it in a similar fashion. If the sun were behind the Earth from our perspective, we would get almost no light. And so it is believed that our ancestors evolved to glow just enough to navigate while continuing to build our society.

It wasn't just us Solans either; plants and fauna also shared this evolutionary trait. When the Earth eclipses the sun, and the stars are barely shining above us, Nalia becomes a diverse light show. Personally, I glow a white hue, similar to the stars or the Earth's moon. Because of that, my mom likes to call me her "favorite Starchild," which is funny, because I am her *only* child. The nickname also came from her adoration of the idea that we all came from the stars—that we were created from the sparkling dust and ashes of the fires that light the night sky.

Now, I am more the region's favorite Starchild. Thanks to my mom's position, the people love our family, and the humans respect her enough to keep us happy. They may take our resources, which I despise, but they know when to leave a hardworking mother alone.

And, as much as I hate the humans' work here, I can't hate all of them. Like my mom's assistant, Veronica, whom I am staring down now. She is human, yet she has a deep respect for our planet, and I appreciate that.

"What did you do this time?" I question.

Veronica yells through her tears. "I knocked over that little vase on your mom's desk. I am so sorry!"

The vase is an old pottery assignment from when I was in second grade.

"It's fine," I reply. "I always thought that thing was ugly, anyway."

"Oh, thank God-"

"Don't get too excited yet. My mom adores that ugly piece of shit. Yeah, I know, poor taste." I bend down and help Veronica pick up the pieces. "We should probably try to glue it back together; it isn't that bad."

"Oh, thank you so much, Lunion, but I can't ask you to do

that. I am your mom's assistant, for crying out loud. I ought to do this alone."

"Yeah, exactly. You're *her* assistant, not mine. Just go get the superglue, and we will be done soon."

She nods and runs over to my desk drawer. "I can't find it, but I did find this... rune? What are you doing with your time?"

I turn red and rush to my desk. "Nothing... mind your business, *assistant*."

I may hate humans at times, but I love some of their creations; YouTube being one of my favorites. I mean, it helped me with a love spell for Marin, the boy I am head over heels for in my Science class. So far, no results. Well, for me, but he did get a girlfriend whom I despise, so maybe it worked for him.

I push aside the thought and turn to her again. "Anyway... let's get to work."

Veronica and I work on the pathetic "vase" for about an hour, placing every little chip back into place. When we finally finish our recreation, we place it under a UV light to help the glue dry faster.

"Yay! I am not losing my job today!" Veronica cheers.

"Yeah, you still have a few hours; don't be too sure," I tease. "We should put some flowers in it to distract from the cracks, right?"

"Great idea! I'll be back in a flash." I don't doubt her. She may be clumsy, but Veronica is a fast worker.

As promised, Veronica bangs on the door five minutes later. "Who is it?"

"I don't have time for this. Let me in!" she pants.

Opening it, I usher her back inside. "Okay, damn, you really meant it when you said 'back in a flash,' but please don't have a stroke."

Veronica throws some white flowers at my face and flops onto my couch. "At least I don't draw runes in my free time."

"Haha. I can get you fired."

"You would never..." Her sarcastic tone switches to fear. "Would you?"

"You never know. It never hurts to be safe!" I joke.

Obviously never would. Besides Maula, whom I rarely get to see, Veronica is the closest thing to a friend I've got.

Veronica sighs and runs out of my room.

Alone at last, it's time to stalk Marin on another amazing human advancement: Instagram. His light yellow hair and pale skin complement his girlfriend's similarly pale skin and black hair. And while this may be the delusion speaking, she is essentially me as a girl, which only makes his love for her hurt more. I can't even chalk it up to him being "straight," because that is a word I only learned when the humans arrived.

"Straight" and "gay" aren't terms we use here on Nalia. History books from the beginnings of Solan civilization included historic recounts of maxims stating that everyone could love anyone, no matter what.

No one gave a shit, and no one did until the humans showed up. Only in the deep city, where the human visitors live, will you find someone who actually cares about throwing labels on sexuality. Thank you to Earth-1 for that.

So his blatant ignorance of my admiration for him can only be explained by him just not being into me. Yippee.

"Hey, Lunion." My mom's voice interrupts my stalking, which is good, because I was seconds away from crying.

"Hey." I move over on the couch, making room for her to sit.

She wraps her arms around me. "Stalking that boy again?"

She can read me so well. "Unfortunately."

"Well, if he doesn't like you, that is his loss. I mean, he is missing out on the Starchild of the entire planet; it sucks to be him." She kisses the top of my head, squeezing me tight as I try to keep my tears from falling.

Obviously, she has to say that stuff; she's my mom, but that doesn't change how Marin feels, or how I feel about it.

I switch the topic. "Thanks. How was your day?"

"Oh, just as crappy as yesterday. The humans are really starting to piss me off. I've given them so much, so many opportunities, and it's never enough." She kicks off her heels, a red pair we picked out together when I was five—it's a moment I still remember. "I have a feeling they want to expand into areas protected as our regional parks, that they are looking into buying that land from our government, and creating more businesses that will benefit the Earth."

"Oh," I whisper, unsure how to respond. I've always loved nature, especially watching it, seeing the trees glow and the animals play. Still, my love for the natural world could never compare to hers.

Her first act as regional leader was to rezone our parks to be even larger, and now that could all be taken away from her by some other planet's greedy businessmen? No thanks.

"Better yet, America's president is visiting with his entire family. I've never had any government leader from Earth-1 come to discuss, well, anything. I have a sneaking suspicion this is about land acquisition, and I won't be threatened into allowing it to happen."

"Good. We need to be on guard. I don't like the sound of this. Is there any way I can help?"

"Glad you asked. I need you to make the President's family feel welcome. I don't want to start off on the wrong foot. He has a son around your age and a wife as well."

Great. I had to not only deal with whatever was going on in these negotiations but also entertain houseguests. "Okay, I'll try my best, but you know how I am with humans."

"Yes, I do. You have made Veronica feel at home, and I expect you to do the same for them, at least until I know what they want." She pats me on the head and begins her exit. "Oh, one more thing. They will be here tomorrow! Good night, Starchild. I'll make sure you're up for your big performance. I love you."

"Love you too..." I blow a kiss as she leaves my room.

Time to stalk a new boy. The wife I've got under control: throw some compliments, insight, and maybe some wine at her, and she will be fine.

That is, if she is anything like Veronica.

It's the son I'll need to figure out. Given my lack of friends, and the two I have both being women, I am not best suited for befriending a boy. Especially one whose father is likely here to turn my planet into a sewage plant or something equally nasty.

I find his Instagram: Luke_Dynire2091. Based on that username, he is only about a year older than me. His profile is littered with a mix of professionally shot government photos and monthly photo dumps of his friends.

The most terrifying thing about him is his appearance. Not that it's bad—he is actually quite attractive—but it's bad for *me*. From his light skin and freckles to his muscular build and light blonde hair, he looks like he could be related to Marin, just... without the chance of him glowing.

I send him a follow request and begin searching into his mom, just to be safe. She is forced to use the official FLOTUS account, so I don't find much there, but I see some cheesy quotes not unlike those on Veronica's account. I can just hope their similarities don't end at optimism.

As I start to fall asleep, I get a notification. Rolling over, I quickly check it.

Luke accepted my follow request, but didn't follow me back.

Selfish asshole.

If he keeps this up, I am going to hate him.

2

LUKE

I despise my father. Well... That may be a little extreme. I loathe his policies, his platform, his lifestyle, and every choice he has ever made.

While my dad is campaigning with his ever-famous slogan, "Climate Change is as real as Pernicky's Privates," I'm trying to get into Georgetown to study Environmental Law. You heard that right, a re-election campaign based on attacking not only the planet, but his opponent's gender as well. The most intriguing part of his little saying is the fact that Molly Pernicky, a California Democratic Senator, is a cisgender woman.

Despite my many pleas, he never listens. I show him the statistics I learned from the elite private school *he* chose for me, and I get a "that's just propaganda" in response. It's like arguing with a stone wall. But not Stonewall, as he also isn't too fond of the gays.

Another part of his extreme agenda that I clash with: homosexuality.

I've never told him, but it's obvious to everyone else—my

voice is a dead giveaway. No matter how hard I fight it, I can't shake off the "gay pitch." I've bulked up, played pretty much every sport I can, and now even tailgate people in traffic. Unfortunately, these evidently straight attributes haven't kicked that twang out of my timbre.

I don't hate it, but I can tell my dad does. That should make me like it more, but it's the one thing about myself that I wish he didn't dislike.

As for my life at school, everyone knows I'm gay. It's not like I try to hide it either. I've had my fair share of boyfriends, but no one would dare to leak it to the press because everyone has secrets at Evelyn Silsa Preparatory School, all of which would only affect the parents, and by relation, their money.

I'm the same way when it comes to money. While I may be an advocate for sustainability, I am, in fact, materialistic. I feel like my affection for private goods is inborn; it's hard not to love things when you've been given them your entire life. But even then, I'm trying to forgo my worldly possessions, but the most difficult thing to part with is my music collection. Carefully cultivated since I was ten, each of my records ranges from oldies like Britney Spears and The Pussycat Dolls to the new wave of Lina Rillis and Trixi Solya.

My CDs? I store them in a small silver box beside my bed. Yes, I know they're so one hundred twenty-seven years ago, but somehow my dad has a way of finding vintage editions of the things I love, even if we have different views on general morality.

Even now, during lunch, I can use a portable CD player to block out my friends' chattering. Sometimes it can be so peaceful to just ignore the drama I would usually fawn over; blocking out the information on my exes can be the best dessert to any meal. At least until that liberty is ripped out of my hands, or better yet, off my head.

"Are you listening to us?" My friend, Chloe, asks with a concerned glare, my headphones resting in her hand.

"No. I have enough issues; I do not need to hear about Danny's antics." I roll my eyes and try to snatch them back.

Chloe resists my struggle and grimaces. "Not so fast, buddy... You need to hear this."

"She's right; it is insane." Renee, Chloe's girlfriend, adds, with a flicker of villainy in her eyes.

Reluctantly giving into their demands, I huff. "Fine! I'll stop listening to *Work Bitch*."

Chloe begins the info-dumping session. "Okay, so first off, you are not an *old gay*, so put down the Britney. Secondly, and more importantly, you know Seth?"

"Yeah, but what does this have to do with anything, like ever?" Seth was my best friend from my childhood through last year; something about Junior year separated us.

"Well, I heard he was caught doing some... things to Danny in the H-Wing bathroom." Chloe replies with a hint of joy, like a proud child showing off a painting.

"Okay." My reply is monotone, disinterested.

Renee and Chloe both say unanimously, "Okay? Just okay? Nothing else?"

"Yeah. I mean, I don't really care. They look like cousins anyway." Both Seth and Danny have super-pale skin and black hair, are tall with little muscle, and even share similar face shapes.

"Oh, so now you admit they looked similar. Wonder if that has to do with Seth's sudden disappearance from your side..." Chloe scoffs.

I wasn't about to admit it a year later, but Chloe was right. I definitely had a type, and Seth fit the description: lanky, dark hair, nerdy. I didn't think Seth was gay until after I got with Danny, and by then, he had gotten distant.

Then one day, he just stopped talking to me, and I was too fascinated by Danny to notice. And now? Well, it sounds like Seth is obsessed with Danny. Which is exactly why Danny is even available to obsess over. I got too clingy, too interested, too giving. He just wanted a boyfriend, but I wanted someone to love. I guess those signals got mixed, and I got too involved.

No matter what, it is over now, and I am honestly glad it is.

"Well... if you aren't going to respond to that, let's move on." Renee clicks her tongue against the roof of her mouth to get my attention.

"Sorry, I just don't really care, must be because of personal growth or something," I reply, more than ready to go back to my old gay music.

"Mr. Dinyre?" The deep voice stops me as I am about to put my headphones back in place, belonging to none other than our headmaster, Mr. Terosa.

My annoyance accidentally slips. "God, what now?"

"Excuse me?" Mr. Terosa lurches back.

"Sorry, how are you, sir?" I flinch.

"I'm fine, but I need you in my office." Reaching forward, he shakes my hand before immediately turning away without another word.

I follow him, my eyes rolling in response to the mocking "ooh" coming from Renee and Chloe. The walk is short as he leads me to his office, a dim room lined with slate blue shelving, before he motions for me to take a seat.

"So... what would this little meeting be about?" It wasn't for anything bad; I had excellent grades and never did anything *too* controversial.

"Oh, nothing; you're just needed at the White House. Legally, I have to keep you safe here before your driver arrives." He looks out a window to his left. "Who, ironically, appears to have just pulled up. Have a good day, Mr. Dinyre." With another shake of my hand, he opens his office door and ushers me to exit.

I walk out to the courtyard: a bright pasture with an ornate fountain in its center, its rims covered in vibrant florals and rich vines. Waiting for me in the sun bleached-drive circle is a black sedan with tinted windows. Hopper.

Hopper has been my driver for the last two years, a luxury I would cherish if I didn't enjoy driving as much as I do. Something about the freedom of being behind the wheel matched with the danger of the road—I want nothing more. As long as that car is environmentally friendly, of course.

"Hey, Hopper," I say as I slip into the car, my head smacking against the low ceiling.

"Hey Luke! How was school?" It's a question fueled by genuine interest. I'd told him a long time ago not to be a stranger, especially with how often my dad orders me around, and he hasn't hesitated since.

"Oh, fine. Do you know what this is about?" I ask, already knowing the answer.

Chuckling, he presses the gas. "No clue. You are about the only person in your family that tells me a thing."

"Well, thanks for driving me."

"Of course, sir." He smiles in the rearview mirror and slides up the divider.

I take out my Calculus homework and begin working on derivatives. How do I have to learn this in the year 2109? As I scan my problem with my phone to get a quick answer, a notification from Instagram distracts me. *Lun_i_on! Started Following You.*

I have no clue who this is.

Tapping on the little window, I prompt the app to open. The profile picture is blank, but from the bio, I learn Lunion is a he, and some Senator's son from Earth-2102. This is the first

I have *ever* seen anything from a Solan, considering how behind they are technologically. I mean, I knew they existed, and even tried to find some on social media, but no one ever showed up.

But, by some strange happenstance, he finds me?

When I first heard about the discovery of Earth 2102, I was enthralled. I grew up on ancient movies like the Star Wars trilogies, and was immediately thrilled to hear about a life-sustaining planet unlike ours. Apparently, it's just some trade stop to sustain our pilots—at least that is what we have been told. My dad is especially secretive when discussing the planet; all he has told me is its real name: *Nalia*. And while I still haven't been, I would love to meet a Solan.

I'm about to follow Lunion back as we arrive at the Capitol, but our arrival draws my attention elsewhere.

Hopper slides out and grabs my door as I'm trying to open it. "No, that is my job." Giving me a short smile, he takes my bags.

"There's my son!" My father comes slinking down the Capitol steps.

"Hi Father," I mumble.

"Why so boring? I came down here excited. Where is that same energy from you?" He rolls his eyes and throws an arm around my shoulders condescendingly.

His grip is always constricting, like a boa. Except boa constrictors are cute, and not naturally evil like him. They only act out of fear, but his life goal seems to be instilling that fear in others.

"Sorry. Why did you pull me out of school?" I question, eager to figure out what he has up his sleeve.

"Oh, nothing serious. Just that we are heading up to Earth-2102 for a few weeks, maybe a month." He says, far more nonchalantly than the fake guys at school.

I escape from his grasp. "What?"

"Don't act surprised; you should be happy! You've wanted to see that wasteful, insignificant planet forever!" Despite his harsh words about Earth-2102, he's not wrong; I have longed to see Earth-2102 since I learned of its existence.

"Okay... What do I need to bring?"

"The staff has already packed your bags. The trip will take about a day with the newly equipped spaceship, thank you Meta." Him and his dumbass tech collaborations; I won't be surprised if that rocket has his face on it. "You can pack one bag with your school stuff. There is Wi-Fi there, and I expect you to keep up with your schoolwork." He slaps my back once before he continues, "Hell, take whatever you want; we've got the space for it!"

...

After Hopper brings me home, I race upstairs to grab anything I might need for this spontaneous vacation. I grab some perfume, not cologne, because cologne smells awful. Some games, CDs, and a few books. Childishly, I pack away my stuffed bunny, Pebble, whom I promised years ago that we would go to Earth-2102 together.

"Hey sweetie." My mom pokes her head into my room.

"Hey Mom, are you excited for this little visit?"

She takes a deep breath. "I'm so sorry, baby, but I can't come along. I think I'm coming down with the flu, and I'll be damned if I pull a Christopher Columbus on the Solans."

I try to laugh, but she is the only parent I genuinely like, the only parent I trust enough to have been able to come out last year. "Without you it's going to be horrible."

"I know. I'll call you every day, don't worry a bit." She blows a kiss, trying to avoid spreading anything to me, and exits the room.

My attention is next shifted to my cat, Samantha. I scratch

her chin for a handful of minutes before passing her a few treats. "I'll be back soon."

She meows in response and rubs against my leg, falling down for a demanded belly rub.

Before I head to my inevitable doom, I follow Lunion back. It would be nice to have someone to talk to who isn't my dad on this trip. His bland Instagram spread does not provide me with a single glimpse into how similar we will be, but my curiosity remains.

I force myself downstairs, dragging my feet at the pace of a garden snail, and return to the foyer. My dad is waiting for me with an entourage of White House staff, each decked out with their own myriad of suitcases, duffles, and even totes—all of which belong to us.

I grip my bags tightly and prepare for my first time traveling by spaceship. And as much as it pains me to be away from Mom, I can't wait to fulfill my childhood dream.

3

LUNION

Okay, maybe I was a little harsh on Luke. He followed me back an hour after I fell asleep, so *maybe* my judgment was a little hasty. I can only hope he was just busy and not hesitant to follow me back. Though I'm not sure why I care so much; he's just some slightly attractive boy I'll have to deal with for like a week. Not a big deal. At all.

I throw my phone down on my bed and slip into a light blue robe—a gift from Veronica after she accidentally walked in on me after I got out of the shower.

I have clothes on, but the robe is oddly comfortable, so I always wear it to breakfast. With one glance over my shoulder, I fixate on my tablet. Mom has a rule against having them out at mealtimes, so I've learned to just leave mine in my room.

Stumbling down the stairs, I trip slightly as I tighten my robe. Right before reaching the floor, I slip on the last step and land face-first on the cold tile. I appreciate our two-story apartment, but the modern, spacious stairs have always given me trouble, especially so early in the morning.

"Hey, Mom!" I push myself up from the floor and stumble over to the table, trying to play off the pain.

"Hey, Starchild! Oh wow. Your, uh, nose is a little messed up..." Her face shifts from excitement to pure horror.

"Oh, come on, it can't be *that* bad." The agony is only surface level, like a scratch. I make my way to the bathroom and check my nose in the mirror. "Mom, can you stop over-exaggerating? It's a slight cut, that's all!"

She rushes in with a first aid kit. "I just can't have you looking all busted when the President arrives, he'll get the wrong idea of this place!" Working with purpose, she rubs ointment on the wound and slaps on a plaid bandaid. "All better! Now, please try to stay safe. You're too perfect to get broken." She squeezes my cheek and slinks back into the kitchen.

I love her, but ever since her new position, she has become emotionally ambivalent. She switches from treating me as her son to treating me as a prop. Which has its perks, of course: some press opportunities and the region's love. But I always find myself wishing we could return to the simple life. Before she was elected, and before the humans came.

I follow her into the kitchen, pull out a small, circular chair, and sit down for breakfast—slaxberry waffles and trucklen juice, my favorite since I was a kid. They offer an ounce of nostalgia in this strange urban world.

Don't get me wrong, I am more than grateful for our newfound wealth, but the city is killing me. Monotone, electric-lit walls and circular furniture are only exciting for a month, tops. Anytime I get to leave to visit Maula, it's a breath of fresh air—literally.

The city is composed of tall, slender buildings that leave almost no room for trees, grass, or even a flowerpot. We had to trade in our hover-cars for bikes because the "roads" between buildings were too slim for our original ride to fit through, and I had to sacrifice my garden for the sweet life of ornate ceiling lights and formal events. But most of all, I miss having Maula around to help with every little dilemma.

"Do you think I have time to hang out with Maula today?" It is the first time either of us has spoken since the stair incident.

"I suppose. The president hasn't given me a specific time of arrival, so just make sure you are ready for them when the time comes." Mom offers me a small smile before returning to her email.

I finish my meal, slowly go upstairs, throw on an outfit, and rush out the door. I straddle my speed bike and blow past the myriad pillars of the city, passing neighbors, strangers, and the occasional stray animal. Finally out of the city, I can throw my hands back and enjoy the openness of the woodlands.

Our region is arranged like a star, with the city at the center. Starting at twelve o'clock the nearest point is the suburban region for middle-class workers. Then, going clockwise, far from the epicenter, we have our main military base.

Next, a vast regional park, rich in flora and fauna. The Naulonem Park, protected by the government since our founding, has been an imprint of vitality and history. The one hundred mile stretch is one of the few remaining protected reserves on Nalia. Left of the park is, unfortunately, a range of air and spacecraft storage units. Several miles more of pointy, metal blocks, all used to store government and private carriers.

The last point contains both the woodlands and, behind those, the lower-class neighborhoods, like the one I grew up in. Until Mom's election, I wasn't able to spot the lights of the city, but now, they're all I can see.

As I enter the dusty clearing before Maula's neighborhood, I breathe a sigh of relief. I am free of the confines of the cityscape, at least for a little while. I park my bike by a broken-down fence and practically skip to Maula's house. I don't even knock, an agreement we made way back when we were kids, and nudge the door open.

"How's my best friend!" I beam at her.

"I think I am your *only* friend." Her sarcasm never gets old. She gives me a quick hug, then retreats further into her house while I stay in the doorway. "You're not coming in?"

"Nope, but I need you to come out here. I need your help."

Her face twists in apparent concern. "Oh no, what happened?"

"I'm actually dead, and this is my ghost coming to tell you what happened," I state matter-of-factly while remaining emotionless. "Okay, obviously not," I relent, "but I need help setting up for some political thing and you're a great decorator."

"As long as I'm allowed to shop, I'm down." She punches my shoulder on her way out of the house and saunters over to my bike.

Where the city has always fascinated Maula—the lights, the architecture, the speed—I always preferred the trees and flowers of the woodlands. We were different in that way, and I guess it was because I realized how constricting it was after having lived in it.

I hop on, rev the bike, and spin around, heading for the city. We pass the woodlands and quickly enter the urban center. Keeping my eyes on the air traffic, Maula oohs and aahs at our surroundings behind me.

We soon arrive at my favorite mall, yet another tall, pillar-like building with stores stacked on top of one another. After I park my bike in the designated area, I lead Maula into the first store.

"Okay, so here's his Instagram." I pull up his account and

hand my tablet to Maula. "I thought we could get him some Nalian clothes that match his style; maybe it'll help him feel like he fits in." Sighing, I shake my head before grumbling, "I have no idea what I'm doing."

"Who is this?" Maula looks extremely lost.

"Oh, my bad." I never filled her in. "He's some president's son from Earth, and he is visiting with his dad for a little while. I'm supposed to make him 'feel at home.'"

"Got it." Maula runs away with my tablet, only to reappear minutes later holding a sweater in one hand and a basket of assorted goods in the other. "Okay, so we've got a large sweater in what appears to be his favorite color, green. And then here we have a candle, a weird-looking lamp, some sort of nature magazine, and some snacks."

"Wow. Where did you come up with these... gifts?"

"Well, this department store has a home section, and his page is jammed with nature-lover posts and trips to art museums. The magazine for the nature-lover, the lamp for Mr. Artsy." She takes the items to the checkout, slides my card, and throws the bag into my arms. "Where to next?"

AFTER SEVERAL HOURS OF SHOPPING, WE LEAVE WITH our final selections: a gift card, a fake plant, a stuffed animal resembling his cat, and another sweater, this time in blue. "I think we did a wonderful job. He should feel at home in no time!"

Maula snorts. "We? *I* did most of this... But you did pay, so I'll let you have it."

I take us to my apartment and track down Veronica. "Veronica?"

She walks out of the kitchen, a cup in hand. "Yes, Lunion?"

"Do you know where the president's son will be staying?" I ask, raising our bags to make my intent clear.

"Oh, yeah, actually I do. Your mom said he was staying in the apartment across the hall, 203, I believe." She checks her phone for confirmation, "Yes, room 203. The one-story apartment."

"Thanks!" With the bags getting heavy, I offer her a weak smile, and progress toward Luke's apartment.

The door is cracked—probably thanks to my mom—and we slide in easily. I place the sweaters on the coffee table, with the stuffed animal on top.

"Okay, I made a spread with the snacks, do you think he'll like it?" Maula looks proud as she makes jazz hands at a basket filled with the treats.

My jaw is on the floor. "You stole the shopping basket from the store?" Maula had taken the store-branded carrier basket and used it for the snacks.

"Oh, lighten up. They don't need it. Did you see how many they had? He'll either find it funny or not notice it at all." She rolls her eyes and takes the abstract lamp she found to the nearest outlet. "Perfect."

Placing the fake plant by his bed, I fluff the pillows and give everything a final once over before returning to my own apartment.

"Hey, Lunion!" My mom returns less than a minute after we do. "And Maula!" She holds Maula's head in her hands, planting a kiss on the crown of her head. "I've missed you, darling."

"I've missed you too!" She gives Mom a hug. "I should probably be heading home; it's getting late."

"Nonsense, you can stay for dinner, at least. Can't you?" Mom gives her a warm grin.

"I will never turn down a meal here, count me in." Taking a seat at the table, Maula struggles with the oddly shaped chair.

"Here you all go," Veronica sets down our meals, then takes her own seat across from Maula.

"Thank you so much, Veronica. It looks amazing."

As we eat, the conversation consists of the basic "How has it been?" and the ever-famous "How is *relative* doing?" with Maula answering questions as quickly as she can.

Mom interrupts her barrage of queries towards Maula to give me an update on the president's arrival. "Oh, Lunion, the president and his son won't be here until tomorrow afternoon. The trip got a little delayed."

"Okay." I didn't really care about the delay. "Wait, just him and his son? What happened to the wife?" *Was I really going to be stuck alone with the son?*

"Oh, yeah, she doesn't feel well, so she isn't coming anymore. I hope that's okay."

Part of me is upset that I will be alone with some strange boy, with no other task to balance it out, but another is relieved. I was so stressed about Luke that I forgot to buy anything for his mom.

"Yeah, it's okay. I'll try to keep him entertained."

We finish our dinner, and I escort Maula back home. The night breeze in the woods makes me feel more at home than the city ever could. I consider staying for a little while, but I have to be ready for tomorrow. Can't have eye bags when you're meeting the president of some country from some other planet, can you?

4

LUKE

To my disappointment, the giant hunk of metal is actually impressive. I hate the fact that I can't help but be in awe. The ship is made of our depleting resources, but its size, shape, and general engineering are sublime.

A small bridge leads to the back entrance, allowing us to wheel our luggage into the spacecraft with ease. I'm the last to board, and the ship is eager for my arrival.

As soon as my back foot leaves the bridge, it zips back to the base of the ship, folding into a slim pocket against the surface of the ship's rear.

"Damn!" I shriek as I cling to my luggage, my body only an inch from the edge of the ship. "I thought these engineers were smart; did they not account for safety?"

"I heard the bridge was made using AI, but I don't really give a shit, so..." My dad remarks, using his inside knowledge of the tech companies in an attempt to provide clarity. His acceptance of this artistic cop-out only infuriates me, so I rush past him and enter the main room of the massive spacecraft.

Several tables, a bar, and some vending machines fill this hexagonal, LED-lit tin can of a room. The ship's walls are pieced together from hexagons, contrasting with the oddly pentagonal tables, another idiotic design choice that I will attribute to AI. Around the tables are rectangular benches, maintaining the diminishing pattern of the room.

Luckily, the vending machines are not triangular, and neither is the bar. The machines are the basic rectangles, and the bar is oblong. Not that I'll be visiting the bar, even if my dad lets me drink, I've always hated the idea of alcohol. So unnecessary, so dangerous, and just downright foolish.

A woman dressed as if she were about to attend a funeral appears in front of me. "Hello, sir."

"Uh, hi?" I have no clue what is happening.

"Allow me to escort you to your quarters." She smiles and takes my luggage.

"Thanks, but just call me Luke, sir is for my father..." I weakly return her expression and follow her past the bar. To my dismay, a triangular piece of the wall shoots up, creating a passageway into a short corridor. "Oh, you've got to be kidding me."

She lets out a short laugh, but I doubt she is allowed to mock her workplace verbally. She opens a door to our left, which is fortunately rectangular. "Here you are! Press the blue button by your bed if you need anything." She leaves me in my room and sways back to the lobby.

The space is an acceptable shape, with four walls for the rectangular furniture to lie against. There's a bed with a night-stand to its right, a dresser, and an armoire with a screen on top of it. A little over the top for a now two-day trip, but I assume we aren't the only people renting this ship.

I look at the large screen atop the armoire. It appears as if it functions like any casting service, allowing me to use the internet, even when I'm out in the emptiness of the galaxy.

As much as I hate the architecture, I could live in it with no other complaints. Finding the remote, I use the keyboard function to enter a single word into the search engine: *Nalia*.

Nothing.

I let out a loud sigh. *Really?*

I try again, this time entering *Earth-2102*.

Bingo. Kind of. Two whole search results appear, one being a two-sentence AI overview: *Earth-2102, a small planet capable of sustaining life. Found in the year 2102, this planet houses many original Earth loading docks.*

So helpful. The other result is tied to my location, and is just a flight tracker from the ship's website.

Begrudgingly, I give up and flop onto my bed. Surprisingly comfortable for space travel, but I don't have anything to compare it to. Booting up my personal device, I open a streaming service and cast *Rupaul's Drag Race: Canada Vs. UK Vs. The World* (season 15)—bringing back two of my favorite queens: Kara Sells and Garlic Breast.

After I finish the new episode, I saunter down the hallway to the main lobby of the ship. There, at one of those horribly shaped tables, is my father.

He's sipping what I can only assume is an alcoholic beverage and sifting through his email. "Hey Luke!" He waves me over. "To what do I owe this pleasure?"

I take a seat across from him, fighting the urge to cross my legs. "Oh, nothing special, just got bored."

"So, I don't warrant a special occasion, even from my own child?" *Typical.*

"I'm sorry, Father." I'm not, because I shouldn't need a special reason to spend time with him. "What are you doing?"

"Oh, *nothing special*, just checking on America. You know it, the country that I'm currently saving day by day."

Under my breath, I mutter, "Humble."

"What was that?" He sounds genuinely confused, not necessarily angry.

"Right on, Dad!" I fake a smile. The last thing I need before setting foot on a new planet is an argument, so I try to stir conversation again. "So, what brings us to Nalia?"

"I am glad you asked." He flashes a grin and closes his email. "I've noticed how hard you've been working in your classes, and thought you could use a vacation."

I wanted to mention that I couldn't afford a vacation, that exams were coming up, and without study time on Earth, my GPA would suffer the consequences. But this was a genuinely kind gesture—a rare gift lent by my crass father to his only son.

"Oh, really?" I say softly to show I'm not being sarcastic.

"Yes, really." He takes a deep breath. "I am very proud of you, Luke."

Now, that was a true first. Almost as strange as a journey to an alien planet is his statement.

Seventeen years on, well, *a* planet, and this was the first time he has been proud of *me*. Sure, I've heard the word, but always in the context of his own accomplishments, accolades, and of course election results. But never me.

I try to hide my pleasure. "Thank you."

"Well, you should try to get some sleep. We'll dock on Earth-2102 tomorrow." He gets up to leave.

"Tomorrow? I thought the flight was two days!"

"Well, basically. I mean, it's going to be late when we arrive, so basically two days of travel."

"Well, I can't wait for that." I'm actually being honest. "I'm going to find some food and turn in."

"Third triangular door to the left, great cafeteria."

I signal a thank you by nodding and pressing my hands together as if I'm in prayer. I enter the cafeteria, a well-lit oblong room with a few more tables and some restaurants scattered about. To my pleasure, there is a Panda Express aboard. The waitress is a robot, because why wouldn't we waste more space in the job market?

I order my Kung Pao Chicken and white rice and head back to my quarters. Before entering my room, I notice a shimmer at the end of the hallway.

It's a window, looking out into a sea of stars. I don't love overused metaphors, but a sea is the only way to describe it. The burning hunks of rock litter the empty region beyond the glass like a bedazzled landfill. I know each one is shedding star dust, carbon outlets used to sustain life.

Life like mine. Probably life on Nalia.

The Earth is not far back, but it is still beautiful from this perspective. Despite centuries of warfare, natural disasters, and erosion, the sea shines through like its own vessel of light. The continents trace the bounds of terrestrial habitation, and the atmosphere provides a facilitating cap of vitality. It is its own gargantuan world, but it seems so small compared to its surroundings. With other planets to support life, "Earth-1" is infinitesimal. It isn't special to anyone but humans. Humans like me.

Seeing my home planet from this angle only solidifies my dream of becoming an environmental lawyer. It makes Earth seem smaller, more fragile, and I must do what I can to protect it.

After this revelatory experience, I finally regress to my doorway. I turn the screen on and watch whatever is on the first channel. Some show about trophic levels, this time discussing the relationship between otters, sea urchins, and kelp. It's mildly interesting, and I hope it can help me sleep.

I finish my chicken, lie down, and force my eyes shut.

Darkness.

Silence.

A buzzing sound.

The vibration of the ship.

I'm still awake.

I toss around for about five minutes, then give up. Social media it is. I fish for my tablet and open Instagram. Nothing special, just some very awful videos that make me question if the internet should have been invented.

I HAVE NO CLUE WHAT TIME IT IS HERE, ANYWHERE on Earth, or even where we are landing on Nalia, but I do know that several hours have passed. I can hear doors opening down the hallway, smell food brewing from the cafeteria, and, most noticeably, hear my dad's texts coming through.

Are you up?

We have a lot to do today!

Better get ready so you're not half asleep when you meet the Senator and her son!

I send a simple thumbs up and throw on some real clothes. I race down the hallway only to spot my dad drinking from a *"World's Best Leader"* mug.

"Hey Luke!"

"Hey," I say weakly.

He puts down his cup, almost violently, and shoots up from the table. "Come with me. I have something to show you." He paces back to the window I was looking out of last night. "Look. Right there!"

Straight ahead, a blue and red orb is in view. "Is that..?"

"Damn right! That's Earth 2102, in the flesh!"

It's different from what I expected. When I heard "life sustaining," I assumed it would be green, with blue waters and maybe some tan desert regions. This planet, however, was primarily red, with purple and blue swirls running through what I hoped were forested regions.

"Wow," I say, with nothing more to add.

"I know, right?" It's so weird! Why can't they just have a green planet, like ours?" He laughs snidely and leaves me alone by the window.

I could argue just how "green" our planet really is at the moment, but I'll leave it alone.

Thanks to my lack of sleep, my ever-prominent eye bags are even more noticeable. I cannot wait to meet a potentially purple boy while I have purple circles under my own eyes.

We are finally about to dock. It has been two long, boring days of space travel, but I am finally going to set foot on Nalia.

It is obvious that my father wasn't referring to Nalia's time system when he said it would be late. First, we enter the atmosphere with only a slight bump, and we are sent barreling towards the planet below. As we near the loading dock, I am swept away by the architecture of the distant city.

Tall, compact spires litter the sky. Lights brighten every section of each slender building, and I can even spot a faint glow flowing inside the urban complex. The forested areas are painted head-to-toe in purple, blue, and red hues. The waters are blue and the air is clear.

Within our descent, we pass over colossal stretches of forest. The forested areas have to go on for tens of miles, if not over a hundred. The ship seems to go one hundred miles a minute, spitting us past the forests at great speed.

We finally arrive at a port, and as the ship sinks to the docking pad, I can tell this vacation is going to outdo any other.

5

LUNION

The ride to the ship dock is bleak. I insisted on taking my hover bike so I could follow closely behind a larger car, driven by Veronica. Selected to carry the President, his son, my mom, and Veronica, there was one remaining seat left for me, but I refused to join them when it was already too cramped. I know I will have to get to know him, but I am not eager to.

We wind around a regional park, following a trodden path that used to outline the reserve. Trees blanket the left side of my bike, flowers line the path, and birds sing overhead.

With my mind settling on the tune, I happen to spot my favorite bird, the Trelor, which is in season. Its pink tail feathers caress an orange body, forming a slight gradient of warmth. Seeing the bird sends me back to primary school when I had to do a project on it, and the time I spent learning about it became the driving factor in my favoritism. My favorite fact is that, unlike many other birds, the Trelor has zero difference in feather coloration between males and females. A rare sign of equality in nature, and a testament to my planet's inclusive regard for all life.

A flock of these sunny avians flies above, migrating in a harlequin formation. The flash of sun-kissed pink takes a sharp left and disappears into the forest.

I wish I could be like those birds. I wish I could *escape.* Not that I'm necessarily scared of the President or his son, I really just don't give a fuck. Who cares about the leader of *one region* from a whole planet? Is America really *that* important?

My thoughts are interrupted as blue brake lights flash ahead of me. Somehow we're here, and my focus on the birds had distracted me from the giant hunk of metal that sat only a few meters ahead.

It was... an odd shape. Circular in some parts, rectangular in others, hexagonal in whole, but its size was impressive. Almost intimidating. Most of our spacecraft are small, compact vessels used to check on nearby disturbances and snap footage of potentially harmful asteroids.

This vessel, however, was at least five times the size of Solan ships.

The front opens slowly, and I almost expect a puff of smoke to emanate from the opening, like in the movies. Thankfully, to spare my nerves, nothing of the sort happens. Two figures stand in the archway: an older man and a slouching younger man.

Immediately recognizable because of his blonde hair and pale skin, Luke's height throws me off guard. Perhaps my social media... *curiosities* had given me somewhat of an advantage in knowing what to expect, but they hadn't prepared me for how handsome he truly was up close.

The two walk slowly down a silver ramp, Luke appearing to watch each step with great care, as if the ramp is about to disappear under him. And it becomes clear that his fear is warranted as soon as he steps off with his luggage, because the ramp shoots back up into the base of the ship.

"Hello, Solans!" The president shouts, with his arms out like he is about to perform a jazz number. "Pleasure to be in your company." He grins, offers a curt bow, and wastes no time to start talking to my mom.

Luke is left alone, his expression twisted in confusion as he kicks a rock.

Mustering up the courage, I approach him. "Hey, you must be Luke?" I pose, more like a question and less like a statement, to ensure I don't sound cocky.

"Yeah-" He looks up from the ground. "Oh, wow." He stares at me for a few seconds, then his expression immediately turns to fear. "I'm sorry! I didn't mean to sound rude, I'm just so surprised, you're not like purple, or green, or even gray."

"Well, no."

"And you look like the boys back home." He says with a hint of distaste.

"I'd assume so..."

"Oh, my God. You speak English too?" His mouth opens in shock, and I can only hope his jaw shoots back up like that ramp.

"Again, technically, yes. Not really, though. You have a lot to learn... apparently." I'm pretty annoyed by his gawking, but I don't feel like confusing him anymore than I already have. *How is it that I know so much about humans, and he knows practically nothing about Solans?*

My mom steps away from her conversation with the president. "Are you boys ready to head into the city?" Her publicity persona is on: chin up, head high, shoulders pointed, smile gleaming.

"Sure, ma'am!" Luke is bursting with energy, and for

someone who just had a two-day flight, likely his first in space, his lack of exhaustion surprises me.

"I guess so." I say begrudgingly as I slink towards my hover bike.

Just as I'm about to speed away, a voice pierces through my ears like a dying bird. "That is sick! Can I come with you?"

Luke. He stares at me, jaw on the ground, hands on his head, eyes wider than the moon.

"I don't think I have a choice," I respond. *"Right?"* Looking at my mom, I can only hope I'm wrong.

She nods in confirmation and smiles sarcastically.

"Okay, get on." I grumble.

Wasting no time, he throws his legs around the spot Maula would normally be, and leaves his hands hovering above my shoulders, obviously hesitant to grab on.

"So... are you going to hold on, or do you want to fly off?"

He grabs on, still very lightly, and gives a blunt "No."

I press the pedal, and we immediately shoot off towards the city. Either I'm used to the speed of the hover bikes or this is too much for Luke because his grasp tightens on my shoulders, a bout of pain spreading throughout my upper body.

"Ow."

"Sorry!" He screams, his voice becoming distorted in the wind. His grip loosens slightly, and I take a deep breath of relief.

"Okay, that's better. Sorry if the jump startled you."

He scoffs as if he's offended. "Startled? No, not that. I'm not scared, this is just *very* new."

"Whatever." I increase the speed, which unfortunately returns his grip to its previous intensity. At least we will get to the city faster.

After a few minutes of awkward silence, we arrive at our destination: the apartment building. Luke and I wait for our parents, and after the car arrives, we all take an elevator to the second floor.

"Okay, so this is your apartment!" My mom motions towards 203. "Lunion, why don't you give them a tour?"

"Sure," I say coldly.

I don't want anything to do with them. I still don't trust the president, his garish ship, or anything about humans. The son is just weird, even if he is slightly attractive.

I give them a routine tour of the apartment. It's slightly different from our own, but it's only one floor, so it isn't hard to navigate. The president and his son split up to look at their rooms after I show them the kitchen and common area.

I can't help but peek in to see if he likes his gifts. He seems to appreciate the plant and sweater, but he stops and stares at the stuffed animal as if he's afraid it might come to life. He must have heard me, because he whips his head around and glances in my direction.

"What is this?"

"So-" I start.

"It's so cute! I love it, it reminds me of my cat!" He hugs the stuffed animal like a ten-year-old, then places it neatly on his bed. "Do I get to keep it?"

"Well, yes. All the items in that basket are for you to keep."

"Yes!" He celebrates with an arm pump before dropping to sit on the edge of the bed.

"I'm going to leave you here to get used to everything. See you later." I wait for him to wave goodbye, and I finally make my exit.

I go back to our apartment and lie on my bed. Staring at the boring ceiling, I yet again wish I was back in my small, messy house from when I was younger. Yeah, I had jack shit financially, but at least humans like these weren't here to disrupt my day.

My mind is once again brought back to the myriad of questions Luke asked me. *How odd.*

Drifting off toward a nap, a knock on the exterior door pulls me from my reprieve. "You've got to be kidding me."

I open the door and find a straight-faced Luke staring me down. "Hi. I am bored."

"Okay?"

"That's it? I thought you were supposed to hang out with me." Rolling his eyes, he turns to leave.

"Okay, wait." My response catches his attention, and he pivots to face me, his eyes lighting up. "What do you want to do?"

"Can we go shopping? I want to add to my collection of Nalian things."

"Impressed that you know the planet's real name, but I don't know. We should probably stay in the apartment building at least for tonight."

"Ugh, okay. That is so boring."

"No way..." I say under my breath. *How spoiled is this guy?* "We have a vending machine and some games downstairs in the lobby?" I propose.

"I'll take it." A smile forms on his lips, and he leads the way to the elevator with glee. Or, he thinks he is going towards the elevator, when in all reality he is actually walking towards a dead end.

"Hey, Luke. Wrong way."

"Oops." He turns around, and this time follows me.

The floor system is vague. There are technically two levels to each apartment on the left side, but one to each apartment on the right. So odd floors only have half as many new apartments as the even floors. It's disconcerting when I am leaving from my second floor, but this is the type of treatment you get when you are of high political status, I guess.

"Here we are." I gesture towards some arcade-style games, a few vending machines, and a small cafe. "Take your pick."

He starts at the cafe, browsing the options. "What are slaxberries? Are they like a drug?"

I laugh, "They should be considered drugs; they are amazing. Anything you try with them will be perfect."

Luke orders a plate of slaxberry waffles, then issues a lengthy investigation process. He sniffs them, licks them, and even listens to them before taking a bite. "Oh, my God. These are amazing. It's like a rich blend of blueberries and cream, but... without cream? I think?"

"I have never had a blueberry, but that sounds like a positive review. I will take it." I grin. It's nice to see someone from a completely different planet enjoy the same things I do. It just qualifies my taste as superior.

"Okay, let's move on to some games, if that's okay?"

Now he asks how I feel? Maybe he was just hungry.

"Sure," I say, my smile widening.

Little does he know these games are all competitive, and I am extremely well-versed in all of them. If he gets bored on his first day in the apartment, imagine how much time I have had to play games down here.

"Ooh, what's this one?" He points to my favorite out of all three available.

"Gal-X-E Crusherz, it's a fighting game. Think Mortal Kombat, but with flashier outfits."

"Okay. I think I've got this then." He cracks his fingers. "Wait, you know Mortal Kombat?"

"I know a lot of things." I leave it at that and get ready to destroy him in Gal-X-E Crusherz. I use my main, Lexi Lovely —a scorned bride who caught her betrothed cheating, then killed him at the wedding ceremony. Her story is insane, but iconic.

I throw some veils, swipe at his feet, and finish with the thorn flurry, and win the game.

"Oh, wow," he breathes.

"You wanted something interesting. Never said you wanted something easy."

"Yeah, I guess I have a lot to learn." He laughs lightly. "I think I'm going to go back to my room. I'm so tired all of a sudden."

"That's alright, I need a break too." Without another word, we both return to our rooms.

Free at last.

6

LUKE

What the fuck is happening?

I've been told that this place is years behind us ever since we made contact with the Solans, yet this planet is the furthest thing from behind. If anything, technology here is leaps and bounds ahead of ours.

While we are still drilling literally anywhere we can for oil, Solans seem to rely solely on electricity. We still don't have flying cars, and they have entire air traffic systems set up for *hover bikes*. Fucking hover bikes.

Not to mention that Lunion is not any color in the ROY-G-BIV spectrum. That man is as white as they get, maybe even whiter than me. His black hair is unsettling, though not in the way that makes him look "alien," but in the way it makes him look familiar. Why does the first extraterrestrial man I meet have to look like every boy I've ever been entangled with? Kill me.

Oh, and of course, the terrain itself. The purple, red, and blue plants? Are you kidding me? I haven't even seen an animal yet, but I'm already assuming I'll shit my pants when I do.

Honestly, forget Earth's environment; let me practice law here. There should be less to worry about, since so much of the natural world remains. Even the Earth-owned docks were minimalist, leaving as much room as possible for trees, bushes, flowers, and other beautiful things.

The city is so compact that plants are comfortable curving around it, and even the paths are eco-friendly. Reminiscent of the Highway Beautification Program from back home, the roads are lined with stunning displays of natural power. Impressive foliage, vibrant florals, you name it, it's there.

It's all too much, and I can't sleep like this, so I don't.

Instead, I head back down to go play Galax-E-Crusherz, a game that I evidently need to get better at. I use a flashlight built into my watch to find my way around the apartment. Trying to shut the door quietly on the way out, I end up slamming it instead, disrupting the perfect silence of the night.

This time, I head the right direction, going down a level with ease. The lights shudder on as I enter the first floor, and I hear a slight creaking sound and stop in my tracks.

"Hello!" A robot pops up from behind a counter, and I shoot backwards onto the floor.

"Goddamn! A warning next time!" I quietly yell back at the white android.

"My apologies, sir. Is there any way I can assist you? Perhaps a muffin, or a drink?" It blinks its cyan eyes at me expectantly.

"Sure, I'll take some juice. Dealer's choice." The robot pours me a beverage that looks like grape juice but tastes similar to orange. "Thanks."

"My pleasure, Mr. Dinyre."

Great, I'm already in some sort of database here.

I make my escape from the creepily knowledgeable robot and find the Gal-X-E Crusherz machine. This time, I pick a different fighter. Her name is Gleam. It's simple, but her skill set seems easy to use.

I initiate a battle with a training bot program and familiarize myself with her moves. She can send a beam of light from each limb, with a kick, a jab, or a punch. Gleam also has the ability to blind her opponent if the light hits their head. If she spins, she creates a tornado of rainbow light, blinding her opponent for longer and giving herself some extra space from them.

Most intriguing is her ultimate: a move that causes her to explode, losing one of her own lives, but taking away two of her opponent's as well.

I experiment with the training program for about ten minutes, then get another scare from that robot. "Why, hello, Mr. Moire, what brings you down at this hour of the night?"

I turn around to see Lunion standing before the robot.

"Oh, I heard a noise." He spins to look at me, rolling his eyes. "That adds up." Shifting his focus back to the robot, he continues without missing a beat. "I'll take some ploberry juice."

The android pours a glass of the same juice it gave me and offers it to him.

"Thanks."

"My pleasure, Mr. Moire." The robot moves back to its stationary position.

"Sorry to wake you, Lunion." My apology doesn't sound sincere, and it's obvious he notices.

"Mhm." He takes a sip of his juice. "So, what are you doing down here?"

"Just wanted to get better at this game. Seems like there is not much to do around here."

He laughs. "I suppose it would seem that way. Let's play again."

"Oh." He beat my ass last time, and I am not ready for that again. "Are you sure? I mean, I already interrupted your sleep."

"I was definitely not asleep, so don't even worry about it." He presses a few buttons and switches the bot to Player 2, selecting Lexi Lovely again.

I put up a mediocre fight this time. He wins the first two rounds, but insists we continue to a third. We load in again, and I am able to get him down to two lives. I race to use my ultimate, forgetting I only have one life left, which ends the last round in a draw.

"Damn!"

"Hey, you did better than I expected. At least on that one. Still a little foolish to use a self-damaging ultimate when you can't afford it, but I digress." Lunion gives me a reluctant high five and turns away from the game.

Part of me doesn't want him to leave; it is more than a little lonely on a new planet. "So... Do you want to do anything else?" I ask, trying to hide my desperation.

He thinks about it for a few seconds. "You looked very lost when you got here. I'm sure you have plenty of questions. Let's just talk."

Lunion doesn't seem stoked to be talking to me, but I'll take the opportunity, if only to be less confused tomorrow. "Really?"

"Shoot." He leads me to a little diner table, orders some food on a tablet, and waits for my first question.

"How do you know English?" That came out more quickly than I thought it would.

"Well, I don't. I know Nalian. We are a small planet with little regional diversity. We all kind of decided on a language. Just because it's extremely similar to English doesn't mean it *is* English. It just means we aren't as different as you'd like to think we are."

That is easier to swallow than I expected. "I guess that makes sense. You look human, too. You even remind me-" I can't finish that thought.

"Huh?" He stares at me for a handful of seconds before shaking his head. "Actually, I don't care. What else?"

The language question was the one I was most excited about, so I need a moment to consider what to ask him next.

"God, hurry up. I know you have plenty; I could see it in your eyes when you landed." He rolls his own eyes at me.

"Damn, okay, fine. Why are all of your plants red or blue?"

He takes a deep breath, almost as if he is disappointed. "Did you not pay attention in science class? We have plants of all colors. Most of them absorb all light waves other than red and blue. Basic science, what isn't absorbed is reflected."

"And they still produce oxygen correctly?"

He stares at me and shakes his head in disbelief. "Well, you are alive right now, aren't you?"

I blush. "You're right, my bad."

"Anything else?"

"Yeah, quite a bit actually. What's up with the hover bikes? We have been trying to do that forever."

"They've been around for a while. Of course, they improve every year, but we discovered electricity a *long* time ago, so we started basing everything on it. The bikes are rechargeable and have fans inside that increase in intensity based on voltage capacity. That is what helps propel them. They don't last very long if you go too high, and they have to be charged fairly often. Still fun though."

"Ooo."

He rolls his eyes at my response. "How do you *not* have hover bikes?"

"Oh, so now you have questions." I think about it and shrug. "I guess we are too stupid to figure it out."

"I can tell."

"Hey!" As I am yelling at him, his food is brought out. It is a single waffle, but my stomach gurgles at the sight , causing him to raise an eyebrow.

"So... I'm assuming you want some."

"Please." He slides the full plate over to me.

"There, have it all, maybe it will slow down your questions."

"Okay, so I saw you had an Instagram." I say while chewing, honestly just to prove him wrong.

"That is fucking disgusting." He looks horrified. "Please, just wait until you're done eating."

I finish quickly, despite my meal only hours earlier. "Okay, I'm done. So Instagram. How long have you had it?"

"Oh, a while. I actually love it. My mom's assistant introduced me to it. Quite a few Solans have it, but it's still pretty underground around here. Why do you ask?"

I know for a fact I look dumbstruck right now. "I hadn't seen a single Solan on there until you followed me."

"Doesn't surprise me. I've seen how behind you guys are. I bet your internet service is awful." He sings the last word mockingly.

"That doesn't explain why I could see you only after you followed me." I look at him, somewhat expecting an answer.

"Hey, I don't know what to tell you. The way I see it, it just makes sense that we can get the connection to work from here. Better tech, better speed." He stops for a second. "That is odd, however. I have been watching reels and liking posts by humans for years now, but really only other Solans find me."

"Well, your account is private, so that could have something to do with it."

He nods his head. "Oh! You guys also made YouTube, right?"

I let out a short laugh. "Yeah."

"I love it so much. So I guess I have you all to thank for that. I would never have gotten a VPN to download that Earth game, Minecraft, without it."

"You like Minecraft and YouTube too? Aren't you supposed to be an alien? You're so human."

"Okay, that is insulting. Don't forget that to me, you're also an alien. Actually, you're more of an alien than I ever will be."

"How do you mean?"

"I think it is obvious. We found inhabitable planets like yours a long time ago, but we never beamed down in military-grade spacecraft, carrying guns like barbarians. That is a *human* thing, not a Solan thing. To come down upon another world from which you are not from matches the common folklore of aliens. Therefore, you bitch, are more alien than I ever will be."

"Despite all of your annoyingly intellectual language, I see that, actually. And trust me, I agree with you. Humans suck in comparison to you all."

He seems taken aback. "Really?"

"I mean, yeah. When I landed here and saw the bountiful forests, I was floored. We have pretty much ruined nature on Earth. Not to mention how energy-efficient this planet is. You have it great here. I just hope our presence here doesn't defile that."

"Okay, so you can be a little intellectual too." He chuckles.

"Oh, trust me, I normally am quite insightful." We share a laugh and begin our trek back up to our apartments.

"Good night, Rillious." Lunion waves at the robot.

It shoots back into its ready-to-work condition. "Hello, Mr. Moire, how may I help you?"

Lunion grimaces. "Sorry, I was just saying goodnight. We don't need anything."

"No problem. Have a great night, Mr. Moire, Mr. Dinyre."

I shudder. "I'll never get over it already knowing my name. Ew."

"Leave him alone; it's not his fault he has facial recognition software. He is still an icon in his own right."

I laugh, "You're right."

We walk into the dimly lit elevator and rise up to the second floor.

"Goodnight, Luke." Before I can respond, his door is already shut.

Lunion really seems to be warming up to me, and I can only hope my father won't ruin my only chance at friendship here.

7

LUNION

Why does that naïve bastard have to look just like Marin? It's unfair. He is extremely annoying, but I can't help but stare at him. I could tell they were similar just from Instagram, but in person? It's uncanny.

At least Luke's personality is nothing like Marin's. He does not have the decisiveness nor the forwardness that Marin does. Luke has a very... odd voice compared to Marin's deep, evidently masculine timbre.

I don't know why, but I cannot stand Luke. Maybe it's because he looks like Marin but lacks his good qualities. Maybe it's because he is human, and I just fundamentally dislike him. Maybe I'm just too quick to judge, and maybe I'm being too crass.

He is an unfortunate mix of entitled and confused, but he isn't all bad. I mean, he does have some things in common with me. At least he can take a joke, and at least he has a sense of humor. Still, I am not fully on board with him being here.

His lack of education about Nalia concerns me. Not so

much to him personally, but those misconceptions could lead to some complications with the President.

I actually have no idea what is going on with Dinyre senior. Just based on my few interactions with him, he is going to be a problem. Ugly *and* Republican? No, thank you.

Today, I am supposed to be entertaining his son, which is my goal for the next few weeks, apparently. I don't love the idea of being a distraction, but at least I get out of school for it.

Rolling out of bed by accident, I collide roughly with the floor in a cocoon of blankets. What a great way to start the day.

Throwing on some clothes, I brush my teeth before I head out to wake Luke. I knock on the door of apartment 203 three times. "Luke?"

Silence.

Three more times. "Are you in there?"

I hear a groan, the opening of a door, and then footsteps approaching the main door of the apartment. "What do you want? It's like 4:00 a.m.."

Opening the door, I'm immediately greeted by a horrific sight—a near-bare Luke. "What the fuck? Put some clothes on!" I slam the door shut to avoid seeing him in his underwear for any longer. "Ignoring that... It is most definitely not 4:00 a.m.. You need to get used to the time difference here."

Chuckling at the absurdity of the situation. He horrifies me, sure, but saying I'm not intrigued would be a lie. Needless to say, I enjoy messing with him.

I wait a few more minutes for a response. Opening the door, this time fully clothed, Luke walks out. "Okay. Fine, what are we doing?" Rubbing his eyes, his body sways as if he is about to fall over.

"I think we should start by getting you sleepwear."

He frowns. "I enjoy sleeping in underwear."

"Well, I don't want to see that, so we will start there."

"Fine." I think he's too tired to put up an actual fight. "But you are driving."

"You don't even know how to drive here!" I yell back, stunned by his pathetic response.

He simply shrugs before turning around to head back into his space. With an exhale, I wait in the hallway until he is fully ready, and we head down through the lobby.

Luke lightly hugs my waist as he gets on the bike, not a glowing sign of his alertness. "Please don't fall off."

"Mhm," he murmurs so lightly it's difficult to hear him.

"Okay, play it like that." Grabbing both of his hands, I hold them with my left while steering with my right. While I don't think it's my job to protect him, I do not want to get sued by the United States government.

I take the trip slowly. Usually, I would drive at my normal speed, but with Luke being tired, I can't risk anything. I am about to round the last corner on the way to the mall when I feel Luke's hands slip from under mine.

"Uh-oh," he mumbles, but there's a slight tease in his voice.

I quickly find a balcony to land on, a charging station that I plug my bike into to give Luke a break. "Okay, let's go into the convenience store."

"Are we at the mall yet?" He says drowsily.

"Well, no. You almost fell off the bike. Like in the middle of the air." I state with what I thought would be annoyance, but it comes out more concerned.

He closes his eyes lightly. "That's nice."

"No. No, it isn't. Come on, we are going to get you an energy drink." Throwing his arm around my neck, I guide him into the store, which isn't an effortless task because, unlike me, he seems to be in shape.

"What flavor?"

So he can follow that he is getting something to drink, but doesn't care that he almost died? Interesting.

"I don't care, just pick one," I grumble, folding my arms over my chest as he slips away from me.

Spinning around, he turns away from the refrigerator and heads toward an aisle of chips. "That one!" It's a bag of salted crackers.

"Okay, so no, again. I'm just gonna pick one." I grab a slaxberry drink, a flavor he seemed to enjoy before.

Practically carrying him over to the self-checkout, I pay for the two energy drinks. One for him to wake up, and one for me to stay awake whenever he inevitably starts to bore me.

I return to find my bike still safe and sound, with a little extra charge. "Okay, drink up."

He sloppily grabs his drink and takes a few sips, nearly missing his mouth with the first. After getting a taste, he practically chugs the rest of the can.

"That was great!" He is immediately back to his normal self, however normal that can be, which cannot be healthy.

"I have never seen an energy drink work that quickly..." I utter in disbelief.

"Oh, that was an energy drink? Never had one, that's so cool." He throws away his can and hops back on the bike expectantly. Clapping his hands together with excitement, he points at me. "Okay, let's go!"

I hop on, let him get secure this time, and whip off the balcony. The drive is quick since the mall isn't far from our pit stop. Parking, I locked my bike, and lead Luke straight to a department store to get him some pajamas.

"Okay, so I don't care what you pick. I'll even pay for it. But please... just get *something*." I grimace.

"Fine. Because you cannot approve of my lifestyle, I will find something." Luke leads me aimlessly around the store, finding the sleepwear section after about ten minutes of confusion. "Okay, how about these?" He holds up a pair of bright yellow pajama pants.

"The color is awful, but at least these touch the ground."

He grabs a basket to toss the pants into, then pauses. "Wait. This looks familiar. Did you steal one of these for my welcome gifts?" He looks up at me incredulously.

"I did not, but my friend did." I brace myself for a fit of panic.

To my surprise, he erupts with laughter. "That is fucking hilarious! I need to meet this friend of yours; they seem a lot more fun than you."

"Thanks," I say shortly, then lead him to more clothing options. We leave after buying five pairs of pants, but not a single sleep shirt. I guess that half of the body was non-negotiable.

"Can we go look at shoes?" His eyes glint with an eagerness that is impossible to say no to.

"Sure, I just want to kill time." I escort him to the nearest store, Nali-Up Kicks, which is tailored to athletic teen boys. Colorful sneakers line the walls, ranging from blue to green to pink, bright trims detailing each of them.

"Woah!" Luke exclaims after picking up a pair of grey sneakers with light blue detailing before turning to the solemn worker to his left. "Do these really add extra height to your jumps?"

At this inquiry, the worker perks up. "Why, of course, sir. And for the low price of 200 Nalian Credits, they can be yours."

I speak up, "Oh, what a load of-"

"Silence," Luke holds up his hand and turns back to the worker. "Keep talking."

Confusion flashes across the man's expression. "I mean, that's really all."

"Great. Do you know the conversion rate of USD to Nalian Credits?"

"Ooh, this is my first time doing that. Let me check." His fingers drum across the screen of his iPad before he glances up again. "Looks like that's about $250, USD."

"Deal." Luke slams down a card and pays for his new shoes. "Have a great rest of your day!" He takes his sneakers and leaves the store beaming.

After his unfortunate purchase, I take him to the food court. "So... what do you want to eat?"

"Do you have Panda Express?"

I don't even try to respond.

"Well?" He seems super excited. Either he loves Panda Express, or that energy drink is still fresh in his system.

"You seem to get dumber every time I talk to you."

"What?" He looks lost.

"China is a country on Earth; we do not have Chinese food here. Or, knock off Chinese food, I suppose."

"Not even in a military base type of place?"

"Maybe, but does it look like we are at a military base right now?" Motioning around the space, I turn my attention back to him with a scowl.

"No."

"Okay, so I will choose, I guess." I guide us over to a shop that sells anything from fruit to meat pies, so I can only hope he finds something to eat.

To my surprise, he scans the menu quickly and orders before I do. "I'll have a quaxie pie and slaxberry soda." He waits for me to order, which, per my luck, is the same thing, and then pays for the two of us.

"Thanks for uh... paying. I was going to." I say, a little caught off guard.

"Well, you drove here, so it's the least I can do."

I laugh. "I didn't really have a choice, but thank you." We wait for our food to come out, and then go sit down to eat. "Well, you seem to be more awake now."

"Yeah, that energy drink really helped." Digging into his pie, he retreats slightly when a puff of steam comes out of the top. He lets it cool before taking a bite. "Wow! That is really good. It kind of tastes like chicken."

"Sure, I wouldn't know."

"That's a compliment, trust me."

"I'll take your word for it." We share a laugh.

"So, where are we off to next?" Luke asks, but my attention is pulled away from our conversation. In the near distance, I see a tall, burly figure with blonde hair and a pale complexion similar to Marin's. "Lunion?"

"Oh, shit!" Before I can think, I leap from my seat and jump behind a fake bush behind our booth.

"Hello? Are you okay?" Luke asks with unease.

"Shut up!" I whisper harshly. Through the leaves, I can see him throw his hands up in surrender. I peek around the bush and see Marin and a girl going down to the floor below. Dammit, I thought I pulled Luke out of bed early enough to avoid, well, *anyone*. "That was close."

"What was close? That was some freak behavior. The whole mall probably thinks you're off your meds."

Despite the terror in Luke's eyes, I calmly reclaim my seat. "I don't know if you saw him, but there was a blonde guy."

"Well, yes. I am blonde. No reason to jump behind a bush."

"Not you, idiot. This guy from my school that I have a huge crush on. He definitely knows it too." I take a deep breath. "I did not want to have to interact with him and his new girlfriend. Not today."

I cannot tell if Luke is even more concerned or comforted by this confession, because his expression has not changed a bit since I leapt behind that bush. "Okay... so we are all a little odd here. Good to know."

"Let's just finish our food and get out of here. I really don't want to see him." I continue to eat my pie, this time taking large bites in quick succession to hasten our escape.

"So, I'll ask again, what are we doing after this?" Luke questions.

"Anything you want, as long as we get to leave this mall."

That response elicits a mischievous grin from Luke.

8

LUKE

That was insane. It was something I would totally do too, but it was insane.

I don't have time to question his confusing actions. I have a store I want to pursue. Once I had woken up fully, I saw a fascinating shop on the way to the mall. It was perfect; out of the mall and away from that *boy*. Better yet, if it goes well, it can get us even further away from here.

"I'm glad you said that!" I grin as we rush out toward the hover bike.

"Uh-oh. That scares me." Lunion replies dryly.

He probably is terrified, as he doesn't seem to be as acclimated to me as I thought he was. Still, he is definitely too preoccupied with his own thoughts to display his fear.

"Don't be. It's nothing crazy." That is kind of a lie, but I'm high off my energy drink, so I'm willing to take a risk.

"Okay, whatever. Just hop on!" He practically throws me onto the bike, gets on himself, and speeds out of the parking lot. "Where am I going?" I can see him glare at me through the side mirror.

"Did you see that bike shop on the way to the mall? I think it was right by the entrance that led to the food court. Maybe across one of those tiny lanes, or streets, I have no clue what they are."

His narrow eyes snap open like eager piranha plants. "Oh, hell no."

"What? I'll pay for my own bike."

"You can't seriously think that is my problem with this? I just watched you spend $250 on shoes. I know you'll drop some cash."

"Okay, okay. I get it, safety is a thing. But you're really good at driving, just teach me."

"And if you get hurt?"

"I'll take full responsibility," I fish around in my wallet. "Look. I even have a driver's license."

"I'm not sure..." He's so uptight it's killing me.

"Oh, come on! I haven't been able to drive for years!"

"That isn't a glowing recommendation of your skills, but fine. You can drive, but no illegal shit."

"Yay!" I shout, my cadence embarrassingly similar to a ten-year-old. I point him to where I thought I saw the store, and within a few minutes of circling the tall buildings of the city, we find it. He whips into the store so fast that I almost perform the Heimlich maneuver on him.

"Okay, we are here." He sighs, "Please don't get anything ugly."

"Oh, my taste is top tier, don't even fret," I say, with an oddly placed British accent.

He doesn't respond, just shakes his whole body out of disgust.

Stacks of hover bikes fill the room, some organized by color, some by size, others by battery use. I look in awe, the rows of what I assume are metal bikes, all reflecting the store's lighting beautifully, each creating its own shine.

"Hello, sir! How may I help you?" It's another Solan, not a robot this time.

Thankfully.

"Wow! You're real!" I exclaim, somewhat jokingly.

Lunion steps in. "I apologize for my... acquaintance. He is used to the robots that frequently work the nighttime shifts, as he doesn't get outside often." He cups his hand to his mouth to say, "They don't like to let the public see him. I'm sure you understand."

"Hey!" I reply, obviously irritated.

"Okay... I'll let you boys look around." A flash of disappointment covers the worker's expression as they walk to the backroom.

"Come on! I don't know anyone here. I don't need rumors spreading already because you're claiming I'm not supposed to be outdoors."

He chuckles, "Oh, lighten up! It was obviously a joke. Do you really think some hover bike salesman is going to air out your business?"

I blush, knowing I made more of a scene than I needed to. "Sorry."

"Whatever, just go find a bike." He shakes his head.

I return to the overwhelming stock of bikes. A bike on a shelf to the top left immediately catches my eye. It has a white base with black detailing that almost reminds me of orcas. Shortly after I started kindergarten, they went extinct, which sucks because they were incredibly beautiful to five-year-old me.

"This one!" I shout at an unsuspecting Lunion.

Covering his ears, he spins around to face me. "Damn.

That was pretty fucking loud." Based on his tone, I can tell he's already tired of me. "Go pay for it."

The bike is 300 Nalian Credits, which, given my previous experience, should be around $375.

Snatching a slip with the bike's number, 061108, I drop it on the front desk. . "I'll take this one, please!" I slam down my card eagerly.

"Great, one moment, and I will go collect your purchase!" The store owner returns to his sunny demeanor, which we had previously ruined. Vanishing to the back again, this time not out of fear, he quickly returns with the model I purchased. "All yours!" He hands me a receipt and pushes the bike toward me. It appears fully charged, and from watching Lunion with his, I know the cord is packed away on the side of it.

"Thank you so much! Have an amazing day!" I waste no time taking my bike to the balcony, throwing a leg over the seat with haste. "Okay, now what?"

"No, no. We are not doing this here. One minute." Lunion takes out a hitch, attaches my bike to his, and flies away.

"Hello? Is this a robbery?" I yell into the city traffic, but he doesn't respond.

In a few minutes, not one, Lunion returns on his bike, which is missing mine from its back. "Okay, get on."

Reluctantly I mount his bike, and we make our way out of the city. He descends into an open stretch of land, filled with blue and red plants, many trees, and sporadic wildlife. "You will be learning here, not in the middle of the city."

"That's a little disappointing, but I guess it makes sense." Throwing my legs back over my bike, I straddle it completely.

Lunion eases up his bike so it is parallel to mine. "You're going to start by adjusting your mirrors how you would want them."

I adjust both so that I can see clearly behind me. "Got it."

"Next, you're going to start the engine." He points to a small, glowing button above the speedometer.

With one press, the bike lights up. "Done." Below its black detailing, white lights appear, adding a slight amount of illumination to the ground below. "Cool." I try to refrain from any more yelling, even though this is sick as fuck.

"Yes, it is. So now, you'll want to pull on the left handle to rev the engine, and the right to help slow down, which is crucial on turns." He gives a short demonstration, doing a circle in the middle of a small clearing.

"Okay, I think I got it." Mirroring what he did, I almost fly into a tree. "My bad." I get off, spin the bike back around to face Lunion, and try again. This time, I'm able to swerve right as I am about to hit him.

"Oh, shit!"

"Sorry!" I yell back, trying to return to our starting place. "Okay, I think I was wrong." We continue to practice until I've memorized every inch of the forest, mainly because I almost crash into every tree.

Above, the sky is turning a pinkish-orange color when Lunion says, "Let's head back." He struggles to find a reason. "We don't want to be out in the dark."

"Let's race!"

"Hmm? You can't seriously think-" And with that, he speeds away.

"Classy!" I shout, trying my best to catch up. I keep the distance between us close, but I never close it. He is definitely better than I am.

I didn't know how far we were, but by the time we return, it's almost dark. We must have been practicing for hours, as I remember seeing a hint of sunrise when we left the apartment.

The electric glow coming from inside the buildings washes out any trace of my bike's lights, and the apartment building is no exception. I didn't realize how bright the building's lights were at night until I had something to compare them to.

I park my bike on a rack next to Lunion's and turn around to find our parents chatting amongst themselves. "Should we interrupt them?" I ask quietly.

"Why not? Hey, Mom!" Lunion bellows, his focus immediately shifting.

"Oh, if it isn't my Starchild," nudging my dad she offers a faint smile, "and your child as well!" She doesn't look thrilled to see us, but she still hugs Lunion. "Where did you two go off to?"

"Well, one of us was asleep for half of it, but we went shopping." Lunion remarks, swiveling to face me.

"Okay, that is not entirely true. But, yes, we did go shopping." I glance at my bike and raise my new shoes to show my father.

His eyes light up. "*That* is what we are here for! Are you happier, son? You know what I always say."

"Yes. Money can, in fact, buy happiness. It is the title of your memoir." I say, blushing out of second-hand embarrassment.

"Well! That is spectacular, but I think it is time to go to bed." Lunion's mom offers, glancing between us.

"I agree, today has drained me." My dad fakes a fainting motion and heads up to the second floor, Lunion and his mom not far behind.

"Okay, well, I'm getting a muffin!" I call after them, but it's not like they would wait for me anyway. After grabbing the ever-addictive slaxberry-flavored muffin, I follow their trail upstairs.

My dad is the first to speak up when I step into our apartment. "Well, I'm glad you had fun today. That was the whole point of bringing you here." He flashes me a smile.

"Thanks. What did you do today?"

"Oh, just boring diplomatic stuff, nothing exciting. Definitely not as exciting as getting a hover bike!" He laughs, the sound echoing off the walls as he retreats to his room. His aloofness is surprising, but welcome. I want to believe he is changing, but it's hard to. "Goodnight, Luke."

"Goodnight, Dad." I wave back and head to my room.

Once I finish my selected treats, I take a quick shower and throw on some clothes to sleep in, per Lunion's grating demands. That boy is certainly stuck up and ungrateful. If I got to see someone as fit as me in underwear, I would be grateful.

I leap onto my bed and try to find the ability to sleep. Apparently, having your first energy drink does not help you maintain a regular sleep schedule. I can't stop tossing and turning. Unable to wind down, I get up, throw some socks on, and go to bother the one person I know here.

I knock on the door of 202. "Hello?"

Scuffling follows before a shadow appears under the door. "What do you want?" He sounds pissed.

"I can't sleep."

He opens the door, "Join the club. Oh, would you look at that, you have pants on. That's a start. Let's find you a shirt."

"You cannot be that insufferable, can you?"

"Actually, yes, I can be, and thank you." He grins and lets me into the apartment.

Leading me to the kitchen, he motions at a stool, and disappears up the stairs to his room. Instead of sitting, I go through his fridge, finding a recipe for slaxberry pancakes and what I think are the ingredients. The milk has a very subtle blue hue, but that probably has to do with the mammals' diet here.

Once I have the ingredients lined up, he returns with a tank top in hand. "I'm assuming that's for me." Looking at the material he holds, I smirk. "Are we sure that will fit? I mean, I'm not a twig bitch-"

"Please, just shut the fuck up for once." He throws the top at me and paces the room.

Obliging, I slide it on with surprising ease. Sure, it definitely hugs some parts of my torso, but it's not uncomfortable.

"Wow, go you! This fits really well!"

He makes a face, throws up jazz hands, and replies, "Stretch fabric." Taking one look at the mess I have out on his kitchen counter, his brows furrow. "What is all of this?"

9

LUNION

I've already had a draining day, and now this brute is emptying my fridge at 2:00 a.m.? What did I do to deserve this?

At least he is clothed, but that's only because I am competent enough to fix the problem myself. "What is going on?" The question comes out just as irritated as I feel—perfect.

"Oh, sorry. I wanted food." He flashes an unsure grin across the kitchen island, but I refuse to reciprocate it.

"Do you even know how to cook?" I ask, genuinely concerned.

"Yeah-" Luke starts, pausing to form the rest of his reply. "Actually, that's a lie. I honestly forgot everything about cooking. I've had butlers and chefs for a while..." He looks disappointed in himself, so I don't drive the shame any further.

"Okay, well, let's start by mixing the ingredients. I assume you know how to do that." His eyes glint with annoyance, and I realize what I said may have come off as sarcastic. "I'm being serious, you aren't *that* stupid."

"Thanks?" He takes a spoon and begins to mix the dry

ingredients, being sure to measure each amount with precision. "I'm not sure what Teliciters are, but I can read, so I'll just hope I'm measuring correctly."

"Yeah, we don't go by the metric or imperial system here, sorry. I guess that is one of the few differences between our planets."

He grimaces, "Well, am I doing it right?"

"Yeah, as long as you use the measuring cups, you'll be fine." I wave it off, hoping to lessen the stress and tension bubbling in the room. Watching intently, Luke gets the hang of the measurements and seems to follow the recipe with ease.

After a few minutes, all the ingredients are combined and ready to be cooked.

"Okay, so you're going to want to use this pan." Motioning to the one he got out earlier, I continue, "Then-"

"I know how to make pancakes. Even if I haven't cooked, I have watched *Top Chef*." He snatches the pan from the counter vehemently, eliciting a judgmental expression from me, which he catches. "Don't be a hater, just watch and be wowed."

Luke pours some of the mixture into the pan. Then, like the main character of some cooking show, he cracks his knuckles and slams the pan down on the stove. "I forgot it has to cook for a little bit..."

After roughly two minutes, he grabs the handle of the pan, glares at me, and flips the pancake without a spatula. Or, he attempts to.

The thin speckled disk flies across the room, landing on a lamp. "Oh my god. I am so sorry." He slaps a hand across his mouth and runs over to get the pancake, pan in hand.

"Just... let me do it." I let out a lengthened exhale, and after Luke retrieves his failed snack, I take over, finishing the rest of the batter quickly.

I set out two plates, both with a three-stack of the

pancakes, at the dining table. "So, anything you want to talk about, other than your cooking failures?"

His face turns red, then his eyes glitter with a sudden realization. "Actually, yes. What is with that boy from earlier? You know, the one you jumped into a bush to hide from."

"Really? That is what you want to talk about?" I sigh heavily, hoping he will sympathize and change the topic.

"Yes."

"Damn, okay, I will talk about it. There isn't much, just that I've been into him for years, and I've tried everything to get with him. *Everything*." My mind immediately goes to those idiotic YouTube love spells, and I cringe inwardly. "Anyway, he got with a girl who looks exactly like me, and I've been pissed ever since."

A flicker of confusion and excitement crosses Luke's face, then he returns to his usual, bland expression. "Ahh, he's straight? That sucks."

"No, not at all. We don't really do that here. If you love someone, you love them. If you don't, you don't. Not so much sexuality based. Anyway, he also used to be with a guy, so he isn't, by your definition, 'straight.'"

"I thought this place was great before, but no pressure on labels? This is a utopia." His brown irises glow with wonder, but then switch to a reflection of deep sorrow.

"Are you okay?" I ask.

"Oh, yeah. Sorry, there is just *so* much stigma back on Earth about stuff like this, even if we've come so far."

"Trust me, I know. When the humans came here, they brought a little of it too. Really only in the deep city, where the business people are, but it is still annoying."

"Wow, sorry, I guess we really do suck."

"Yeah, I won't argue with you there. You're not as bad,

though." I regret saying it as soon as it comes out. I've been a stoic and guarded figure this entire time, and until I learn what his dad wants with us, I can't let him get to me.

His smile returns. "Well, because you shared that, I'll share my own embarrassing romantic history."

"Please do, I can't be the only fool here," I respond.

"So, I had this best friend and also this boyfriend, and they both basically looked the same. Anyway, I grew distant from my friend, then later got broken up with. And to make a long, embarrassing story short, they are together now..."

I stare at him with horror stained on my face. "Does that not look weird?"

"Oh, it definitely does. They look related." He fakes vomiting only to start laughing. "But I'm over it, honestly. It's just hilarious thinking about it. How could you ever date someone who looks almost exactly like you? Talk about narcissism."

"Right." His story enthralls me. It's nice to know his life is even more dramatic than mine. It makes me feel a little more sane.

"Anyway, my friends keep trying to get me interested in all of this, but as I said, I really don't give a shit."

"I don't want to overstep, but your friends sound annoying." I can't tell if this comment bothers him. "Sorry, it just seems like they want to use you for entertainment or something."

He ponders it for a moment. "Yeah, I don't know. They've been like that for a while. Do you have any friends?"

"Wow, rude. But yeah, my childhood friend, Maula, actually helped pick out some of your welcome gifts."

His smile widens. "Yeah, you mentioned that she stole that basket! That is hilarious. I have to meet her."

"That can be arranged." I laugh lightly, thinking about what she said about how he'd react, and how she was completely right.

Silence fills the room as we run out of easy topics to discuss. Sure, that was somewhat of a deep conversation, but drama is always easier to bend with the intent of hiding the more personal aspects.

After a painfully awkward couple of minutes, Luke speaks up. "I kind of hate my dad."

"What?" His comment catches me off guard.

"Yeah, I know, that sounds so bitchy. We just have opposite views on literally everything."

"Really?"

"Sorry, I shouldn't have brought this up. I'm going back to bed, thanks for the pancakes." He begins his departure, taking his messy plate with him.

I get up from my chair and grab his hand. "Wait."

"Hm?"

"We can talk about it. It's okay." Part of me is genuinely concerned, and another wants any information I can get on his dad.

"Really?"

"Yeah, no problem." Realizing our hands are still connected, I frantically shake them apart.

He sits back down and begins. "First off, I can tell he hates me, too. The things I like, the way I act, the way I sound. I even started working out and playing sports to make him like *something* about me, but it is never good enough."

I don't respond, I just nod along.

"Let's not even begin to discuss his political views. Super right-wing, the opposite of everything I stand for. I literally want to be an environmental lawyer, and he is at the podium preaching that 'more fake trees keep the city green,' because artificial landscapes never wilt, and purchasable oxygen is great for the economy."

"Fake trees and oxygen? Huh?"

"Luckily, Congress has been bipartisan on not passing any of those efforts, as even his supporters don't want the Earth to get too *Loraxy*."

"I have no clue what that means, but I can tell I should be glad they're stopping it."

"Yeah, but I am afraid he is just too rotten to give up. But enough about him, what about your mom?"

I take a deep breath. I have little to say about her, but the 'juicy' details I want to share aren't things I would want her to hear, and she is sleeping only a few feet away. "Can we talk about this tomorrow?"

"Yeah, I guess so. Sorry." A flash of unease coats his expression, as if he's concerned he may have offended me.

I suppose it is unfair that he opened up to me, so I concede. "Actually, follow me."

When he gets up, I lead him to my room, which is the furthest we can get from hers.

"Very nice, fun posters and all." He obviously has no idea what to say. "Why are we here?"

"I just didn't want her to hear us talking; her room was close to us over there."

He lets out an "ooh" and nods in understanding. I motion towards a chair at my desk for him to sit in.

Once he's comfortable, I take a seat at the foot of my bed, facing him. "I don't know, sometimes I just feel like I am a political prop. She has a kind of sporadic personality now that she is in office."

He leans in, trying to appear attentive.

"I love her, and I know she loves me. We have the same views on everything, but she will make sure I am a certain way when the cameras are around. Which is why I have sort of enjoyed having you around." Shit. Shouldn't have said that.

"Thanks!" He looks deeply flattered.

"What I mean to say is, if I am distracting you, I don't have to deal with her team, or the press, or the interviews."

"Well, you say she has the same views as you, and you obviously have a deep connection, so why don't you talk to her?"

"I just feel like I owe her so much that I can put up with it for a little longer. Her term is almost up, so we will return to a normal life soon. Her salary covers this apartment, and she has also implemented many of the policies we thought of together. She sanctioned so much new land specifically for preservation, which is one of my passions as well."

"I'm glad your relationship is so strong." Despite his cruel relationship with his father, this appears to be a genuine remark.

"That's why I didn't want her to hear me. My complaints are so petty."

"It's okay to be upset," He tries to comfort me. "But I'm sure she will understand. It seems like she truly values your opinion. I personally wouldn't let a seventeen-year-old, or even younger, I guess, influence my policymaking, but she does. That means something."

"Let's see, she was elected when I was ten, and we immediately started brainstorming together, so yeah, much younger."

"That's insane." He laughs incredulously. "Still, I applaud your love for nature. I guess that is something we share, despite our many differences."

It kills me that we aren't that different. I wanted him to be annoying, naïve, and unintelligent. Instead, he is slowly becoming less confused, is sympathetic, and even demonstrates some eagerness to learn.

"Well, thanks for the visit, but I think we need to sleep." I laugh lightly and get up, trying to push him out silently.

As he is about to leave the apartment, he stops. "So, how are you distracting me tomorrow?"

"I have an idea. Just make sure your bike is fully charged." When he nods and wanders off, I close the door with a stupid, irritating, and unfortunate grin on my face.

10

LUKE

I did it. I actually did it. I was able to get up on time today. No more screaming from Lunion, no more shame. I was finally awake before 3:00 p.m.

"Lunion!" I knock on his apartment door repeatedly. "I'm awake!"

The door opens slowly, with a slight hint of hesitation. "Hello?" It's Ms. Moire.

"Senator, I am so sorry! I was supposed to do something with Lunion today. Is he here?"

She looks me up and down, frowns, then cocks her head in confusion. "It is 4:00 a.m., you know that, right?"

"What? No, he usually wakes me up around this time and yells at me to get ready. I promise I'm not crazy."

I wasn't crazy, right?

"I'm sure you aren't, but my son definitely is. He probably got you up this early before to screw with you. Or maybe your biological clock is messed up, I don't know. Come back later."

I never even checked my clock. Not once on this entire trip had I checked the time. Racing back to my room, I hunt through the cabinet for an alarm clock of any kind, and come up short.

I shift my attention to the screen, a large white rectangle much like the TVs on Earth. Searching for a remote, I eventually find a slate blue oval with very few buttons. I press all of them, and the screen turns on. Up in the corner, it does, in fact, read *4:00 a.m.*

That son of a bitch. I knew he didn't like me, but damn. I can't be too upset, though. We didn't do anything until around 7:00 a.m. the last time he woke me up, and I got payback by almost dying on his bike anyway.

I am up now, and I'm proud of it, so this time is not going to waste. I scroll on the TV, or whatever it's called here. After a few minutes, I find a gaming section.

Besides the familiar *Gal-X-E Crusherz,* there is what appears to be a racing game. Above a graphic of a small frog-like animal, blocky text reads "RIBBIT RACE EXTREME: RACE FOR THE UNIVERSE." It's a little long for a title, but the premise is cute.

I load it up and quickly find myself choosing a bright teal frog as my character. It hops into a car shaped like a firework, and the race begins. It starts on Nalia, steering my frog past extensive forests of blues and reds. Then, a ramp appears with a boost pad. My frog goes soaring through the sky, evading pink and yellow birds and bursting out of the clouds with intimidating force.

Before I know it, my teal racer is on the moon. His little firework runs across the rocky, porous ground of the silver rocks, each turn giving him a little extra bounce. To my surprise, I see the Earth to the left. My home planet takes up a great amount of space, and I can barely see Nalia before it. The race ends back on Nalia, but I am too enthralled to end here.

I play even longer. My frog spins, drifts, and glides across planets I'm not even sure are real until I hear a voice awaken me from my trance. "Luke? Are you dressed? I'm not coming in unless you actually have clothes on this time."

Pushing myself up, I quickly pad to the door, opening it swiftly. "Hello, Lunion. To what do I owe this honor?"

"Hi." He looks at me, clearly impressed that I am fully ready for the day. "It's almost 11:00, so we are gonna have lunch."

"What? It was just 4:00 a.m...."

"Yeah, like seven hours ago, come on."

I disregard the amount of time I wasted on that game and follow him to his apartment.

AFTER WE FINISH OUR LUNCH, WHICH HAS EVOLVED into a long, multi-family discussion, Lunion is ready for whatever he had planned for us. "Grab your bike and meet me in front of the building," he says, already heading for the elevator.

I catch up with my bike, getting on the elevator before he descends to the first floor. "So, what are we doing today?"

"We are going to see some... nature." He says plainly, void of animation. Following him to the front of the building, I straddle my bike and he glances over at me once he's seated on his. "Okay, follow me until I stop."

Lunion begins what turns out to be a very lengthy trip. We start by leaving the city, and soon those tall white spires are far behind us. We reach the clearing that I first practiced in after a few minutes, then take a dirt path. It extends beyond the clearing, leading us inside the forest itself. The tall red trees cast shadows over our bikes while blue bushes nip at the ground beneath us, magenta flowers springing from the path.

Despite it only being about 5:00 p.m., the sun is already nearly gone. Orange streaks illuminate the sky, and I can't help but wonder if Lunion is planning to kill me. I mean, maybe I heard too much. This is how all murder mysteries begin; all episodes of *Law and Order* start with the victim dying in some remote location. And while I don't think he would do that, I still don't know him *that* well.

After about an hour of speeding through thick forests, small outposts, and flower fields, we land in a deeply isolated clearing. On one side is a small hill; on the other, a lush range of foliage. The path ended about a mile ago, but that doesn't stop us from making our own path to the top of the hill.

"Okay, we will park here. Now help me so I can spread out this blanket." Lunion grabs the plush fabric, some drinks, and two white blocks out of the back of his bike. "The blanket and basket are for us, the white blocks will charge our bikes back to at least two-thirds battery."

I oblige, taking the basket and chargers from him and letting him throw the blanket down. The sun is still illuminating the sky, creating a stunning blend of oranges behind the forest. "It's beati-"

"Just wait." Lunion cuts me off and pats on the blanket, motioning for me to join him.

We sit there for about half an hour, watching the small animals of the forest play in the clearing as the sun sets. All traces of light are nearly tucked away from view when Lunion finally speaks up.

"Make sure you are watching the forest. Just wait." There it was again, "just wait," like that wasn't what we had been doing for the last thirty minutes.

Still, I listen. I continue to watch the forest edge with a

strange intimacy. Following each bush, each tree, each flower along the clearing, and peering deep into the forest, looking for where each tree obscures another. I get lost in the intricacies, and I don't even realize that the night sky has fallen until I take a drink.

Lowering the bottle, my perspective shifts.

Everything seems to be glowing, radiating vibrant colors, and illuminating the night sky in, well, an extraterrestrial fashion. The tall, red trees sparkled, and the blue bushes twinkled, and small bugs danced atop the gleaming purple flowers and glistening magenta grasses. Each piece of the forest shone uniquely, all working in harmony to create an almost fluid mosaic of faint, yet strong lights that unified the natural world.

It was stunning, beautiful, and still somehow so very... natural. Not to me, but to the wonderful atmosphere of this planet. This planet, where the technology was radiant. This planet, where the personalities and efforts of the people shone like a billion bright, brilliant stars. This planet, whose essence relied on the light inside its inhabitants.

For a while, I am left speechless by the beaming, swirling landscape of bright vermillion and periwinkle. I'm silent until I can finally say something, anything to show my appreciation of this wonder.

"It's marvelous. Really, Lunion, it's-" I turn to him, my breath catching in my throat as I gaze upon his figure. "You're-"

He, too, was glowing, filling up the blanket around us with an ever-so-faint beacon of white light. Maybe he wasn't that vibrant, but his beauty was blinding to me.

His skin was painted with the colors of the moon, emanating moondust with every second. His blanched radiance complemented his night-sky hair, illustrating a bewitchingly lunar scene. He was stunning, even more so than the natural world itself.

"What?" He takes a second to yawn, continuing in an attempt to calm me down. "Never seen a boy glow before?"

"Sorry, it's just..." I can't find the right words. "It's just that you're-" Stopping myself, I pan my hand across the sparkling forest. "It's all so beautiful."

I must look like an idiot, gawking at something he sees as normal. Still, there is something incredibly alluring about not only his glow, but the light of the entire planet, that makes it impossible for me to stop.

Damn those city lights for washing this out. I can't believe I've been deprived of this cosmic resplendence for so long. *This* is the type of environment I wish to protect. *This* is the type of natural vitality worth pain, sacrifice, and hardship.

I turn away from Lunion, but it isn't easy. The only incentive to pry my eyes off of his body is the reward of looking back on the rest of Nalia. An insignificant amount of time passes. I don't care how long, because nothing truly matters to me when I'm faced with *this*.

I finally rest my eyes back on Lunion, but find his body, still emitting soft white light, curled up on the blanket, a light snore coming from him. I hadn't noticed how tired he was today, but I wasn't surprised.

Slipping back into my trance, the chime of my phone deters me—my dad.

WHERE ARE YOU TWO? IT'S GETTING LATE. PLEASE come back to the apartment.

. . .

I SEND AN AFFIRMATIVE MESSAGE BACK AND NOTICE that Lunion's tablet is also exploding with similar messages from his mom. I try to wake him, but he is too knocked out to notice.

I put the empty bottles in the basket, take the chargers off our bikes, and hook his bike to my own. I sit him up softly and wrap the blanket around his shoulders.

Luckily, I am strong enough to pick him up. I lift him lightly, trying not to disturb him, and sit him on the back of my bike. Taking my seat, I make sure he is safely leaning against me, holding his hands around my waist securely.

Then, I leave the glimmering grove behind and make my way to a dissonantly shining city. I pass by more glowing trees, this time noticing birds perched on the branches, their sunrise-colored feathers outlined by an innate dim glow. I elapse cerulean peaks of shimmering pines, softly radiant specks of chartreuse flowers, and even less noticeable encroachments of luminescent lavender vines.

In what seems like no time, I'm back to the artificial glow of the bright city, a stark contrast to the soft, natural glows of nature.

Lunion's light fades into the backdrop of harsh LEDs, and what I had once seen is now only a fresh memory piercing through my mind.

I park our bikes in the apartment lobby, and as I am about to lift Lunion, he begins to stir. Groggily, he says, "Oh, I'm sorry. Did I fall asleep?"

"Yeah," I reply.

"Well, thanks for getting me back." He reaches out a hand for me to help him off the bike.

I lift him out and guide him to the elevator. Once he is safely in his room, I head for my own, and crash on the bed, finally not tossing and turning for the first night since I've been here.

11

LUNION

Luke's father is standing in my living room, hands on his hips, and a smile beaming across his crude face. "Boys, we have an announcement." He motions toward my mom to make the proclamation for him.

My mom hesitates, then speaks. "We are shipping you two off to Earth for a week."

"Oh, Madame Moire, don't make it sound so dark. It is going to be super fun! Luke, you'll get to show Lunion around your home, just as he has so graciously shown you his own."

This is coming entirely out of left field. I was supposed to entertain a few humans for a little while, not the other way around. They were supposed to come to *my* planet, not the other way around.

"Okay, but why?" I ask, making sure my tone carries an acknowledgment of how superfluous this is.

My mom shoots me a look, almost as if to say, "Your guess is as good as mine."

Mr. Dinyre's voice fills the gap, "To strengthen the bond between our planets, of course." The reply comes with such aloof optimism, like he knows we are all contesting this decision.

"So, I am supposed to show off Lunion, a Solan, to everyone on Earth?" Luke questions, the irritation in his voice evident.

"Yes," His father responds definitively.

"You do remember that *no one* on Earth, except some very select businessmen and government workers, even knows what Solans look like, right?"

"Yes, and this will be a wonderful way to educate the masses. Just go and enjoy your time. I want you two to have fun!" He gives Luke a thumbs-up and exits the apartment.

"Okay..." I mutter, still stunned.

"You two will have fun! Luke can let you meet his friends, and you'll get to say you are an interplanetary jet setter!" My mom says, trying desperately to convince me that this isn't absurd.

"Woah, I have to meet his friends? I haven't even introduced him to Maula."

"Oh, well, I guess you can do that later." She starts back into her room.

"Wait," I cut in, stopping her retreat.

"Hm?"

"I want to bring Maula with us," I remark.

"Okay, that is fine." She shrugs indifferently before continuing her path.

Luke looks at me, confusion lining his features. "Okay, so I guess we have to pack now. Or should we go grab your friend? I'm lost, this was supposed to be a vacation..." Wincing, he scratches his head.

I give it some thought. "Let's go see if Maula even wants to go, that way she has equal time to pack and all."

I signal Luke to follow me down to the lobby. He obliges,

and we get to our bikes. "You probably shouldn't bring that with you to Earth," I joke, hoping to add some light to the situation. "So, if you want to drive both of us around today, that is fine."

Laughing, he nods. "Yeah, that works. I'll just need directions."

I climb onto his bike, wrapping my arms around his waist, because I'll be damned if he accidentally throws me off. We head out of the building, and I signal for him to follow a direct path out of the city.

A left, a right, straight for a while, some more lefts. All the basic directions I drill into him as we make our way to Maula's house.

Past the lush trees and bleak paths, we reach my old neighborhood. I tell Luke to stay back, and I go up to her house.

I attempt to knock three times, but an excited Maula opens the door on the second. "Hi!"

"Well, that was quick."

"I was actually about to leave. You aren't special." She grins, a mischievous glint blooming in her eyes.

I chuckle, but only for a second. "I have an... odd proposal."

"I am not marrying you."

"Ha-ha, very funny. No, that is not what I'm here to ask." Pausing briefly to ensure she's listening, I only continue when she dips her chin. "Would you like to accompany me on a week-long trip to Earth?"

She ponders my offer for a second, shrugs. "Sure."

My shock is evident in my countenance. "Really? Just like that?"

"Yeah, I mean, classes are out, I have nothing else to do. It would be nice to spend more than a day with you, because you've been missing for a bit."

"Yeah, sorry about that." I blush.

"I assume he is the reason?" She points at Luke, who is staring at the ground beneath his bike.

"Yep. That is the President's son. He is coming too, so you'll have time to get to know him."

She smirks. "Wonderful, I kind of feel like I know him already."

"How so?"

"Well, besides already being his personal shopper, you can't deny that he looks exactly like Marin-"

"I wouldn't say *exactly*." I cut her off. I don't want to hear about it. "Anyway... We leave tomorrow, so make sure you have everything packed!"

"Short notice, but that's fine. I'm not lazy like you, so I should be quick." She hugs me goodbye before she closes the door.

I jog back to Luke's bike and quickly hop on. "She seems nice!" He says, a smile beaming on his face.

"Yeah, she is great." She truly is, which is why I don't want to leave the planet without her. If I have to deal with a whole planet of humans, I can't do it alone.

I guess Luke had to do it alone, but at least he had his dad. No matter how strained their relationship may be, his dad was here. And yet, for some reason, my mom is sending me alone.

ONCE WE ARE BACK IN OUR RESPECTIVE APARTMENTS, I begin packing. I lay out seven different outfits, complete with accessories and all. I start putting them into my suitcase when I hear a knock at the door.

"Hey! Can you help me out?" It's Luke.

"Sure... What can I do for you?"

"I seem to be missing a few days of pajama tops, and I am doing my best to take your advice. So, if you have any of those stretch-tops, I'd be extremely grateful for them."

"Do you need *that* many? I mean, we will have a washer and dryer, right?"

He looks at me with horror. "I never repeat an outfit."

"Well, I mean, it's just pajamas."

His brow furrows in disbelief. "Just pajamas? Every outfit can be a fashion statement."

"I guess that's why you go virtually nude every night. Fashion." I mumble.

"Hmm?" He glares down at me.

"Nothing, just come and pick some." I let him in and send him to my room.

He selects a few shirts, then heads back to his room. I quickly realize I'm almost out of shampoo, so I go bother him to return the favor.

"Can you put some shampoo in this bottle for me?" I learned earlier that he uses real shampoo, not that nasty five-in-one stuff, so I know I'm safe with it.

"Fine." He pours some in and promptly shuts his door.

The day continues in this fashion: one of us realizes we don't have something, then we run to the other begging for scraps. This relay race of trip-prep would be comical if not so stressful, but it could be a funny story for the future.

Once I'm finished packing, I return to my living room. My mom is drinking a cup of tea while reading something on a tablet. "Hello, Mother." I say, taking a seat next to her.

"Hello, Starchild." She caresses my face with her free hand and pats my back. "I saw your little circus with Luke just now; that was cute to watch."

"How do you mean?" I'm honestly disgusted by that comment. Us, cute? I don't think so.

"I mean, both of you scrambling to get your stuff together for this trip, helping each other out and all. It shows me that maybe we can all get along here."

"Oh, okay."

"So, did Maula say yes?"

"Yeah! I'm really excited she will come along."

She smiles. "You should be. Luke didn't get to come with anyone, so I'm glad you get to bring her."

"But he did come with someone. His father."

"That's true, and I am so sorry I can't come with you, Lunion." She grabs my hand. "We still have some stuff to sort out here, so I'm not quite free from work just yet. I promise it will all be worth it, so just enjoy life until they leave."

Not the work-abandoning act I was hoping for, where she comes along to Earth and we have an equally jarring and exciting family vacation. Still, I'll take it.

I get up to leave, but she stops me. "I love you, Lunion. And even if you are out in the galaxy with millions of stars, you'll still be my favorite Starchild forever." She kisses my forehead lightly.

"I love you too," I respond. Through all the flash and pizzazz of senatorial life, I often forget she is still a mother at heart, and motherly she will be.

I retreat to my bedroom, mentally preparing for my trip before eventually falling asleep. Tomorrow, I will be en route to Earth.

I awake with a start. Something feels off, like I woke up too early. I check my alarm, and I still have three hours before I am supposed to be awake. I toss and turn for about an hour, but still can't fall back asleep.

Giving up, I start getting ready instead. With a simple shrug, I throw on a robe and head for my shower. It takes no time for the warm water to cover my body, lathering it in a steamy embrace. I actually prefer colder showers, but I'm too tired to change the temperature. And while the heat is starting to make me tired, it's too late to go back to sleep.

Maybe I'll get to sleep on the ship ride to Earth. Or maybe Luke will be annoying and keep me awake for too long. I make it through my shower without falling asleep, and throw on some clothes. Returning my soap and hair products to my bags, I make sure everything is together one last time.

Hygiene products, clothes, and any unnecessary items I personally want, like stuffed animals, are all packed, so I go to my living room.

Not wanting to start my trip hungry, I make some pancakes. With the sweet scent still lingering in the air, I eat them quietly, standing at the kitchen counter to stay awake.

I still have about an hour before I need to be in the lobby, so I watch a show on my tablet, *The Singing Vision*. It's a singing competition show where everyone appears as a virtual version of themselves before getting judged by a panel of celebrities. Not the most stimulating form of entertainment, but I don't have anything better to be doing.

After two episodes, I hear a knock on my door. Opening it, Luke greets me, but my expression doesn't match the dumb grin on his face.

"Are you ready?" He asks excitedly.

"Sure." I grab my bags and follow him down to the lobby. We walk out to find a car waiting for us. It has two rows and an open back, which appears to be for our luggage. Some U.S. personnel take our bags and stow them in the trunk area.

The car follows some sort of navigation system, which takes us down an even longer route to get to Maula's house than the one I'm familiar with.

We reach the neighborhood, and the driver gets out to get Maula. She comes bursting out of her house, bags in hand. A worker takes her luggage and, as she makes a mockingly dignified expression, he places them in the trunk.

"Hey, Lunion!" She slides next to me, pushing Luke and me together before she offers him a wave. "And Luke."

"Hi Maula, it's very nice to meet you!" He shakes her hand, having to reach over me to do so.

"Likewise!" She smiles at him, then returns her focus to me. "So, when do we get to see this ship? I'm really excited!"

Luke speaks up, "I think we are nearing a ship field! I just hope it isn't an eyesore like the last one..." He sighs, then stares out the car window dramatically.

Maula cocks her head in confusion.

"The ship he arrived on was fucking ugly." I clarify.

"Got it. Well, here's to hoping this one isn't hideous." She laughs, making a fake cheer motion with a handful of air, and I can't help but grumble.

12

LUKE

"That is so fucking ugly," Lunion says indignantly, almost sounding offended. The ship before us is practically a smaller version of the one I came here in. It has the same confusing shape, with a mix of circular and rectangular protrusions, now just slightly diminished.

"I agree." Maula mimics a vomiting action and chuckles. "I can't wait to see the interior!"

"Oh, it's not any better," I add, remembering the inconsistent structure of literally everything onboard.

A team of attendees leads up to the loading zone, bringing our bags with them as we follow closely behind, crossing the ramp that'd nearly killed me last time. Out of fear, I run into the ship, leaving Maula and Lunion confused.

"What are you doing, Luke?" Lunion asks, then is almost immediately answered as the ramp snaps back. "Oh, shit!" He jumps onto the ship before nearly falling. "Who built this? I'm suing."

"AI," I respond. "Almost killed me last time."

"Ew, that is just wonderful," Lunion grumbles, taking his bags from an attendant and moving further into the ship.

We enter the lobby, and the space mirrors its larger counterpart. The interior decor features a mix of rectangles, triangles, and polygons up to decagons. It is truly atrocious.

"What the hell am I looking at?" Maula asks, stunned.

"I don't-" Before I can finish, she cuts me off.

"How stupid are you humans?" She begins pacing and yelling "What the fuck?" every time she finds a new shape hidden in a wall, door, or table.

An attendant grabs our attention and takes us to the lodging areas as he points at Maula. "So, we didn't exactly expect you to be on this trip."

"Sorry?" She frowns, clearly unamused.

"Anyway, that just means that the boys will share a room. We were able to grab an extra bed, and there is plenty of space for your belongings."

Lunion and I look at each other and sigh. "Fine," I mutter before turning to her.. " Look at you Maula! You get a whole room to yourself." I offer sarcastically.

"I may be visiting you at night, fair warning," Lunion remarks desperately.

"I am not that bad!" I shout. "Sorry, that was loud."

Lunion throws a look at Maula as if to say, "See what I mean?"

Lunion and I retreat to our room, and I race to throw my belongings on the bed I want.

"I'll take this one." Lunion and I state unanimously.

Of course we both want the same one, which happens to be slightly more elevated than the other.

"You can have it." I turn toward him with a shrug. "See, I'm not so bad."

Lunion rolls his eyes at my display of valor. Ignoring his

annoyance, I put my bags down on the other bed and begin taking out the clothes I will need for tonight and tomorrow.

Some pajamas I borrowed from Lunion, or stole, depending on who you ask, and an outfit for tomorrow. Grabbing my shower bag, I place it in the bathroom we are sharing. Once satisfied with my set-up, I wander over to Maula's room and knock on the door.

"Come in!" She shouts, her voice slightly muffled.

Nudging the door open, I peer inside, glancing around her room and noting the single bed. "Hey Maula! Thanks for coming along. You seem cool, and I'm sure you'll help Lunion feel comfortable on Earth."

"Yep, no problem. I can't tell if Lunion likes you or hates you, so I'll withhold judgment. Well, for now, anyway. You have a week to make me like you, so I suggest you use the time wisely!" She hums, walking toward me.

"Oh yeah, I can't tell either," I respond, following her.

"I can. You're really annoying." Lunion exits our room, smiling. Even after the time we spent together on Nalia, I still can't tell if he is joking or being serious.

"Anyway," I grumble, heading towards the lobby. "We should get food."

We reach the cafeteria area, which is significantly down-sized on this ship. Based on my last flight, it appears they chose the ship with *only* a Panda Express on board.

"Oh. Looks like we only have one option. You guys will love it!"

They both agree to order the same thing I do, and we find a spot to sit down and eat.

"You've got to be kidding me." Maula stares at the table. "Why is it shaped like that?"

Lunion laughs. "I think we've learned to stop questioning it."

I don't eat immediately, and instead wait for them to, their reactions priceless. "What the hell! No, this is from hell! It's so hot!" Maula yells, her face heating.

"Oh, come on. It's just orange chicken." I say, confused. "It's like the mildest thing on the menu."

Lunion comes to her rescue. "I can handle my spice, and this is nowhere near mild; try it for yourself!" Shoving his plate toward me, he fans his mouth.

I take a bite, and I can immediately feel my face getting hot. Flames engulf my tastebuds, almost like I've tried to be one of those fire-breathing entertainers but failed horribly. "Oh shit! I think they fucked up the machine."

Running to get something, *anything,* to stop the feeling, I settle on a glass of soda, which isn't the best thing to offset the spice, but it's better than water.

Once the heat dies down, we go back to the cafeteria to order teriyaki chicken instead, which, fortunately for us, isn't messed up.

"Okay, this is actually good," Lunion says between bites.

"Yeah, I'm glad this came out right." Maula rolls her eyes.

We finish our meals quickly and head to our rooms. Lunion takes a shower first, so I wait on my bed until he's done. He comes out of the bathroom in his pajamas, which are covered with small pink birds. Somehow, his black hair is even darker when wet, and hugs his head like a helmet. Some curls stick out, giving it a cartoonish look.

"Love the birds." I tease, raising my eyebrows.

"Don't even start," he scoffs, flopping on his bead. "At least I wear clothing."

"Whatever."

I go take a shower. To my surprise, the water is warm, well, until it isn't. The heat only lasts for about ten minutes before abruptly switching to a cold so jarring I jump out of the shower.

"Shit!"

"Are you okay?" Lunion questions from outside.

"Yeah." I throw on my pajamas and brush my teeth, then head out to the bedroom. "The water temperature suddenly decided to plunge me into an icebox."

"Nice, I love cold showers." He says, without a hint of sarcasm.

"You are a freak," I huff incredulously.

Falling down on my bed, I try to go to sleep. All the lights flicker off on their own, but Lunion is still slightly illuminating the room. I'm about to ask him if he is still awake, but his snore from above answers my question. Tightly closing my eyes, I turn over, covering my head with the blanket.

A YELL WAKES ME.

"Bitch!" Maula shouts from the lobby.

Forcing myself out of bed, I stumble down the hall to investigate. Rounding the corner, I spot the two of them, one of the tables now serving as a surface to play ping-pong on And, to my surprise, they're using actual paddles and a ball.

"Where did you get this stuff from?" I ask, rubbing my eyes.

"I brought it with me," Lunion scoffs, like it should have been obvious. "I'm gonna beat you again, Maula. 7-0!" He bounces back and forth in anticipation of her hit, and acts swiftly once the ball is on his side. Returning it with great force, he leaves Maula unable to act fast enough, and wins.

Maula throws her hands up in surrender before tossing her paddle at me. "You try."

"Is that necessary? I just woke up." I question querulously.

"Yes," they both say definitively.

With a groan, I take the paddle and serve the ball. Lunion returns it with shocking force, but I'm still able to send it back. We volley the ball back and forth for a good while, but I get the upper hand. Slamming the ball to the side opposite where he was standing, he fails to return the hit.

"Excuse me?" He seethes, unable to believe that I beat him.

"Is that all you have got?" While I may have won, he put up a fight, and I am not eager to play him again.

"No! Let's do it again." So we do—for five more rounds— and I beat him every single time. Each game shortens as Lunion grows more tired. "Maula, grab my extra paddle."

"What are you going to do with another paddle?" Wiping the sweat from my brow, I cock it in his direction.

"We will both be playing you. Yes, she sucks-"

"Hey!" She yells back.

He continues without bothering to address her. "But she can be defense or... *something*."

I shake my head. "I don't think there is defense in ping-pong."

Maula quickly returns with the third paddle and takes Lunion's side of the table. He spikes the ball at me and I send it back with ease. They both scramble for it and end up smacking into each other and falling to the floor.

"I got it!" Lunion shoots up and tries to hit a ball that is no longer airborne.

"Maybe you two should formulate a plan before you try anything..." I joke, trying to hide my smile.

"Yes. Okay, so Maula, you take the left, I'll take the right."

The two of them work somewhat well together for another

five rounds, all of which I still win. It's getting pathetic, so I "slip" when trying to hit a serve from Lunion and lose.

"Yes! We did it, let's quit while we are on top." Lunion puts his paddles away and sits down at another table, his grin something I find myself focusing on.

THE SHIP MAKES A *DING* NOISE, AND WE ALL LOOK out of a window. Earth is in view, and the ship slowly descends into the atmosphere. Luckily, we have discovered how to minimize heat-related issues in the atmosphere, so the spacecraft runs no risk of burning up during landing.

After about half an hour of Maula and Lunion gawking at the rows of buildings below, we land on a strip near D.C. The ship speeds down the landing strip, slowing rapidly as its wheels drag against the rough asphalt.

We stop moving, and the ramp unfolds onto an open lot. A car waits for us, and with it about five dozen U.S. soldiers. "Lots of, uh, backup."

"I am the President's son, so you'll want to get used to it." I laugh nervously.

This is actually unusual. Do they have fears outside of my safety?

The three of us, with our bags in hand, follow the ramp down to the car. A man in a black suit takes our belongings and stows them in the back of the large black van with highly tinted windows—a bulletproof layer.

The vehicle drives onward, taking us out of the ship port and towards downtown D.C. We wind past shops, oddly parked cars, and homeless camps before arriving at the White

House. Upon our arrival, we are led through a back entrance and to our rooms.

I return to my space, which feels nothing but sweet due to my time off-planet. My music collection and stuffed animals bring comfort with the familiar curtains and ornate windows. After a few minutes of lying on my bed with Samantha and staring at the ceiling, I go to check on Lunion.

"How's it going?" I say melodically while wrapping my knuckles on his door frame.

He finishes putting his things away. "Fine, I guess." He walks towards me. "I didn't realize it would be so... lavish here. I kind of assumed all of Earth was a hell-hole."

"I mean, it kind of is. We have huge housing and healthcare problems. Honestly, don't even get me started." I sigh and look at him. "I'll try to find something fun for us to do, but it won't be as amazing as buying a hover bike."

He chuckles nervously, obviously trying to process the new environment. "Yeah, Nalia is pretty amazing."

I nod and we exchange a handful of words before I decide to head back to my room. We got in late, and sleep calls for me, but one thought settles in the back of my mind.

I hope I don't disappoint him.

13

LUNION

I awake in a sea of crimson, soft blankets hugging my body as I stir. Sitting up, they fall, and behind me are silk maroon pillows traced in sumptuous gold trim. The ceiling above is draped in whipped cream, and the floor below is covered in a deep blood-red carpet, and the curtains hang elegantly on metallic beams. From the windows, a soft beam emanates, illuminating the room wholly and without discrimination.

So this is how the President lives, in garishly regal, grandiose, and gratuitous flair. The room is lined with intricate embellishments, exotic insignia, and paintings of past Presidents; it's only a guest room.

A soft knock sounds on the large, white door before me. "Lunion?" *Luke.* "Rise and shine." Without warning, he opens the door, and to my surprise, he is fully decked out in slightly elegant daywear.

"Hi," I groan, rubbing my eyes.

"Sleep well?" he asks, brown irises shimmering as he tries to hide his laughter.

"Yeah." Focusing my vision on his face, I notice the restraint that contorts it. "What?"

"It is 12:00 p.m.."

"What?" I shoot out of bed, throwing the red comforter and duvet even farther from my body.

"Yes, now if you want to eat, get dressed and come down-stairs. I'll save a seat for you." He says quietly, backing out of the room. This new poise in Luke is jarring, but I do as he says and quickly go downstairs.

"Oh, hey Maula, did you get up on time?" I ask, looking at Maula as she eats a burger.

She yawns, "Nope. I woke up about ten minutes ago. The adjustment is crazy."

"So, you can choose between McDonald's or what the staff has made, which is a salad bar and some pizza." Luke offers, slowly taking his seat at the grand table.

"What's McDonald's?"

"Some fast-food chain. His dad loves it apparently, and I can see why!" Maula hums, trying her best to clear my confusion.

"Okay." Ignoring her enthusiasm. I go for the salad bar instead. I don't need to gain weight on this trip, and I've heard plenty of things about American food.

Once I have my plate, I take a seat next to Luke, still leaving plenty of seats along the table. The three of us don't talk much during our meal, so we end up finishing pretty quickly.

Luke leads the two of us out of the house and toward a small black car. He waves at the side mirror until a window is lowered, then yells, "Hey, Hopper!"

A strong-looking man with dark hair and sunglasses exits from the driver's side and waves back at Luke. "Hey, sir! How's it going?"

"Great!" Luke responds as this newly-named Hopper opens the back door for us.

We all slide in, ending up in the same lineup as in the car on Nalia.

"Where to?" Hopper asks.

"The bowling alley!" Luke's reply carries excitement.

Hopper laughs, "You know you have one here, right? Am I just doing a circle around the lawn?"

"No, I want to give these two the true American experience, so I want to go to a *real* bowling alley."

"Okay, whatever you want, just know that those can be kind of nasty."

Without another word, Hopper starts the car and begins driving. We pass many buildings, some of which appear to be residential, and head to the highway.

From the middle seat, I can't see much, but I notice sparse trees and a river beside the road. The water seems murky, almost mahogany-colored, and the trees look sullen. It's not a vibrant display of nature—not like back on Nalia.

After a dull ride, we arrive at a building titled *Lucky Strikes Bowling Center,* a flashy sign lined with balls and large white shapes marking it.

"Come on!" Luke motions for us to follow him inside, and all three of us do so. I assume Hopper is also some form of security, which makes sense given his frame.

We enter *Lucky Strikes,* and the noise of heavy objects pounding the floor fills the entire room. Large lanes lined with luminous bulbs lead to a cluster of white, oddly shaped... things.

"What are we doing here?" I groan. "Is this some sort of art installation? I've heard about modern art, and this seems like one of those weird interactive pieces."

Luke looks at me with a visage of terror-infused glee. "What? You don't have bowling on Nalia?"

"Nope," Maula and I say in unison.

"Okay, so what you want to do is go pick out some shoes and a ball that has a weight you're comfortable with." Luke guides us to a counter, where I grab a pair of size ten shoes and a twelve-pound ball.

I feel accomplished with my selection until I see his fifteen-pound ball.

"Now, you want to roll the ball with enough force and precision that you hit the pins." He explains, then quickly adds, "You get two rolls per frame, and your pins don't reset until the next frame."

"Uh, okay... I think I've got it." Walking up to the kiosk, the screen demands that I enter our names. I want to put something annoying instead of "Luke," but I struggle to think of anything else.

Strategically, I put myself last and Luke first, so I can learn the game before I even try to play. Luke walks up steadily to the first row of arrows on the floor, lines himself up with the two to the left of the center, and gracefully strides to the lane. He softly, yet forcefully, throws the ball, sending it flying towards the cluster of pins.

The ball tucks between the middle pin and the second row, and all the pins come cascading down one by one, like rapid dominoes. "Yes!" He yells, spinning around and doing a little twirl in the air. Immediately, his cheeks heat, and he deepens his voice, quietly saying, "Strike."

"Good job!" Maula screams, "Shit! I have to follow that?"

Walking to the line with a confident swagger, she rolls the ball and watches disappointedly as it falls straight in the gutter, missing every pin. "Aww, dammit!" Maula cries as she walks toward us. "Oh, I get another turn! That's right!" She storms back up, a new ball in hand, and practically tosses onto the track.

She only hits one pin, but that is good enough for her. "Yes! Perfect. You two have nothing on me." Laughing, she takes a seat next to Luke.

Luke, for some reason, starts a chant. "Lunion! Lunion! Lunion!"

Maula joins in, "Lunion! Lunion! Lunion!"

Unable to stop laughing, their chanting distracts me, and I only hit one pin. *"Oh."* Waiting for my ball to come back, I try again. This time, I carefully aim just next to the middle, and knock down the remaining pins. "Yes!"

"You got a spare! Good job, Lunion!" Luke congratulates me before continuing onto the next frame. He dominates the rest of the game, and I do surprisingly well.

We maintain our general skill sets throughout the round, and our scores end with Luke at 250 points, Maula at 54, and me with 168.

"You know what, I'll take it. As a first-time player, I think I did pretty well!" I give myself the accolades that Maula also imputes to herself, declaring herself the bowling champion.

Luke shows us to an arcade in the back and gives us cards charged with points to play the games. "Guys, check this one out first!" He leads us to a giant machine filled to the brim with stuffed animals, a giant claw dangling from the ceiling of it.

"Oh yeah, we have these on Nalia. The crane, right?" I ask.

"The fuck? It's *the claw.*" He says it like it should be obvious, but starts laughing like I was in on the joke the whole time.

I chuckle nervously and swipe my card. "Okay, I want that thing." It's a large green animal with some sort of shield on its back.

"Okay, get that turtle!" Luke grabs my shoulders in excitement, which sends a shudder through my body. I'm already on edge, and I can't tell if I welcome the gesture or if I'm going to be sick.

Still, I power through and fish for the... turtle. The claw grabs perfectly around the creature's body and carries it most of the way to the dispenser bin before the turtle flies from its grasp. "You've got to be kidding me!" Sighing, I give up.

"You're just gonna leave it?" Luke questions.

"Yeah, I mean, did you see how many points that one attempt took?"

He glances down at the scanner. "Shit! 25 points?"

"Ew, yeah, Lunion is right." Maula chimes in. "Let's try this one." She leads us to a two-player machine, which allows one player to be a duck and the other to be a chicken. It reads *Crossy Road* in large, blocky letters.

"You two have got this one," Stepping back, I let them play, watching as they try to avoid cars, trains, and buses. They both do poorly, but Luke beats Maula's score by 24 points.

"Hey, Lunion!" Luke yells from a game across the room. "Do this one with me. I can pay for it!"

He waves me over to a machine that reads *BLADES*, and has a knight on the cover. He swipes his card for both slots, illuminating two identical characters, one blue and one pink. We fight corrupted lizards, each with plants protruding from their eyes, chests, and open, dangling organs.

We clear levels 1 through 19 with ease, but we lose once we reach level 20. With the lizard creatures too great in numbers, they overtook us far too quickly for us to react.

"Good effort. But let's go get some food." Luke slides his game card into his pocket and finds Maula in the labyrinth of machines. "Hey, do you want to come get snacks with us?"

"I'm good! Just get me a drink. I think I tried Dr. Pepper earlier, so I'll have that again. Come get me when the food is done! Thank you!" She throws a hand heart at us and continues playing *Crossy Road*, trying her best to beat the high score.

Luke and I reach the concession counter, and the worker happily welcomes us. "Hey boys, what can I get for you two?" she asks with a smile.

"Hey, Ma'am! Could we get two Dr. Peppers and some fries?" He turns to me. "What would you like?"

"Oh, I'll take a Dr. Pepper, too, and we can just share the fries?"

"That works with me. Okay, so we need three Dr. Peppers and an order of fries!" he says, correcting his order to include mine.

"Wonderful, just tap here, and we will have that food out in no time!" Luke does as she says, tapping his card on the tablet, and pays for our food.

"Thank you so much," He says, smiling at her as he takes a number to mark our order. We drift to an empty table and stick the piece of paper in a metal holder for the waiters to see.

"Thanks for the food, Luke," I mumble, taking a deep breath to decompress.

"Of course," he replies with a smile. "Would you excuse me for a moment? I am going to go find the bathroom." He waits for my confirmation, then leaves the table politely.

Alone with my thoughts, I am left to unravel. My mind processes the entire day from the bottom up. From drowning in drapery to getting a private car. Going to unfamiliar places to play unfamiliar games. The confusing feelings about everything, the confusion as a whole. Earth is nothing like Nalia, and no amount of research could have prepared me for it.

Staring at the empty table, I begin to cry.

14

LUKE

The bathroom is the least of my worries, honestly. I've had very little to drink today. What is on my mind is that turtle that Lunion wants, and I intend to get it. It's obvious he's on edge, and at this point, I'll do anything to calm him down.

To be fair, he is doing a pretty good job of hiding how he feels, but I know when someone is using their publicity skills to hide their emotions. I know what it means when someone jolts at a fundamental touch, and I know what it means when someone with as much tenacity as Lunion gives up on small tasks.

I also know that, despite being separated soon, I am doomed. Doomed to run out of time getting to know him, and more importantly, doomed to fall for him. That night at the grove solidified my attraction towards him, and my feelings have only grown since.

So maybe, once I can make the grand gesture of winning him an insanely expensive turtle, he will understand that I'm more than just a dumb human. Maybe he can realize that I could be a dumb boyfriend, too.

I tap my card against the giant machine and drop the claw. It contorts around the turtle, and again, drops it at the last second. I try again and again but no progress is made. A worker walks by, and I capitalize on the opportunity. "Hey!"

"Can I help you? I'm about to go on my vape break," he mutters, clearly annoyed.

"Yeah, how much can I pay you to get that turtle out for me?" I point at the stuffed animal.

"Forty bucks."

"Okay, that was a... fast decision. Here." I load $40 onto my tablet and tap it against his, transferring the money seamlessly.

"Got it," he confirms, as if he doubted my honesty, and bends down to unlock the machine. In much less time than it took me to try to win the turtle, the worker hands it off to me and locks the machine.

With the stuffed animal secured, I am ready to return fraudulently victorious to Lunion. I pace back to the seating area and find him sitting at a table in silence. "Lunion!" I wave at him as I approach, so that I don't startle him. "Look!"

Smiling weakly, he takes it from me and hugs it, a weak smile growing on his face. "Aww, thank you." He closes his eyes and lays his head on the table, and I can't help but notice that he looks... sad.

"Are you okay?" I ask.

He looks up, wiping a tear from his face and putting on a performative grin. "Yeah, I'm fine. Sorry, this is all just a lot. Like, a lot, a lot."

"Yeah? I felt the same way about Nalia." I laugh, trying to lighten the mood. "If it helps at all, I can say that you definitely made me feel at home, and I hope I can return the favor. Though I doubt Earth can beat Nalia."

"Is that so?" He raises his head a little more.

"One hundred percent yes. If I could move to Nalia, I honestly would. It's perfect there."

This seems to bring him some comfort. "Yeah, my planet is definitely better than yours." He smirks, returning to his normally cheerful and sarcastic self.

Going to tease him further, I stop as a realization settles in my gut. "We never went to get Maula..."

"The food isn't out yet, and she said to get her when it was. I think we are okay," he says, but I don't think he even believes his attempt at reassurance.

"I can keep our table; you should probably go find her."

"Yeah, you're right." Lunion sets down his turtle and goes to find Maula. Within a few minutes, they both appear at the table. Quickly after their arrival, the food we ordered is set down in front of us.

"I love Dr. Pepper," Maula groans matter-of-factly, taking a long swig. "What do you think, Lunion?"

"Can we take five tons of this stuff back with us? Please?" He looks at me pleadingly. "I will give you my life savings, just please smuggle some onto the ship." He grabs my hand to continue his entreaty, and I try my best not to react.

"Okay! Fine, I will try to get some on the ship." I sip my Dr. Pepper dramatically, as if to show that I am exhausted from the craze. Though I didn't mind the careless contact with him, even if it was in jest.

We finish the fries quickly, then get up to throw away our trash. I'm about to suggest leaving when I hear a shrill voice from behind. "Luke?"

Another piercing timbre yells, "It is you! Where have you been?"

I turn around, annoyed at the sight. "Hi Chloe, Hi Renee."

"Well, don't leave us hanging! Where have you been? And

who are they?" Chloe asks, scanning Maula and Lunion for flaws.

"I've been off-planet, on Nalia," *Father said I should introduce people, so why not start here?* "This is Lunion," I motion towards him. "He is a Senator's son, and this is his friend, Maula."

"Oh. My. God." Renee drags it out, like a smoky cigarette that she wants to let linger in the air. "So nice to meet you two…" She shakes their hands hesitantly, like she is picking up someone else's trash.

"Yes, a pleasure," Chloe adds, keeping her distance.

Renee's eyes light up, like she just found a creative solution to world hunger, or at least her own thirst for drama. "Let's all play a round! What do you say, Luke?"

She looks Lunion up and down, from his hair to his pale limbs, then sends me a "really?" look.

"Fine," I concede. "Let's all play a round." We follow the pair to a new lane and enter our names. The lineup places Lunion after me again, but puts Maula first.

"Oh, guys, I am wonderful at this. I'm going to beat you all." Maula laughs, but only Lunion and I reciprocate.

She gets a few pins, but not a spare, and sits down with a huff.

I'm up, but I am extremely off my game, and I only get eight pins. "Damn," I say, trying to act surprised.

"You'll get 'em next time," Lunion chimes in, trying to cheer me on while maintaining his carefree attitude.

A few more rounds go by, and we lose interest. After my turn, Lunion finds the ground far more enticing, and I can't help but wonder if he may have even spaced out.

Chloe's shrill voice fills the room. "Seth, it's your turn."

"Huh?" Maula says, oblivious to Chloe's little game.

"Oops, sorry," Chloe whines. "This one is Lunion, my bad." She grins mischievously, and tries to get his attention one more time. "Lunion!"

"Oh, sorry." He gets up to take his turn. .

I take this break in chatter to excuse myself. "I'm going to head to the bathroom. I'll be right back." As I turn away from the group, I can already feel tears welling up in my eyes.

I dash into the bathroom, find a stall to hide in, and lock the door poorly through my tears. All I can do is lean against the wall, hands on my head, crying like an idiot.

I hear a knock on my stall. "How did you get in here? Whoever it is, Chloe, Renee, I don't care. Please leave."

"Well, I got in because I am a guy, and I am also neither of them." Lunion's voice flows in from behind the door.

"What?" I open the door slowly with the question, and Lunion looks at me with heightened unease.

"*What?* You can't be crying! I am the one falling apart. You can't take my job."

"Sorry," I mumble, trying to get the tears to stop.

"What happened?" Lunion asks, genuinely concerned.

"Those two. They are always trying to start drama; they don't care about me at all. They ridicule me for everything I do, and keep jumping down my throat until I crack." I am crying even more now, tears running down my cheeks. They fall onto my sleeves, darkening them with a sorrowful hue.

"Oh." Lunion isn't the best at being serious, but he tries. He hugs me, which only makes me cry more, and he retreats in shock. "I'm sorry! What did I do?"

"No, you're okay." I hug him again. "I just don't want to deal with them anymore."

"Then let's leave," he states, a hint of decisiveness in his tone.

"How? They are probably out there waiting like lions stalking their prey."

"One moment." He takes out a tablet, sends a message, and turns back to me. "Tell Hopper to get the car ready."

"Okay..." I do as he suggests and message Hopper.

"Come on, you're the strong one." Lunion moves toward a window, nodding at it with increasing speed.

"Really?"

"You want to leave, right?"

"Yeah." I push the window up and get out first. Lunion climbs out after me, and I try to catch him, even if the drop is less than two feet.

"Hey guys!" Maula waits for us in front of the car, Lunion's turtle in her hands. "Hurry up!"

"Okay, this is not a police chase," I laugh through my few remaining tears.

We all file in, and I take the middle seat.

"Thanks, Hopper!" Lunion says, giving the driver a tap on the shoulder.

"No problem, but that was a little dramatic, right?" He asks, obviously ecstatic by the humorous escape.

"No, it was completely necessary," Maula huffs, indignant terror prevalent in her tone. "Those were *piranhas*. You two left me alone with them." Pausing, she puts a hand up. "Actually, I don't want to talk about it."

We follow the highway back home, passing the same sights as before, but this time with a more colorful sky, one painted with the vibrant pastels that can only come from factory pollution.

As we enter the house, a familiar voice yells, "Luke! I've missed you so much!" My mom kicks off her heels and comes running down the stairs, hugging me tightly. She steps back, then looks at me. "Oh no, baby, what's wrong?"

"We can talk about it later," I respond, smiling lightly in her direction.

"No, you two go discuss. Maula and I can play games or something," Lunion offers, patting my arm reassuringly.

"Thank you." I say, and watch as he follows Maula to her room.

"Okay, let's go." My mom links her arm in mine and takes me to the living room. She fluffs some pillows and sits down, holding my hand. "What happened?"

"We were bowling, and that was great. But then, Chloe and Renee showed up."

"Oh." She pointed out their bullshit a *long* time ago.

"They immediately decided that Lunion was a carbon copy of Danny and Seth, and were judging me the entire time. Until Chloe finally just called Lunion 'Seth.'"

"That bitch!" My mom exclaims, a new fury in her eyes.

"I ran to the bathroom and started crying. Luckily, Lunion found me, and we escaped through a window."

"What?"

"Yeah."

"Okay... interesting." She pauses. "Why couldn't you just tell them to fuck themselves and leave through the door?"

"I don't know."

She looks at me, like she isn't getting the whole story. She has always had a skill of knowing exactly when I'm holding out on her, which is one reason I refuse to play poker with her.

"Mhm, so it doesn't have anything to do with you, I don't know, maybe, liking Lunion?"

"Uh-"

"Because it's okay to have a type, Luke. Just make sure you don't hurt his feelings." She hugs me and stands up. "Come on, we are going to go socialize."

"Okay, fine. Please, just don't make me talk about it with anyone else."

"Okay, but let's go socialize." She winks.

She takes me to the lobby and calls for Lunion and Maula. By the end of the day, we are all sitting around a TV, watching her favorite show, Law and Order, in complete silence.

15

LUNION

I'm in a space shuttle, hurtling away from Naila. The planet is still for a minute, then it begins to break out in ruptures, spilling fire from every crevice. I can't help but watch as my home folds in on itself and bursts like a shattered asteroid, littering space with burning soil.

All I can do is cry, cry, cry until I feel a tap on my shoulder. "Lunion? Are you okay?"

My eyes flutter open to see Luke standing over me, fear plastered on his face.

"Are you okay, Lunion?" He takes a step back.

"What?" I shoot up, trying to find a mirror. Tears stain my face, my nose is runny, and my eyes are bloodshot. "Oh, wow."

"I came in to wake you up and found you curled up, crying incessantly." He places a hand on my shoulder and takes a spot next to me, glancing into the mirror with sorrow.

"Sorry, I'm fine. Just a nightmare," I respond, slinking out of his touch to sit back on my bed.

"Do you want anything for breakfast?"

"I guess... Maybe. Uh, I don't know." Taking a deep breath, I run a hand through my hair. "I'm starting to get a headache."

"I can bring you something." He offers me a weak smile and leaves the room.

I feel as if my skull is a broken mirror, each piece reflecting another shard of pain onto itself, maximizing my peril in an endless loop of suffering. Softly holding my head in my hand, I lie down. I pull the covers over my body and curl up again.

"I'm back." Luke sings. He appears in the doorway with a tray of pancakes and a tall glass of what appears to be soda. "Dr. Pepper, you might have a caffeine headache."

"Thank you, Luke." I sit up and begin to eat. After making sure I am stable enough to balance the tray, he gets up to leave. "You don't have to leave," I practically whisper, hoping he will turn around.

"I wish I could stay and talk, but my mom wants me to finalize some plans for today. I'm sorry," he says, leaving the room with a solemn wave.

I finish the pancakes surprisingly quickly despite my headache, but drink my Dr. Pepper more slowly, trying to avoid brain freeze. After about ten minutes, my headache dissolves, and I am convinced that Dr. Pepper is a hallowed beverage.

I get dressed and head downstairs, following a trail of voices into the living room. "Hey," I say to announce my arrival.

"Hi, Lunion!" Luke's mom beams, running over to hug me. "It's so nice to finally, officially meet you! I've heard a lot about Nalia from my husband." It's hard to believe that a woman who would call Nalia by its real name would marry Luke's dad.

"Hi! Sorry for abandoning you two last night," I apologize, my hands holding her own.

"That's my fault, sorry." Luke looks oddly embarrassed.

"Yeah, I blame him, don't worry! And as for our Law and Order time, that's all me. I need silence to consume the drama," his mom teases, then lets go of my hands and sits back down. "Okay, so today, I believe you guys are going to New York," she looks at Luke for confirmation, and he gives her a thumbs-up to answer.

"Cool!" Maula says, excitedly. "Why?"

"Well, going to the city is a very American experience!" His mom continues, "You'll start with a Broadway show, then head to Coney Island!"

"So, musicals and then festival games," Luke explains.

"Great!" Maula responds, growing more anxious to leave.

"Yeah, that sounds amazing. Thank you both so much," I say, surprised that there are actual events planned.

"You guys will probably want to get ready. The flight leaves soon." His mom pushes herself up to exit the room. Stopping briefly, she smiles. "Have fun."

"We will!" Maula runs upstairs to grab her things, and I follow. Luke is ready and has been for what I suspect to be hours.

WE ARE LED ONTO A RUNWAY BY A LEGION OF government agents, travel planners, and security personnel. The plane is actually a small yet roomy private jet filled with mini fridges and rows of individual cushioned seats.

We all take our seats, forming a triangle so we can all talk on the flight.

"Thank you, Luke. This is really exciting!" Maula claps her hands together.

"Yeah, thank you," I agree, talking softly to avoid regaining a headache.

"Of course, you guys deserve it." He's only looking at me when he says it, but quickly turns away after.

The jet takes off, propelling us from the ground straight into the cloudless sky. Despite the lack of clouds, a tint of gray lingers behind the jet's circular windows, filling the sky with a somber note of disparity.

"What's up with that?" I ask, pointing at the slightly darkened atmosphere.

"Air pollution, we travel *so* much by air now, and it isn't good for the environment at all."

"Wow," I exhale, because we, too, are contributing to the smog.

We travel for over an hour, and the three of us pass the time quickly. From card games to personal anecdotes, our airtime is practically cut in half by the entertainment we create ourselves..

The jet touches down on an obscured strip at LaGuardia, and a car is already there to pick us up.

"Mr. Dinyre." The driver nods at Luke, "Your mother ordered you three Levain." He hands a bag back to us and begins his venture to Broadway.

"I love these!" Luke opens the bag and doles out chocolate chip cookies with the ecstatic edge of a hungry badger. "Go ahead, try one!" he tries to yell, a cookie already in his mouth.

"You are disgusting." I take a bite, "But *this* is amazing." I dramatically grab Maula for support as I linger on the flavor of the cookie.

"What the hell? This is the best cookie I've ever had." Maula mumbles, her eyes wide.

"I'm glad you two have some common sense," Luke teases, finishing his and returning to a normal state.

"Tell your mom thank you, and to order some more..." I say, staring at the last piece of my early dessert.

Luke laughs. "Oh, for sure."

We are quickly past the landing strip, and the skyline of the city is in full view. Tall buildings reach desperately for the sky, and lights struggle for notice under the sun, while a light dust invades the surrounding air of the city.

Soon, we are in the heart of the city. Cars blast by, emitting puffs of smoke and dripping oil as they roll along the one-way streets. Bikes, motor and manual, plague the streets like swift urchins, cutting pedestrians off and weaving between grid-locked cars. The buildings cage us in, covering our view from every side and allowing only a small looking glass up into the sky.

We move begrudgingly through the outlets of Times Square, taking in the screens plastered about the buildings, each advertisement fighting for space in a wild fashion. Lingerie conquers liquor over a museum, 3D illusions distract visitors from the bleak, flat advertisements. Powerful fashion brands are held higher than the lower, less intriguing protest pieces.

Each ad is perfectly tailored to match the diversity of city life. Potential is carried out through spontaneity, and profits are made sporadically, depending on the flow of tourists.

The city is one giant mosaic of desperation and vigor: the desire to pursue something greater, and the strength to make it happen. This consistently inconsistent image is reflected in the car window, entrancing me until we are ushered from the car to a secret entrance of the theatre.

Five guards pile out of a van that parked beside us, and they cover our trio as we venture into the theatre. Once we are inside, three stay behind, and the remaining two flank each side, like we are precious cargo being protected from thieves.

"What show are we seeing?" I ask, realizing I never found out.

"*Wicked*!" Luke says excitedly. "It's the 106th year on Broadway!"

"Wow." I'm stunned. "Really? It hasn't been taken off, like ever?"

"Nope, it's just too good," Luke states matter-of-factly, crossing his arms. "And, my favorite music artist, Lina Rillis, is playing Elphaba for a few more weeks!" His already wide smile grows, and he shakes me up and down, as if I am also a superfan of Lina.

"That's wonderful," I offer, looking at him like he is a crazed toddler.

"Well, I am excited! I don't know what an Elphamo is, but I'm sure it will be great!" Maula speaks up, matching Luke's energy.

"Sir, your seats are ready. Follow me," a guard says, opening a door and leading us through. We are in a private box, kept hidden away from other attendees. "You should be safe here, but I will be around if you need me." The guard nods and tucks himself into a corner.

"Thank you!" Luke says. "Could you get us some Pepsi?" He turns to Maula and me. "They don't have Dr. Pepper here, sorry."

"Sure, sir. I will notify a team member to go and acquire those." He taps an earpiece and mumbles something. In less than five minutes, we have three Pepsis, some themed shirts, and even some bag charms in our hands.

The lights begin to flicker, and Luke motions with his hands for us to pay attention. Suddenly, a jarring trumpet blares, and the opening number commences. What I learn to be munchkins are singing, glorifying someone's murder.

In a blink, Elphaba and Glinda have met, despised each other, slowly warmed up, and have become inseparable. Something about the play feels familiar.

Elphaba and Glinda sing *Defying Gravity*, and my body almost defies gravity, flying to the edge of my seat. My attention is entirely on Elphaba. Lina's vocals are alluringly striking. Every note is hit, held, and mixed to perfection. She approaches each scene with marked deftness in her motions and expressions. Her performance is flawless.

Elphaba flies towards the audience, pulling a large cape behind her as she sails around the theatre. Wires are attached to both her and her broom, lifting her effortlessly as she soars through the auditorium. She belts with sheer perfection, even through the turmoil of flying.

She returns to the stage, the curtains close, and the lights are turned on impromptu.

I get up from my seat. "What? Is that it?" I look at Luke in desperation.

He laughs. "No! This is just the first act."

"Okay, good." I release a great sigh of relief and sit back down.

Maula leans over, offering her two cents. "The flying was impressive!"

"They sent her into the audience around '60," Luke explains. "They decided to spice it up so people would continue to come to shows during the Broadway recession."

"'Broadway recession' sounds absurd, but that's nice," I reply, my face contorted in disbelief. After a short while, the lights flash again, and the musical resumes.

I watch in zealous awe as the rest of the story unfolds before me. Fiyero goes to Elphaba, Glinda cries a lot, and Lina demolishes *No Good Deed*.

Then *For Good* happens, and my jaw is on the floor. Their voices blend in harmony like never before. Even when singing different lyrics, they sound like one unit. A few tears trickle from each of my eyes, and I place one hand on Maula and one on Luke.

The story comes to its finale, and the lights return for the last time.

"Wow. That had an effect on you... I think." Luke says.

I wipe the tears from my eyes. "I don't wish to speak about it."

Maula hugs me. "I love you."

"Damn, emotional as fuck." Luke looks at us, stunned. "Maybe it's just that I've seen this show so many times, so I'm not-"

"Your eyes are red," I say, locking onto his puffy eyes.

"Fine. Lina brought me to tears. I'm not strong enough to survive her siren song." He surrenders. "She was spectacular."

"Time to go, sir." The guard says, emerging from his dark corner.

"Okay." Luke follows him out through the door and we tail them into a wide hallway. "Oh. My. God." Luke stops in his tracks.

"Hey! I don't have much time, but I wanted to give you guys these!" Lina Rillis, still caked in green makeup, is barrelling toward us.

"Lunion, pinch me." I obliged Luke's request. "Ow."

"Here you go!" Lina hands us signed albums and posters and gives each of us a hug. "I've got to go, but your support means the world!" She blows us a kiss and heads back down the hallway.

"She's real." Luke stares at the hallway, even after she is gone.

"Yes, now come on, we have to get to Coney Island," I say, trying to hide my excitement, because I have definitely been converted into a Lina Rillis superfan.

Maybe Luke is right about some things, because that was spectacular.

16

LUKE

I'm talking quietly to a worker at the park, and I can tell Lunion is nervous. Why would I tell him what's up now when I could get a humorous reaction by throwing him into it instead?

"Three karts, please," I whisper.

"Okay," the worker mutters back. "But why are we whispering?"

"Shh." He looks traumatized, but at least he's cute.

"Here you go." He hands me some tickets, then opens the gate to the go-kart track.

"Thanks! Lunion, Maula!" I call them over. "Pick a kart, any kart!"

"Huh?" Lunion looks confused, but there is also a small glint of terror that coats his features.

"Yeah, what is going on?" Maula asks.

"So, we are all going to get into a kart, then we are going to chase each other around with the goal of hitting each other," I beam, ushering toward the track. "Let's go!"

We all find our preferred karts; mine is deep navy blue, Lunion's is bright yellow, and Maula's is a striking lime green.

I hop in, secure my seat belt, and familiarize myself with the controls. The pedals were placed like those of average cars, the ones I never got to drive, but the wheel was much slimmer in width, yet larger in width.

The signal light flickers on, and we go. "Wait!" It's too late, and no one can hear my shout.

I had mistaken the rules for Go Karts and Bumper Karts, so now Lunion and Maula are screwed.

Abandoning the starting line, I zip through the course with ease. As I am about to begin my second lap, I see Maula and Lunion caught, their karts intermingled, wheels locked in a contest—the result of them running into each other.

"Guys! I'm sorry, I got this confused with Bumper Karts. Detangle and finish the race!"

"What?" Lunion yells, not like he didn't hear me, but to indicate that I will be sorry that he *did* hear me. "You are screwed."

"Oops, bye!" I drift past them, hugging the wall to give myself distance. I hear cars getting closer and glance back to see Lunion only a few feet away.

"I'm gonna catch you, Luke!" He somehow gains speed and clips the edge of my kart, pushing me into the side wall. He throws up a middle finger and passes me, completing his first lap.

"Hey bitch!" It's Maula. She is nearing me with enough speed to rival a cheetah, and I'm still stuck against the wall, trying my best to reverse out of the situation.

"Hey..." I reply quietly, hoping she won't hit me.

"Here you go!" She rams into my side, reorienting my kart in my favor. I leap at the opportunity and speed ahead on the track.

In only a few moments, I am back. Lunion matches my pace, and Maula is still on her second lap. Lunion and I continuously pass each other, struggling for power in this silly game.

The finish line is in sight, and all I can do is hope I beat him. I slam my foot against the gas, using all of my weight to cross the line, but so does Lunion.

"I won!" We shout simultaneously.

"Actually..." The worker points at a board. "Same time, 5:01:11."

"Oh," I sigh, glancing over at Lunion. "That's nice, I guess."

"Yeah, so I basically won. I mean, you gave yourself a little head start back there," Lunion argues.

I lift my hands in surrender. "Okay, sure. You are the winner, Lunion."

"Actually, I am!" Maula spins into view. "Seven minutes, and a lot more seconds. That is a winning number to me!" She is always proud of herself, I'll give her that.

"Okay, where are we going next?" Lunion questions, calmed now that I've conceded our tie.

"The aquarium. I've always wanted to go, and now is the perfect time to do so."

"What do you mean?" Lunion cocks his head to the side with the query.

"The Orca, an ocean animal, went extinct a while ago. It preyed on many different animals, which helped balance the population. Without Orcas..."

"The other species will continue to reproduce unchecked and run out of producers to support their populations," Lunion finishes my thought. "Wow, how did you let that happen?"

"Okay, rude. *I* did not let that happen; everyone else did.

Also, very impressive that you know that." Clapping, I give him a little round of applause.

"Well, we have sea life on Nalia too, but we take better care of it," he states without the expected hint of condescension.

"I won't argue that, we kinda suck here."

"Well, let's go!" Maula lifts us from our sullied moods and we leave the main park, heading to the aquarium.

The building is ornate, with intricate yet minimalist architectural details. One white portion bears the word *SHARKS*, but anyone from Earth would know that sharks are rapidly losing enough status to warrant an entire area wholly dedicated to their species.

We enter through the main entrance and are immediately thrown into a room lined with cushioned benches, all facing a large screen. A video collage of sea animals plays behind a voice-over detailing protective measures for sea life, including which species primarily live in captivity.

The narrator points out that sea lions are rapidly declining in number and that the dozen here are among only two thousand left in the world.

"Wow," Lunion sighs after the video finishes, shaking his head as he follows the crowd into the next room. "That's just sad."

Each wall is plastered in glass that holds thousands of gallons of water. Behind it hundreds of different forms of sea life flow among one another. Stingrays are dancing with manatees, both fighting for the spotlight. Jellyfish push against the water, and clownfish dodge them while starfish lie stagnant below. It's as if each creature is struggling for attention, attention from the crowd before them, but also attention from the entire world.

"That's so beautiful." Maula points to a jellyfish, its pink frills emanating from its white bulbous body like a couture gown. "What is it?"

"That is a jellyfish." I gesture toward the info card. "This specific one actually reproduces asexually, budding off to create identical forms of life."

"That's so cool." Lunion is fixated on the jellyfish now, watching it dance around its enclosure with the grace of a trained ballet dancer. "Are there any other types?" he asks, looking at me for assistance in this quest to discover more jellyfish.

"Probably, I mean, they do exist. I haven't been here before, so I wouldn't know where to look." I turn to scan the other walls of the room, my eyes meeting a tank filled with them. "Lunion-"

He's gone from my side and has a worker practically pinned to one of the tanks. "Where can I find more jellyfish?"

"Right over here." She slinks out of his trap and walks the three of us over to the case I had already noticed. "So here we have a bluefire jellyfish, which is part of the Scyphozoa, or 'True Jellyfish,' family of these creatures." Smiling, she walks away, leaving us to gawk at the animal.

Its cup-shaped body covers a bright white glow beneath its blue exterior, making it appear almost chimerical. The mystical sea creature hauls itself past us, flowing quietly to the top of the tank, and receding from our view.

Only after a couple minutes pass do I dare ask, "Are you two ready to move on?"

"Yeah, I am. Maula?" Lunion glances at her for approval, and she nods in return.

I lead us to a circular entryway that opens into a tunnel.

"Woah," I utter near breathlessly, stopping almost as soon as I enter the burrow. "Look at that."

Above a shark swims over us, and I watch as every other

animal moves aside for its approach. It's not aggressive, nor intimidating, just beautifully striking and noticeably confident. It moves upwards, twirling and arching back into the flow of animals, taking its place in a lined loop of constant motion.

"Can I take one home? That thing is so cute," Maula squeals, breaking the silence that overcame our group at the sight.

I laugh. "Maybe a stuffed animal at the gift shop."

"I'm gonna hold you to that." She points at me assertively and starts down the tunnel.

We continue throughout the exhibit, making our way through the various enclosures of sea creatures. As we venture further into the aquarium, we pass starfish, sharks, belugas, stingrays, and a handful of sea life I don't recognize. Finally, we wind up outside in a circular enclosure. The area is covered in concrete, and a large pool sits in the middle. Behind the pool, the surrounding floor is littered with theatrical wooden backdrops of waves. Against the backdrop stands a woman in a wetsuit, holding a cooler. The microphone she wears is wrapped around her ear and positioned near her mouth, making it look as if she is about to begin a speech.

We all take a seat, and the woman speaks up. "Welcome to today's sea lion show!" On her cue, a sea lion darts out from beneath the pool's surface. "This is Harvey, and he is one of just an estimated two thousand remaining sea lions."

Harvey stares up at the worker briefly dipping back into the water. A few moments later, he is back, closer to the audience.

"Well, as you can see, Harvey is excited to play today." She opens her cooler. "So, I am going to throw this fish." Taking one out, she displays it for a few seconds, allowing the crowd to observe. "And Harvey is going to do a trick to catch it."

She takes a few steps back, whistles, and throws the fish

high into the air. Harvey dives deeply into the pool, speeding to where his preferred meal will drop. Suddenly, with a large splash of water, Harvey jumps out of the pool, catches the fish, and does a flip as he falls back down. He hits the water, sending an aqueous ring up as he falls, then he resurfaces.

Harvey and his trainer continue their routine for about ten minutes, and we watch the sea lion leap, flip, turn, and twist for food.

Lunion leans over to whisper in my ear, "Okay, I want one of those."

"Gift shop," I mumble back, chuckling lightly.

Luckily for Maula and Lunion, I keep my promise. After the show, we find the gift shop. The room is filled with turnstile shelves of stuffed animals, ranging from flashy and tacky to natural and realistic.

Somehow, we all split up.

I find Maula gawking at a bright-pink shark tattooed with foil strips of gold. With a smirk, I use this opportunity to my advantage.

"Hey, Maula."

"Hi. Look at this!" She shoves the shark in my face.

"That is wonderful. Can I ask you something?"

"Uh-oh, serious. Sure."

"Do you think Lunion might, I don't know, like me?"

Her eyes widen. "What? Why do you want to-" She nods. "Oh! Got it. Hmm, maybe? I haven't really talked to him about it, but he is super comfortable with you, and you are *definitely* his type."

"Really?" I'm shocked by her somewhat positive response.

"Yeah, maybe it's trauma bonding or something, but you two have been closer than he and I have been this whole trip. If you want, I can find a reason to leave you two alone later?"

"Really?"

"Yeah, you just have to pay for this shark." She says it plainly, like it's nothing more than a business transaction.

"Why not? Okay, sure." I take her shark, tucking it under my arm, and we go to find Lunion.

"Hey, Lunion!" Maula yells across the room.

He stares at a giant wall of sea lions. "Hey, guys."

"Gonna pick one?" I ask, confused.

"They're all so different; how can I choose?"

"They all look the same to me," I state matter-of-factly, looking at the unremarkably identical toys.

"No, look. This one has a messed-up nose, but that's kinda cute. Then this one has a misplaced ear," he sighs. "I can't choose. Each of them are so unique in their own right."

"Can I choose for you?" I question, hoping he will say yes for various reasons.

"Please," he answers desperately.

I scan the shelf, finding one with almost perfect features. Somehow, the placement of the eyes reminds me of Lunion, so it's kind of perfect.

He confirms that this sea lion will do, and I take us all to checkout. I end up paying for both of them, one out of business, and one out of affection.

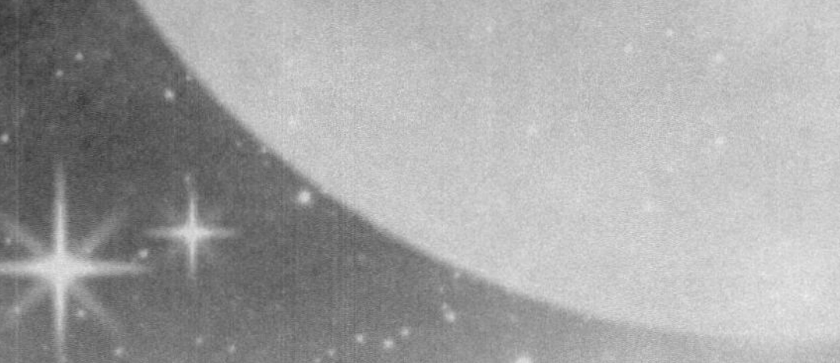

17

LUNION

We leave the aquarium behind. All the endangered animals, the fortified glass that holds them, and the shoddy replicas of their characters all disappear as we return to the boardwalk.

"Thanks for paying for us, Luke," I say, nodding at him in gratitude.

"Oh, of course. I mean, I didn't want you two to waste any of your money on souvenirs anyway," he responds, referencing the American money we were given for our trip. Maula and I each got $500, most of which I still haven't used.

With Luke around, he's just kind of bought things for me, and if it didn't come from him, the White House Staff pre-purchased it before our arrival, or his mom had sent it as a gift. All of the things we wanted, even wanted to buy for ourselves, were already taken care of.

Don't get me wrong, I'll take it. Still, I feel bad. I made Luke pay for his own things on Nalia, and now he is paying for everything for *me*.

He's been acting weird recently. Swooping in to buy me

things, running away from his evil friends, and bringing me breakfast. Maybe he just wants to make me feel at home because he knows I never wanted to come here. Maybe he's just a better person than me, because I never gave him the same hospitality when he visited my home.

Maybe it's something more, and I can't for the life of me figure out what.

I snap out of my trance when Maula shrieks. "That is so cute!"

She points to a large round tent. The tent is made of metal and painted in soft pastels. At the base of the structure is what appears to be a turntable covered with horses. I saw a post about Earth's horses on Instagram a while ago, which sparked a week-long obsession with them.

Some are shrouded in metal fittings; some go with only saddles; and in the place of some horses are detailed cars, traced with flames.

"Oh, that?" Luke looks at the machine. "That's just a carousel."

"Just a carousel? That gives me zero information. What does it do?" Maula asks.

"You take a seat, and you spin around. Crazy, I know." Luke tries to downplay what seems to be a complicated mechanism.

"Oh. Well, I'm too committed to the bit of me caring now, so let's try it!" Maula replies, skipping towards the ride. "I want this one." She takes a seat on a white horse traced in pink detailing, not unlike the jellyfish we loved at the aquarium.

Dozens of children rush the carousel alongside her, leaving only one car available. "I guess we are taking this one," Luke says, pointing at the bright red two-seater.

"Boring," I huff, slumping into the vehicle.

The ride starts, and we watch the horses go up and down as

the ride completes its circular route. Never getting close to each other, never getting too far apart. Like a plan that you can formulate but will never work. Like a romance that reaches no end, but no beginning.

"Look at me!" Maula shouts as she passes us, her horse on a separate track from our little car.

"You're doing great, sweetie!" I yell back, mimicking the excitement of a mother watching her child play a recreational sport.

After a handful of circles, the ride ends, and we all hop off.

"Well, that was thrilling..." The exhaustion in Luke's voice is apparent.

Seeing a sign that reads *"Fire Dancers,"* I turn back to them. "Ooo, let's go check this out!"

"Okay," Luke mumbles, following me into a darkened room.

The space is filled with circular rows of seats, all benches that curve toward a stage at the center of the room. The only light that is allowed to breathe in this room is the stage spot; illumination in its most natural form—fire.

Two men appear on stage: one with a stick burning at both ends, and the other standing still, with no props in sight. The staff master spins his flame stick, and the fire erupts in a blazing wheel. Each end circularly follows the other, just like the carousel. The flames emit a trail, but their ends never truly meet, chasing each other eternally until they are extinguished.

Suddenly, the dormant dancer snaps awake, sliding something into his mouth in the near-darkness. He comes to the front of the stage, parts his lips, and the blaze spills out of his lips like a geyser. Like an aggressive waterfall, the inferno burst out of him, warming the room intensely for a few seconds as the flames dangle from his tongue. Each second, I can imagine him feeling more and more pain, the fire engulfing his body whole and sending us all home crying.

No such thing happens. Instead, the man lets out one final puff, and the raging blaze disappears. The lights follow suit, and the dancers take their bows, safe and sound.

"Wow," I practically whisper, dumbstruck.

"'Wow' is right," Luke agrees, his jaw hanging closer to the ground than my own. "It's time for something *I* want to do."

Did he forget the aquarium was his idea?

"Lead the way," is my reply, beyond excited to see what he has in store for us.

Luke pulls us out of the theatre and towards a large structure held together by metal supports.

Throwing his hands up at the massive thing, he shouts, "The Thunderbolt! It's a roller coaster. Let's go!"

The coaster is grand not only in height but also in length. A nearby sign tells me that it spans 2,233 feet. Between its intimidating zenith and its horizontal stretch, that number does not send a single ounce of disbelief through my body.

A crowd of park-goers is currently using The Thunderbolt, and from the looks on their faces, this isn't going to be enjoyable.

After waiting in line for several minutes, we are allowed entry. This is the first ride where I notice the security presence. The control operator is next to a government security guard watching over us. Part of it is comforting, another disconcerting.

We board the coaster, and I brace for the most traumatizing experience of my life.

But it never comes.

People can be so dramatic. The ride is nothing compared to the tricks I've taught myself on my hover bike. Let these people try flipping around on something *not* attached to rails, then we can talk.

Maula and Luke, however, seem a lot more affected than I am.

"No way you two thought that was bad..." I glare at them.

"Oh, stop the judgment, Lunion. That was awful," Luke spits back.

"Fine, whatever you want to believe," I respond mockingly.

Interrupting our banter, Maula looks up. "Oh wow, the sun is going down fast. You don't think we will be distracting or anything, right?"

I hadn't even considered that we would stand out at night here. Now, it consumes my every thought. I don't want to reveal myself as a Solan, no matter what Luke's dad says about enlightening the general population.

"Do you two want to show people that you aren't human?" Luke quietly asks.

We both shake our heads.

"Okay, I have a plan. The lights should already drown it out, but if anyone asks, just tell them it's glow-in-the-dark body paint. People always do costumes around here," he reassures, and I trust him. Oddly enough, I've started to trust him more than myself.

"Thank you," I say, grabbing his hand so I don't get lost. Under the setting sun and orange-pink sky, I can't really tell, but it looks like he is blushing.

"Let's go to the Ferris wheel," Maula offers, but both of us merely offer her a look of confusion. "Oh, I read a sign earlier."

Leading us to the large circular mass, Maula acts like our trained tour guide.

"Here we are!"

"Wow, you're like a real New York Native!" I reply sarcastically.

We start to get on the Ferris wheel when Maula stops. "Oh no! Looks like only two can fit in one carriage!"

Lifting a brow, I challenge her. "Really? I think we could all fit."

"Oh, it will be cramped. You two go! I'll go in alone." She shrugs, but there is a mischievous glint in her eyes.

Luke and I step into a white car. By the time the ride starts moving, the sun has fully set, and the night sky is perfectly visible.

The wheel slowly starts to spin, lifting us off the ground and carrying us backward.

"It's beautiful, right?" Luke asks, a soft smile forming on his lips.

"What is?"

"The moon." He points at the bright white orb, its luminescence stark against the rough black sky. Small stars litter the space around the moon, acting as a pathway to the giant leap pad into the galaxy.

"Yeah, it is." I reply quietly.

"It kind of reminds me of you," he states casually, keeping his gaze settled on the moon.

I can't help the laugh that falls. "That's funny."

"How so?" He shifts his attention to me.

"My mom," I say, shifting my focus to the sky. "She always calls me her 'Starchild.'"

"I don't know about that, you're more the moon to me."

"Why?" I question softly, flattered at the discrepancy between his perception of me and my mother's.

"There are billions of stars, always new ones appearing. They all burn and burn, always under intense pressure and heat. I couldn't point out a single one of those stars and name it. The moon, however, is different. There's only one for this planet, and it helps us so much. At night, it provides light, helping us find our way around. It controls the seas temper, steadying them when necessary, and making them flustered more often than not."

"Is that all?" I look at him now, my eyes wide in disbelief.

"Uh, no. Just look at you. Your glow may be faint, but your light is more than that of just some star. Lunion, I could point you out in a crowd of a hundred people, maybe even a thousand, because you're that unique, you're that special. You aren't just some misplaced star; you are the moon."

The ride is almost done, and our cart is nearing the exit. "Thank you, that's really nice, Luke," I whisper, quickly exiting as tears well up in my eyes.

"Hey guys!" Maula says, and I wipe away any trace of my many emotions. "I think the car is here; that guy came to get me." She points at a security guard.

We all follow him to our car and get in. As we leave the island behind, fireworks boom in the distance. Yellow and white sparks litter the sky, falling like tears upon the convivial sight below.

The seating arrangement is a little different from usual, Maula settling between Luke and me, and I take the opportunity to stare out of my window. The tears begin to fall, and I allow them. I cry for myself because I know I'm not good enough for him to be describing me in such a fascinating way. I was horrible to him, and yet he always maintained a cheerful attitude, and now it's clear he holds feelings for me.

I cry for him, too, for if he asks me out, because I don't know what I'll say. I can't say yes, because it feels like I would probably just be using him to get over Marin, but I can't say no, because I would be lying if I told him I felt nothing for him.

I cry because it's too much.

Too much to not know.

Too much to know.

Too much to deal with on a different planet.

Too much to suffer through on my home planet.

Maybe it would be best for everyone if I fell out of the spaceship on the ride home and was lost forever to the coldness of space.

Still, that coldness could never rival the coldness I forced Luke, the warmest boy I've ever met, to endure.

18

LUKE

Only a few hours after pouring my heart out to a boy who ran away, we are both staring at that familiar ugly hunk of metal. It's time to return to the place I wish I could call home.

Lunion heads up the ramp, acting quickly to avoid getting thrown off, and Maula follows closely behind. I pause, waiting for my mom to say her goodbyes.

"I can't wait until your trip is actually over," she cries, a glossy sheen coating her eyes.

"Nalia is amazing, are you sure you can't come too?" I ask, tearing up.

"No, I have to hold down the fort until you two return. Don't let your dad get out of control, we both know how rash he can be," she warns, her voice darkening.

"He's actually been a lot better. At least before I came home, he was pretty good. I'll keep an eye on him though." My response carries authenticity. He had been getting his act together. He was eating dinner with all of us, being nicer, and even saying he was proud of me. Maybe he was changing.

I hug her goodbye and watch as a slick black sedan escorts her out of sight. Some workers approach me, a pallet of Dr. Pepper behind them. "Where does this go?"

"Oh wow, okay! So, that can go anywhere in the ship, I guess." I shrug, pointing the duo towards the ramp.

I wait for them to finish their task and finally enter the spaceship, throwing jazz hands towards the Dr. Pepper stash. "Ta-da!"

"No way!" Lunion leaps at the boxes of sugary liquid.

"Thank you, I am speechless." Maula bows, shoots a hand heart my way, then hugs the pallet.

"I am glad you two are excited. I'll see you later." I move to head for my cabin.

"Where are you going?" Lunion questions with a slight hint of concern.

"I need a nap." My reply is short, and I give him a carefree expression before retreating to my quarters.

There is actually no way I could sleep right now. I am such a fucking idiot.

How could I let myself say all of that bullshit last night? I mean, it wasn't really bullshit, because it's how I feel. Actually, no, it was bullshit. Why can't I just be normal? I could've said, "Oh, Lunion, you look great tonight!" But *no*. I had to go on a tirade of moon metaphors and celestial connections that went absolutely nowhere, had no merit, and lacked any definitive purpose. Maybe I just need to get my poetic ass up and tell him how I feel, plain and simple.

That is exactly what I'll do.

If all goes well, I have a boyfriend.

If it fails, we can turn around right now and they can leave me on Earth. I'll hide in my room and cry for at least three months, but at least I'll be on my own planet.

I get up and stumble to the lobby of the ship. Maula and Lunion are playing a card game.

"Uno!" Maula screams.

"You still have seven other cards, I checked under the table." Lunion replies dryly.

Laughing, she shakes her head. "Damn, I thought that would trick you."

"Hey, guys." I take a seat on the other side of the table. "How's it going?"

"I'm about to beat Maula's ass, so pretty great," Lunion replies, not looking at me.

"Oh, shut up." Maula throws down one of her two remaining cards, and actually wins. "Loser. I mean Uno!"

"Oh no. Whatever will I do?" Lunion softly sets down his cards. "Now that's over... I guess we should put our things away, right?"

"Yeah, I was just about to," Maula states, getting up from her seat.

I wait for her to leave, and watch as Lunion picks up his bags. "Hey."

"Hi," he mumbles, still not looking at me.

"Can I talk to you?" I ask with an evident edge of anxiety in my tone.

He looks up at me. "Sure."

"I was wondering-" A chime sounds from one of his bags.

"One second, sorry." He fishes around for his tablet. "Oh my God." His face transforms rapidly from shock to fear to excitement.

"What?" He doesn't respond. "What happened?" My entire body feels like an empty shell, each limb shaky, as if air were pulsing through each tendon, ligament, and blood vessel.

"Marin just asked me out, I think." He throws a hand on his head in disbelief.

"Oh," I reply, my mind racing with every emotion but happiness.

"Look!" He throws the tablet in my lap.

LUNION, I KNOW WE HAVE BARELY TALKED, BUT you're really cute. My girlfriend just broke up with me. I need someone to talk to. Can you see me at Slaxil's Cafe someday soon? I really need to talk to someone like you.

A WAVE OF DISGUST WASHES OVER EVERY INCH OF MY expression. "So, you're telling him no, right?" I look at Lunion incredulously.

"I don't know..." he responds shyly.

"Are you serious? He's not even hiding it!"

"Hiding what?" He looks clueless.

"He only wants you so he can get over his girlfriend!" I yell, suddenly filled with untenable anger.

"You don't know that. Don't make assumptions, Luke."

"Are you stupid, Lunion?" I regret saying it the second the words leave my mouth.

"What is wrong with you? Why are you so mad?" he asks, tone filled with genuine confusion, but his eyes deceive him. Tears are forming, and his saddened pupils reveal that he knows the truth.

His quivering lips say everything. They relay the words he will never be able to utter, at least not now, which would disclose that he knows how I feel. That my words last night, intended to be comforting like therapeutic needles, instead acted as everyday needles, sewing a thread of confusion and pain through his heart.

"I'm sorry. Do whatever you want, it's none of my business." I hiss, turning to leave.

"Wait." The single syllable is soft, and I ignore it.

He can go to his doom, which, any other time, I would gladly save him from. I can't make him love me, and I won't hurt him or myself anymore by trying.

Storming to my room, I fall on the bed, and cry.

LUNION NEVER SHOWED UP THAT NIGHT. I ASSUME HE spent the night in Maula's room, likely gossiping about Marin. How attractive he is, how perfect this is, how Lunion's dreams are finally coming true.

Because, of course, just because I look the part, doesn't mean I'm good enough. I may be a carbon copy of that man, but my appearance isn't enough to save me. Not enough to sway Lunion my way, not enough for me to find love myself.

WE DON'T TALK FOR AN ENTIRE DAY.

My words, meant to protect him, instead acted as small, poisonous blades. They cut deeply through his soft skin and into his already hurting heart, severing our tie forever.

The ship touches down midday in Nalia. The car ride back to the apartment building is silent, Maula creating a wall between Lunion and me.

Unfortunately, she is taken home first, and she leaves with

an awkward wave, Lunion and I left to suffer alone, in complete silence.

The car drives past the trees, bushes, flowers, and paths. All just like they were when we left. The forested areas remain intact, and no new buildings have been erected, proving that a trip to Earth was all it was.

Not a plot to take over Nalia, just a way to distract us from ourselves, and an unfortunate attempt to make us bond. An attempt that worked, if only for a week. An attempt that worked, all the way up until Lunion's potential feelings for me were shattered by Marin. A crude mace of a man, who swings his weapon of charisma around without regard for others. An action that hurt me, and ruptured Lunion's mind into a million fissures of palpable indecision and torture.

19

LUNION

The flight home was hell.

I spent the last moments with Maula, not because we would soon be separated, but because I wanted to avoid Luke. Our argument was pointless. He was right.

I knew that Marin's request was too good to be true, but what was I supposed to do? How can I ignore what Marin said?

I suppose I could have left him on read, blocked him, and run into Luke's arms—into the arms of a man who is not going to be around for much longer.

I could have run away from Marin to a love that can only last for a few more days.

Sure, it's not fair to Luke. It's not fair to discard him, especially after everything he's done for me.

But it's not fair to me, either. He is going to leave Nalia, and I'll be alone again. Why would I want to deal with the pain of losing a *lover* when I could just lose a *friend?*

In some strange, twisted way, it's also not fair to Marin. I don't know the full story. Maybe he just wants to get to know me. Maybe this isn't some opportunity for him to rebound, and he simply doesn't know who to turn to for help. But who am I to judge him prematurely, especially when I've wanted this for so long?

The opposing thoughts ring through my head as I stare at my bleak ceiling. I hated the White House ceilings, but now I miss them—the building's decadent, excessive flair, as well as the personality it carried.

Returning here just feels sad. It makes me realize we aren't any better than humans. While they have air, water, and pretty much every other kind of pollution, we have our own: light.

The city's illumination drowns out our very essence; it disguises what is natural and abandons the true beauty of our world. We are no better, so why can't I let myself love a human?

I try to shake these ambivalent feelings aside as I stretch to get up for the day. I throw on some nice clothes, not too nice to where I seem desperate, but nice enough so I don't look like a bum.

Leaving my apartment, some part of me yearns for Luke to pop up and ask for a shirt, food, or anything, honestly. But he never does.

I grab my bike, grimacing as I glance at his own next to mine. It was Marin's presence that led to him getting that bike, and it's Marin's presence that leaves it here. Hopping on, I head toward the address Marin gave me just a few nights ago. The city is bright, gleaming blue and white against the bright sky. The sun is in view today, and its small size glows prominently upon our smaller planet.

The cafe comes into view; a large sign, dotted with small pink bulbs, lights its landing pad. Hover bikes litter the strip, so I know it's busy.

It's 11:55 a.m., but I see Marin waiting on the dock. I slide to the side opposite him and lock my bike.

"Hey!" he yells across the dock.

"Hi," I whisper.

He's still stunning, I'll give him that.

"Follow me, I have a reservation," he states smugly, like he deserves praise for booking a table.

"Okay," I reply, keeping my head down as I follow him across the large room, full of life. The number of customers is disconcerting. I don't want anyone here. I don't want any witnesses to this crime I'm committing against Luke.

"Here we go." He pulls out my chair, waits for me to sit, and pushes me toward the table.

"Thanks," I say, still on edge.

We order some drinks, and he begins the conversation with shocking ease. "So where have you been?"

"I was on Earth actually." Cringing internally, I think of how I left things there.

"Really? That's so cool! How was it?" He feigns excitement, his facial expression betraying his truth.

"It was actually pretty cool, we got to-" He cuts me off mid-sentence.

"Who's we?"

Shock consumes my features as I inch away out of confusion. "Maula and a boy from Earth, he's the U.S. President's son. Why?"

He rolls his eyes. "No reason."

"Well, moving on..." I mumble, slightly disgusted by his response. "How have you been?"

"Oh, just great." He says sarcastically, grabbing a napkin tightly in his right hand.

"Are you okay?" I question, a little scared of the response.

"No, Lunion, I'm not. Why else would I need you here? Use your brain, please, *God.*"

"Sorry." Now I'm just pissed off. *Who the fuck do you think you are?*

"Anyway, yeah, so Liesa broke up with me."

"I'm sorry to hear that, Marin. From what I'd seen, I thought you two were pretty close."

A demoniac smile curls on his lips. "Stalking me, huh?"

I blush, forgetting that we had barely interacted in person and that most of my knowledge of him comes from social media.

"It's fine, it's nice to know I have admirers." He smirks.

I don't know how to respond. "So..."

"So... she's a bitch, moral of the story."

"How so?" I'm getting more upset by the minute.

"She said I was a bad boyfriend, then left me! Can you believe that? *Me? Bad?*" His brows furrow with seriousness as if what he said just made perfect sense.

"No, not at all," I lie, rolling my eyes.

"Why'd you do that?" he asks, staring at me with anger in his building glare.

"Do what?"

"Roll your eyes at me. Why did you do that?"

"Oh." I think for a moment, settling a pitiful fib. "I had something in my eye."

"Okay, thank you for understanding. I knew you would get me."

A waiter brings out our food, and I am saved from talking to him for a few minutes. He eats like a rabid dog, shoving large forkfuls of his food into his mouth aggressively, savagely.

I eat my meal calmly, actually cutting up my meat, unlike him. We finish up, and Marin speaks up again.

"Should we take this to the arcade?" He asks, getting up from his chair.

I can't think of a safe way out, so I agree. "Sure."

He gestures to his bright yellow ride. "Would you like to get on my bike?"

"I don't want to leave mine behind. We can go separately."

"That makes sense, meet me at the one in the mall."

I nod and unlock my bike, taking it to the invisible streets of the sky. Part of me wants to give him another chance, and another, larger part of me is disgusted by him.

I return to the mall where it all started for Luke and me. The same mall where I bought him his welcome basket, and the same mall where I made him run away from Marin. If only I could run away from him now, too.

Again, Marin is waiting for me at the parking lot. I slow down, carefully lowering my bike onto the landing dock, and hop off. After locking it up, I meet up with Marin.

He leads me inside, past the food court, the shoe store, and the department store. We make our way around a kiosk selling flowers, which he doesn't offer me.

We reach the arcade, and I couldn't be less excited to be here with him. He buys a card for himself, leaving me to purchase my own. Which is fine, but I know Luke would have at least offered.

"Let's play this." Marin stops at a racing game—where we play as frogs—and the game's thematics fail in helping keep my mind off of Luke.

Our races take place in outer space, sending us past Nalia and into the vastness of the universe. I can see the Earth, Saturn, Mars... every planet as we tour the galaxy. Every inch of my body wants to land on Earth, but the track never leads there. Instead, we do a circle on Saturn's rings and venture back to Nalia.

The return isn't all bittersweet, however. I beat Marin with a large margin. He finishes seventh, and I finish first. Still, one victory over him isn't enough to make up for that awful lunch.

"Wait, I have an idea." I lead him to my favorite game, "This looks cool. I saw it on the way in."

He reads the title out loud. "Gal-X-E Crusherz? Okay..."

"Have you played it?" I ask.

"Nope, you?"

"No," I lie, hoping to shock him with my abilities.

We load the game and pick our characters. I select Lexi Lovely, of course, and he chooses Rip Ranger, an interplanetary conqueror.

"Good choice." I joke, not really caring about it. If I can get into his head, maybe I'll have an even better chance at winning.

"Thanks. Your character is a little girly, though."

"Whatever." I've stopped hiding my distaste for him because it's too potent to discard. How can one person, someone I once thought to be perfect, be so awful?

We play, and I demolish him almost immediately. With kicks, throws, jabs, and spins, I defeat him three times consecutively. I don't even have to use my ultimate because he is just *that* bad.

"Yay!" I celebrate my sweeping victory.

"Ugh," he groans. "This is boring. Can we leave?"

"Not yet, I want to do one more thing." I walk up to a crane and slide my card.

There is a bird in the back I want, just like the Trelor, its pink and orange hues softly caress the fabric of the stuffed animal. The stuffed animal is jammed in the back, slightly covered by a pile of frogs and other birds.

I aim for it, grab its leg, and watch as the crane carries it near the collection shoot. Just before it drops, the crane shakes, sending the bird flying towards the back of the machine.

"Dammit!" I yell.

"It's not that serious, calm down," Marin hisses, bitter that I'm keeping him here.

"Sorry." I throw up my hands in feigned surrender, disagreeing with his curt attitude.

I try again, and again, and again. Using all my credits, each attempt brings the bird closer to the bin, but not my hands.

"Okay, let's go," Marin says, sliding his card in his pocket before leading me out of the arcade.

I know he still has plenty on his card, and he could at least have offered to use it. Not that I would have accepted, because I don't want shit from him, but the offer would have been the kind thing to do.

But I guess he is never thinking of what the *kind* thing to do is.

He walks me back to my bike, his words coming out with enthusiasm. "That was great!"

"Sure," I mutter in disbelief.

"So... Do you want to take this back to my place?" he asks with a smirk.

My jaw drops, and I stare at him incredulously for a good minute. "Excuse me?"

"That sounds like a yes to me! I'll send you my address."

"Are you fucking crazy?"

"I know, I know, you've wanted this for so long, and it's finally happening. Pretty crazy, huh?"

I know he isn't going to back down, so I flash a fake smile and reply. "Sounds like a plan."

"Great! Meet you there." He grins, then tries to walk away seductively.

I wait for him to leave, then hop on my bike. I don't even bother checking the address he sent me; I just run away.

I run to *my* place.
I run to Luke.

20

LUKE

It's 11:30 a.m., only a half hour before Lunion goes on a date with Mr. Nobody, and I'm still a bawling mess. I lay in my bed on a foreign planet, a planet I wanted so desperately to call home, and a planet where I thought I could fall in love.

I was so excited to leave Earth at first. To come back here, where the trees grow into what I could have only ever seen in a fantasy movie. Where the city is fuel-efficient, and the environment is protected with the utmost respect. Where the most perfect boy I've ever met lives.

Now, I don't care where I go. Back to Earth, here, it doesn't matter. Lunion has Marin now, and I don't want anyone else. Not yet, at least. Maybe after this interplanetary rift in my heart is sealed, I can find someone else. Preferably someone who doesn't look and act exactly like him.

A knock sounds on my door, and I sit up immediately, hoping it's Lunion. Maybe he had a change of heart, maybe he realized Marin isn't the best option. Maybe he wants *me*.

"Come in," I respond, my voice shaky and my breath tight.

The door opens, and to my disappointment, it's my dad. "Hey, Luke."

"Hi."

He sees my red, puffy eyes and all the tissues strewn about. "Wow, that upset about leaving home again?"

"Yeah." I lie.

"Okay, well, stop moping around, and come to the kitchen." He wraps his knuckles on the door frame and leaves.

Pushing myself up, I follow behind, snagging a few tissues on the way out. As we round the corner, a spread of food sits on the dining table, all of which appears to be from Earth.

"Come enjoy some food from home; that should stop whatever *this* is." He waves a hand at me, or the mess that is me, then takes a seat.

I sit down, looking at the spread. Of course, there is McDonald's, which he probably got from the cafeteria of one of our ships. Next to the McNuggets and Big Macs are some salads—just like our first day on Earth.

"I know you like that healthy shit, so you can have that if you want," he mutters, disdain clinging to his voice.

His verbal blade has no effect on me, however. I'm too distraught to care about being healthy, so I pound down a Big Mac, some nuggets, and a Dr. Pepper, holding off my tears with each bite.

Breaking the silence, he offers a statement I could've gone without hearing. "Wow. I haven't seen you eat like that since you were... fat."

"Thanks." My jaw feathers as I glare at him.

Of course, he had to mention that I used to be "fat." Which I wasn't, I was actually a normal weight for a twelve-year-old, he just believed I was overweight. In part, the constant reminders of my weight led to my affinity for working out, so I don't know why he's complaining.

While I may have been "fat" per his definition, he isn't healthy, either. He is very frail and only eats fast food. We have a full kitchen staff, but he prefers drive-thru meals and sugary drinks to anything remotely healthy. He doesn't gain weight, but he doesn't gain muscle either. He is a very skinny, *weak* man. So he has no right to make me feel bad about myself, when I have ten times the amount of muscle he ever will.

"So, what are your plans for today?" he asks as if forgetting the insult he tossed at me.

"I have no idea," I reply quietly, desiring to slink back to my room and hide.

"That sounds sad." Judgment drips from his timbre as he continues, "You kids need to get out more."

"Well, I can go wander around if you want me to," I mutter sarcastically.

"Sure, but I have another idea after you do that. I have a meeting with Ms. Moire later. If you would care to get off your ass and do something productive, you could join."

My jaw twitches as I narrow my gaze at him. "What a lovely way of putting that!"

"Don't get smart with me, but consider it. It's a pretty important meeting, I'm sure you'll enjoy it." He says, getting up from his seat and tucking the chair beneath the table. "It's at her apartment, so meet me there at two if you wish to join."

"Okay."

With a couple of hours before the meeting I am somewhat interested in, I decide to get dressed and head downstairs shortly after. My bike is alone, so that means Lunion has already left for his little rendezvous with Marin.

I head out to the trees, though I'm not sure where I am, aside from the fact that I went north. I pass all the familiar views: the red and purple trees, the bright blue and magenta grass, and small violet flowers. It now feels normal, as if this type of light reflection were common, and the green hues feel alien.

It's like Earth-1 isn't the original Earth, but that Earth-2102 is.

Again, I feel an innate need to protect the peace at work on this planet. Like this world is a monolith of perfection, a symbol of what could have been on earth.

What could have been if we hadn't drilled for oil. If we kept the air and water clear and didn't pollute our own cities and parks with toxic chemicals. Nalia was an example of everything I wanted Earth to be, and a reminder of why I wanted to be an environmental lawyer in the first place.

Even if it is home to the boy who broke my heart, Nalia is a haven in its own right, a haven that must be protected.

I continue a little further out, finding myself in a grove surrounded by tall, looming mountains. Flat, desolate rocks jut out of the ground, and on one side, foliage takes over. On each peak is a large tree, each a different hue. I try not to get distracted by the area's beauty and check the time.

1:30 p.m.—I need to head back.

Luckily, I had just been working my way in one direction the entire time, so I easily retraced my way back to the apartment.

Ms. Moire and my father are standing around a kitchen island, the very one that Lunion and I had made pancakes on together. That night was when I first felt truly connected with him, despite his sarcastic comments and light stabs at my flaws.

"Hello, Ma'am," I say, looking at the senator.

"Hi, Luke!" She gets up to hug me. "Long time, no see. Huh?"

"Yeah, it's nice to see you."

"How was Earth? Did Lunion enjoy it?" She asks, her eyes wide in anticipation.

"I think so. I don't really know."

"Well, I sure hope so. I know you probably did a wonderful job showing around, didn't you?" She has more confidence in me than I do myself. That, or she is just trying to continue the conversation.

"Yeah, I guess so. We went to a Broadway show. He seemed to enjoy that."

"That is amazing! I've heard so much about Broadway from my assistant, Veronica-"

"Should we start the meeting? It's 2:05 p.m.," My dad chimes in, cutting her off.

"Oh, I suppose so." It's clear she's upset by his interjection.

My dad pulls out an easel and sets down cards to go over his points for the meeting.

"Dad?"

"Yeah, Luke?" Agitation drips from his timbre.

"Where did you even find these things? We've been using Google Slides for over a century."

"If you are going to be rude, you can leave."

I throw my hands up in surrender, backing away a little.

"Okay, so if you look here." He begins, ignoring me. "You can see a map of this region." There is a star shape made by paths, each leading to a different location. The center of the star is the city, and the top point is marked by the suburbs. Radiating clockwise from there, we find military bases, a regional park, some aircraft storage units, and unprotected woodlands.

"If you look here," He takes off a panel, revealing a more in-depth look at the forested area. "This is a lot of space that you aren't using. Valuable space that could be leveraged to, maybe, get some money flowing into the economy."

"Our economy is excellent. I don't think that will be necessary," Ms. Moire responds.

"Okay, just hear me out." He returns to his presentation with determination. "So, this area, just off from the woods, is full of pointless slums. We could dissolve these houses, give the few inhabitants some money to move, and set up some very profitable exploits in the region."

"Why there?" Her voice breaks slightly, giving away her unease.

"Are you kidding me? There are barely any people in these neighborhoods, and the buildings are very poorly made."

"I used to live there, you know. Lunion grew up in that very neighborhood. I'm not sure you understand what you are asking of me, Mr. President." Her voice grows colder, more demeaning. "I'm sorry, but that is not happening."

"Can I at least explain what I would like to do in this area?" he asks, his eyes glimmering with a harsh rejuvenation.

"Fine," she breathes.

"I would like to set up oil drills, because to my knowledge-"

I cut him off. "Are you crazy?"

"Quiet," he snarls in my direction, his true colors surfacing. "Anyway, to my knowledge, Solans have never once drilled for oil. Just imagine the bounty underneath you right now."

"We've been avoiding drilling oil for a reason. Why would I ever agree to start now?" she questions rhetorically.

"I am so glad that you asked that." An iniquitous grin curls onto his lips as he motions around the apartment. "Do you enjoy this lavish lifestyle?"

Her brows narrowed, confusion lacing her reply. "I guess so?"

"Does *Lunion* enjoy this lifestyle?"

"I'd probably say yes," she concedes.

"As I am sure you are well aware, your office is almost up. A little less than a year, and you are out of here." He hums, that devilish smirk still plaguing his face.

"Yeah, why does that matter?"

"Well, that means that this apartment is no longer a guarantee for you. Sure, you might have some money in savings. You can go rent an apartment for a few months, but then what? What will you do? What will your son do?"

"I..." Her utterance fades.

"What does this have to do with boosting the economy through oil drilling, Father?" I pose, intercepting the conversation once again.

"Thank you for the prompt, Luke! You're doing great." He puts his hands on my shoulders, and hovers for a second like we are getting a father-son portrait taken. "Just as Luke has pointed out, a government deal for oil wouldn't help you too much once you're gone. But don't you worry! I have a little subsection, 45C, to be exact, which entitles the original signers, you and I, to a nice share of the profits."

I look at Ms. Moire. "You can't really be thinking about doing this, right?"

She glances at me innocently. "It would just be the woodlands?"

"That's the best part!" my dad interjects. "If all goes well, we could keep expanding! Imagine how much we could do in that nice section you zoned as a regional park!"

"And Lunion would be able to stay comfortable for the rest of his life?" There's a desperation to her question, a plea I know my father is leveraging.

I shoot out of my chair. "Hell no! Ms. Moire, you know he wouldn't want this."

"Luke, shut up," my dad hisses through his teeth.

"No! I'm tired of you acting like I don't know what I am doing. I am smarter than you, stronger than you, and better than you. If you had treated me like a human being every now and then, maybe I could have helped you with this contract, maybe it would have benefited us more!" I scream, my chest heaving.

"Oh, save it! How would we benefit more from this? It's flawless!"

"We could have, I don't know, asked for help on electric energy?" I snarl, jutting a finger in his direction.

"I've had enough of your attitude. Go back to your room while we finish this," he orders.

"No, I won't sit by and let you ruin this planet too." Years of unchecked rage towards my father bubble to life. All of the times he called me a fairy, every time he screwed over someone else, or me, to help himself. It comes back in a flash of bright, blinding light.

Before I can tell what is happening, I have him pinned against the kitchen counter.

"Nice performance, Luke," he spits condescendingly. "Now let me down."

My grip on him tightens, and I spin him around, putting him in a headlock.

He struggles, kicking free from my grasp and running to the counter. "This deal is happening no matter what, and you can't stop it. I mean, look at you. How is someone like *you* going to stop me?" He turns around, and as I go to grab him, he quickly reveals the kitchen knife in his hands. "Don't try it again."

I grab his wrist with ease, disarming him. With the hilt in hand, I spin it between my fingers and, without hesitation, press it to his throat.

21

LUNION

I need to find him.

I need to hold him.

I need to apologize for my idiocy.

I need to tell him that I want him, that I need him, and that I love him more than he could understand.

I made my mistake, but I won't let it last. I won't leave him alone, and I won't leave myself regretting my decision forever, having lost the perfect love for a fallacious chance at an illusory love.

The traffic is heavy, the buildings are tall, and the sun is slowly setting—on Nalia and on my future with Luke. A chapter that could've begun if I had just been a little smarter is now coming to a premature close.

I weave between zipping hover bikes and sluggish cars, clipping the mirror of a small van as I spin out of a cluster of tall, now intimidating, white, stoic buildings.

Their structures seem to close in on me, working with time itself to prevent me from reuniting with the boy I hurt. Every second, I know his hatred for me grows. Every wasted minute out in the city, his undying affection towards me wilts, its evergreen thistles erupting into unlikely brown spires of abhorrence.

It feels like a video game, where I am racing against time in a dark backdrop to save a damsel in distress. Except I'm the damsel, and I'm racing to the prince to save myself from my own troubles.

I'm so consumed in my thoughts as I drift through the city that I almost smash directly into a convenience store. Luckily, I weave through the charging stations, sending me back out onto the main driving area of the city. I speed across the gap between buildings for another few minutes and finally reach the apartment building.

Ditching my bike in the lobby, not caring to plug it in or even park it properly, I check the charging station. Promisingly, Luke's bike is still here.

I race to the elevator and smash the button to take me to the second floor. Repeatedly moving to the one responsible for closing the doors, I press it incessantly, drumming my foot against the ground impatiently. I don't have time for anyone else to join me on this lift—a lift to a bundle of love, fear, and regret.

As soon as the doors crack open, I practically leap to Luke's apartment, his door wide open. I don't take time to be polite; I burst into the living room area, tears forming in my eyes.

"Luke?" I scream, looking around the common area frantically. Not here. All that lies before me is an unfinished bowl of cereal, a TV remote, and a stack of books.

But not *him*.

I race to his room. "Luke?" No answer. "Luke? I'm sorry, can you let me in? Please?" Still no answer.

I twist the handle and use all my weight to open the door as quickly as possible. It flies open, and the pressure I exerted sends me tumbling to the ground. My head spins from the excitement, sending me dizzily crawling around the bedroom.

Disoriented, I yell again, "Luke?"

I get up and survey the room. Luke is nowhere to be found. His bed is unmade, his floor littered in stuffed animals and old clothes—clothes that I had lent to him, or clothes we bought together.

Tears erupt from my face like a cold, vicious volcano as I rush to my own apartment. "Mom?"

"Yes, sweetie?" She looks terrified, she's shaking as she turns to face me, and her eyes widen.

"Where's Luke?" I utter between sobs.

"Oh, Lunion-" She begins.

"I think I can handle this one, Madame Moire." Luke's dad appears from behind me as he places a hand on my shoulder, fingers digging into me with aggression. "After what happened between the two of you, it was too much for Luke to handle. He is heading back to Earth now." He offers me a sly smile, but his eyes reveal a hint of malice.

"What? No, no, no. I love him, please-" I fall to the ground, silently begging for him to call his son back to Nalia, back to me.

His eyes widen in surprise before instinctively returning to their routine cruelty. "I'm sorry, Lunion, but he has made up his mind." He taps my shoulder again, this time with slightly less strength. Helping me from the ground, his assistance is patronizing, a display of false pity, of power, of authority.

"Mom? Did you know about this?" I breathe, my question barely audible through my tears.

"Yes, I am so sorry, Starchild," she replies frankly, her eyes sorrowful.

I turn back to the president. "Is there any chance he hasn't left yet?"

My query catches him off guard. "Hmm. I doubt it, kid. To check every dock would be a waste of time."

"I don't care. I've already wasted enough time."

Pushing him out of my way, I bolt for the elevator. The ride feels too sluggish, but everything feels slow when he could be off the planet. Nothing moves quickly enough, because I will never be fast enough to make him stay.

I jump on my bike from feet away, somehow landing and immediately spinning out of the building. If he is taking any ship, it has to be the one we took to get back to Earth.

The one small enough for a minuscule crew. The one with his favorite restaurant. The one where we shared a room. The one where I broke his heart.

I pass the forest where we shared our most intimate memories. The forest where I showed him the secret of my planet. Where I physically glowed before him, despite the days of him shining brighter than me with his beautiful personality.

I follow the same trail I took when I first met him. The path that led me to him, and the path that we took together when I visited his own home. In the distance, I can see the loading dock where I first saw him in the flesh. Where I originally saw that hideous spacecraft, and where I met the perfect boy that stepped out of it.

The plants lining the path glow more intensely as the sun continues to set. Another reminder of the time I'm losing.

I can see the first loading dock, but the sudden tug on my bike draws my attention instead. The bike tosses me from the seat, and I feel my ankle contort as I fumble to catch myself. I slide down, hitting the ground and spinning, a sharp pain boiling through my entire foot.

But I can't let it stop me.

I check my bike, and the battery blinks red—*dead*. Still, I can't give up now. Through the pain of my twisted ankle, I hobble to the docks. Running with as much speed as I can, I can only hope the amount of regret I hold converts to energy and propels me forward.

The dock only seems farther away when traveling on foot. I can't notice the flowers, the trees, the now visible moon, or anything else except for the distance between the landing platforms and myself. If I'm fast enough, I can enjoy this view with him, the only person I'd ever want to share my secret outlooks and luscious groves with.

To my surprise, the docks, only a few hundred feet between one another, house identical ships. Each spacecraft is identical in size, shape, and color to the one I took on my voyage to Earth. I have to start somewhere, so I begin with the ship on the far left.

Guards litter the loading dock, but appear unarmed. They only carry flashlights, key rings, and their identification cards.

Stepping forward, I greet one of them with a simple "Hello?"

"What are you doing here? Do you have clearance?" He squints at me, shining his flashlight in my direction, which temporarily blinds me. "Oh! Mr. Moire, what brings you here?"

"I-"

He cuts me off before I can finish. "You know, you really shouldn't be out here alone at this time of night."

"Whatever, anyway-"

"I'm serious. I could get in major trouble if anything were to happen to you," he interjects again, not letting me answer his question.

"I think I'll be okay, seriously." I finally get out a full

sentence, to which he puts his hands up in surrender. "Where is Luke?"

"Who?" he questions, confusion overtaking his expression. "Oh! The President's son, right?"

"Yes..." I take a deep breath.

What a dumbass, seriously. How can you call yourself security and not even know who is supposed to get on one of the docked spacecraft? As the guard delays my reunion with Luke, my sadness splits into two lines: deeper sadness and growing anger.

"Why do you ask?" he interrogates, his eyebrows narrowing.

"Mr. Dinyre told me that Luke would be flying back to Earth tonight. I was hoping he hadn't done that yet. And based on the amount of empty docks, which is zero, I assume he is still somewhere on this planet," I reply with a trace of venom in my tone.

"That is true, I think. None of these ships have taken off yet, so if you want to talk to him, you'd better act fast."

"Okay, thanks. Can I have that flashlight?" I hold my hand out expectantly.

"Oh, uh, sure?" he hesitates, but hands it to me anyway.

I storm up to the first ship, prompting it to light up. The spacecraft ejects its loading ramp, and I climb into the vessel.

"Luke?" I investigate the main room first, checking the tables and benches for him. No luck.

The cafeteria yields a similar result, only making me miss him more as I see the Panda Express insignia catch the shine of my flashlight subtly in the dim lighting of the ship.

He isn't in the rooms either. I even check the showers, under the beds, and inside the cabinets. I know he's too big to fit inside a drawer, but I can't help but pull out every single one trying to find him.

I scour the ship once more, but my conclusion doesn't change.

Each ship is exactly the same. I yell his name over and over, but every spacecraft is just an echo chamber, carrying only the cargo of my voice, and returning it to its sender. My message will never be received by Luke, so I crumple in despair on the dock outside the last ship.

A small part of me had hoped that the last one would be different. That somehow, we were just different enough to have chosen opposite sides of the dock. That maybe my intuition was wrong from the beginning, and Luke was actually in that last ship.

He wasn't.

Luke was nowhere to be found. Not on Nalia, not in space, not on Earth. He had disappeared.

Like the sand enclosing my eyes from my drying tears, Luke had been brushed off this planet, this world, this plane of reality. Now, he is missing. Missing from these ships, missing from my life.

I can't bear it.

I spot a stout guard tower overlooking the range of landing docks and slowly limp over to its entrance. The tower is more of a hut, gaining its height from the hill it sits upon.

I reach the door, and it immediately opens. "Where is he?" I beg.

"Who? Where is who? Are you okay, child?" a woman asks frantically, holding my shoulders to keep me from falling.

"Luke. Luke Dinyre. Where is he? You have to know." I'm crying again, my eyes wide with fear.

"Oh." Her eyes drop.

"So you do know!" I yell, my tears forming pools on her leather boots.

"Um-" She looks panicked.

"Please. I just want to know." I'm holding her hands now, gripping them with the desperation of a hundred hungry animals.

"Okay, I'll show you, but don't try to pull anything funny." A glimmer of sympathy returns to her eyes, and she leads me to a tall, dark door.

22

LUKE

I can't hear a lot of anything, really, aside from the faint buzz of the lone light above my head, the drip of some exterior rain pipe, and the... The panicked footsteps approaching?

A door swings open with tremendous force, revealing a tall, slender silhouette. "Luke?" Even in the darkness, there is no mistaking who it is.

"Lunion?" I call back, waiting for him to rush into the room.

He does, and when he comes into view, his face is a fractured mosaic of emotions. His tilted eyebrows display his confusion. His quivering lip reveals his sadness, and his wet, shy eyes provide a window into his regret.

Aside from his complex countenance, the fact that he is standing before me is a testament to his feelings for me.

He looks so scared, so concerned, so hurt.

All I want is to embrace his moon-toned skin, to feel his night sky colored hair, and eclipse him with a comfort warmer than the sun itself.

But I can't. Not from behind these bars.

"How did you end up in here?" Lunion asks softly, fighting off any noticeable fear as he talks.

"It's a long story," I mumble.

"I spent a long time looking for you. I expect a long story." A small smile curls on his lips, but as soon as it appears, it vanishes, and his sorrow reappears. "I thought you had left. Left Nalia, left me."

"What? I love it here, and that's part of my... issue."

He looks at the ground. "And I... I think I love you."

"Really?" I ask with a pointed, oddly sarcastic tone.

"Yes. I think so, at least. I know that stuff with Marin was a huge fucking mistake. I just want to be with you." He looks up, tears streaming down his face with the speed of a thousand waterfalls.

His expression carries the countless apologies he wishes to utter, and I'm too enraptured by him to care. "I think I love you, too, then." I flash a smile, hoping to calm him down.

"Okay, wonderful! Now that we have that sorted out, what the hell happened to you?" He's still crying, but his eyebrows tighten to reflect a more poised version of himself.

"I may have put a knife to my dad's throat."

His head swings towards the cell, his eyes widening in disbelief. "Excuse me?"

"Yeah, I should provide a little more backstory."

"You think?"

"Anyway, my dad brought me to a meeting with your mom. He was pitching these crazy ideas about setting up oil drills in the area," I explain, the anger I felt in that room returning.

He shakes his head, his response immediate, "My mom would never go for that."

"I know, but he didn't really care. He kept finding ways to

make it appeal to her, practically threatening her with factors that he really didn't have any say in. It escalated, and I got a little hostile."

"So you pulled out a *knife*?" He folds his arms, his stare blank.

"No! My dad did, and I spun it back on him. I guess that's what he wanted me to do, because well..." I gesture to the cell.

"Do you know if they signed anything?"

"I'm not sure, to be honest. She seemed close to signing, though," I reply, looking down to hide my shame.

"No, there is absolutely no way. She would never go for that, *ever*." The determination in his tone makes it clear that he believes what he is saying, wholeheartedly.

"He started bringing you into it, and that woman will do anything for you. I've only known her for a little while, and I can see that clearly. I'm so sorry, Lunion, I really tried to stop it."

He puts his hands on his head and starts pacing outside of my cell, breath heavy. "Shit."

"What did they tell you?" I ask.

"They told me that you were going back to Earth, that what happened between us was too much for you to handle, and you had to leave," he recounts.

"What? I didn't even tell him about the whole Marin situation."

"I could tell. He seemed to make things up, but I had to check myself. That's when I begged a security guard to let me see you. I didn't think you would actually be at the docks, but here you are."

I think for a moment. They don't want Lunion to know about any of this. Their deal, me, anything. "You have to act normal when you go back."

"What? No! I'm definitely screaming at them. I have to

hear them say it, say that they will trade my world for your own. And, I will make sure they let you go," he yells back, a hint of aggression in his voice.

"Listen, please?" I beg, the calmness in my timbre wavering slightly. "Act like you were too late to find me, say that you think I'm gone. While you're there, look for signs of a deal, then decide what you want to do from there."

He sighs, notably defeated. "Okay, what about you?"

"I'll be fine for now, I doubt I'm getting out of here, really ever. I mean, I threatened the President, *and* I opposed his entire plan. They have no reason to let me out. I'll just be a problem, a mess to clean up."

"I'll get you out," he whispers.

"Thanks, but it won't work."

He lurches back, almost comedically. "How insulting! Have a little faith in me."

I roll my eyes, "Whatever you say, just don't do anything stupid."

"I am actually quite the intellectual-"

"You know what I mean. The second you break me out, we are both fugitives, we both have to flee, and we both have to figure out what the hell to do."

"I'll figure it out. As I said, I'm not stupid." He shrugs and comes closer to the bars. "I'll be back soon. While this is awful, I'm glad you aren't headed back to Earth."

"The cell could be worse, it's just me, so no weirdos." I chuckle, trying to lighten the mood before he's alone again.

"I'm off, I guess." Bowing, he exits through the same door from which he came, and I am left alone in my dim imprisonment.

The night is long, the bed is hard, and the light remains on, halting my sleep. At least I got to see him, and that gives me some hope.

It's obvious I can't stop him from acting rashly, but if he does, we both become targets for my father. His mom likely wouldn't hunt us down, but the moment he goes missing, and I'm not in my cell, search parties and armed guards will flood Nalia.

Not just this district, but the entirety of the planet will become my father's hunting ground, a playground in an interplanetary struggle for wealth and control.

It's hard to sleep when on the precipice of involuntary rebellion, but as I toss and turn, I muster up some ounce of exhaustion and crash.

"Mr. Dinyre?" A soft, feminine voice wakes me from my tumultuous slumber. "I have your breakfast."

I stir, forcing myself to sit up and look at my attendant. It's the guard that brought me down here, a tall woman with short brown hair, dressed in loose black clothing, her legs cut by tight boots.

"Hello, ma'am. Lovely day, right?" I offer, the words filled with sarcasm.

"Well, yes, actually! The skies are clear for now, and it isn't humid outside." Her head lowers. "I assume you won't get to check that out, though, my bad." She opens a small window and slides in my meal: a plate with two pancakes, a glass of what looks like orange juice, and some fruit.

"Thanks..." I grimace, taking it from her.

I don't have much of an appetite, but what I do have is ruined by the sound of the door opening again, this time revealing the last person I want to see.

"Well, well, well! This is so... quaint!" My father's voice echoes throughout the small room, echoing off the ceiling and cutting through the bars.

"Hi," I huff, not hiding my boredom with his annoying character.

"Aw, we can be warmer than that! How are you doing, son?"

"Don't pull that bullshit. If I were your son, I wouldn't be locked up in here."

"Actually, I will concede, if you were actually my son, you wouldn't have pulled a knife on me. So I guess you aren't, congratulations, Luke."

"You pulled the knife on me first!"

"Details..." He shrugs it off and pulls a chair up to my cell. "So, here is a little status update for you."

Rolling my eyes, I clench my jaw. "Oh, yippee."

"The senator took a little more convincing, especially after your little stunt, but I got her to sign off on the woodlands. She still won't budge on that park... In time, in time." He grins, holding my glare. "I can't wait to transform this little planet into something real!"

"Are you dumb?" I snarl, my agitation only growing. "Look around, they are so much better than us."

"Whatever. You know, you should be a little more patriotic every now and then." He exhales dramatically before continuing, "Anyway, I may have told your friend a little lie."

"What?" I do my best to feign ignorance.

"I might have told him that you are on your way back to Earth. Oh, and that it was his fault. He didn't like that part, but he does love you apparently, which disgusts me."

"Why would you do that?" I beg, finally able to confront him and his lies.

"I can't have him interfering, obviously." He sighs in frustration. "A little sad to know I've been right all of these years, though, you really are a little fairy. Now, at least, you're stuck in a cage, and you can't buzz around ruining my plans."

"Fuck you."

"So colorful! Didn't know you had that in you. Or maybe I did, I don't really listen to what you say. Enjoy your confinement!" Without offering me anything else, he takes his chair, sets it against the left wall, and leaves.

Great. So I am never getting out of here, legally at least. And on top of that, he got the confirmation he has been waiting for since I was in elementary school, so he can justify everything he does to hurt me.

Lunion is in trouble, too. They think he's in the dark, and they know that with knowledge, he's a problem.

I'm split down the middle, almost exactly. I want to see him again so badly, but I also want him to stay safe, and those two realities cannot coexist.

I'm about to fall asleep when I hear a light creaking sound come from the opposite end of the room. The light never turned off, so I can see the two figures approach from the doorway.

"Hello?" I say, a little too loudly, because I hear a shushing sound come from one of the two.

"Luke, it's me." Lunion comes closer to the cell, the guard following him closely behind.

"Nice to see you, but what is she doing here?" I ask.

"I'm helping you two out. I have a son, and if he had to go

through this, I know I would want someone to rescue him," the woman says quietly, shuffling to find a key.

"Wow, thank you so much. That seems a little too nice," I reply, stunned.

"This job also sucks, so if I get fired, I won't care too much," she admits with a shrug of indifference.

My brows narrow. "But wouldn't you get put in prison for helping us?"

"We have that covered," Lunion answers. "She is going to take some sleeping pills to make it look like we used force to escape; that way, she won't get in too much trouble."

"You are one brave security guard. Wow." I offer her a curt bow to display my gratitude.

"Yeah, let's get you out before I regret it." She slides a keycard across the pad and opens the door.

I go to hug Lunion, but he pivots to make his exit. "We'll have time for romantic shit later, we have to go *now*."

Our bikes are waiting for us on the grass before the tower, both baskets filled to the brim.

"Let's go." Lunion jumps on his, and we speed away from the tower.

Away from the district.

Away from the mess we've made.

Together.

23

LUNION

"So, are you going to tell me where we're going?" Luke questions, trying to keep up with me as I race towards the forest.

"I'll get there, just give me a second. We don't have many of those, if you weren't aware," I reply curtly, trying to keep him as quiet as possible.

His laugh erupts from behind me. "Okay, you're lucky I trust you. This is some serial killer behavior."

"Ha-ha. Too bad your career as a comedian will never happen." I grumble, doing my best to make up for my previously rude tone.

From where we are, the tower and landing pads are no longer visible, instead we can make out the woodlands up ahead. "Take a left!" I instruct, spinning quickly into the shrubbery. He follows, and we work our way into the heart of the forest.

I check for landmarks as we go: the grove, an icy-blue-topped tree with purple vines, a clearing void of any foliage aside from grass. We take a right, passing by a family of birds, and I see my final marker: a mushroom-ridden log tilted at a forty-five-degree angle. This oddity has always amazed me, and from how long I'd studied it, I know we are in the center of the forest..

I call over my shoulder, "Check the back of your bike!"

"Okay, I'm still very confused." He searches, finding a small shovel I had planted in his basket. "Uh... are you going to kill me?"

"No, dummy. Hand that to me." Handing it over hesitantly, I snag it, struggling to dig a small hole. "I forgot how fucking skinny I am, you do it."

"Sure, but just let me know why as I'm doing it." He accepts the shovel and digs with uncertainty.

"I pulled some trackers off our bikes. I think I deactivated them for now, but I'll try to get them working again. If we bury them here, they might think we set up shelter in the forest." I explain, simultaneously working to reactivate.

"Why would we want to do that?" Luke asks, one eyebrow lifting with his confusion.

"Two reasons. One, if they think we are in the forest, they'll spend a while searching it, instead of where we are going to be. Two, the longer they search, the less time they have to set up any drills here."

"I would like to believe that last one, but I don't think he would care about our safety in the forest." Luke's admission comes with a sigh.

"Oh, I know that. But if we are near, we can mess with their construction sites more easily. He wouldn't want that." I hum as a smirk rolls across my lips, my consideration for his father's apathy driving my mischievousness.

"Great. Second thought: where is it that *we* will actually be?"

"I'll discuss that later. We need to make sure we are as far away as possible." Watching him shovel dirt out of the ground with enviable ease, I can't help but admire him.

After a few minutes of my ogling, he raises the shovel dramatically, settling his other hand on his hip. "Is this good?"

"Yes, diva." I look him up and down with a smirk.

He studies his own posture. "Shut up."

I hand him the trackers and reach for the shovel. "I think I am competent enough to cover it."

"Enjoy!" He throws in the trackers and steps back, allowing me to haul the clumps of dirt back into the hole.

Sweeping the last signs of our presence back into place, I pose triumphantly, tossing the tool back into his open hands. "All done!" I pose triumphantly, throwing the shovel to his open hands. "Let's go!" Without rebuttal, he follows me back to our bikes. Securing the items we brought, I hop onto mine and lead us out of the forest.

After a few minutes of traveling, Luke speaks up. "Okay, so where are we going?"

"So, you see the shoreline, just there?" I point at a lightly reflective surface in the distance.

"Sure."

"We are going to cross the sea. There is a nice town we can hide in."

"What?" He practically shouts.

"Why are you yelling?"

"Crossing an ocean will take days!" He replies, obviously growing more anxious.

"It's like a day and a half, Luke," I say, rolling my eyes. "Plus, there is a small island on the way there with an Inn to stay at."

He sighs. "Okay, that's not that bad. But what about our bikes?"

With both of our bikes half-charged, I offer reassurance.

"We can charge them at the Inn, and if we need to, I brought some portable chargers for the road."

"What road? We are literally going to be crossing over water."

"You know what I mean." I throw him a smile and speed up. We need to reach the Inn before the sun rises if we want to remain inconspicuous.

The way to the shore is troubling, a myriad of natural barriers in our way. Tightly-closed treelines, low-hanging branches, and tall rocks all create an obstacle course as we rush towards the sea.

Once we are past the treeline, a new story unfolds.

"Can we please go up there?" Luke begs as he stares at a hill that juts above the shoreline.

"Why? That's too much extra-"

"Please."

Unable to tell him no, I release a breath. "Fine."

We follow Luke's path, which takes us up a ramp of sorts and spits us out onto the water. We are lucky we have hover bikes, because instead of sinking as we reach the water's surface, we bounce slightly, then glide seamlessly above the sea.

Our bikes leave a faint illumination atop the water, but it is nothing compared to the view below.

Corals, seagrasses, and fish alike glow below the surface of the water, each living entity adding to a slightly blurry backdrop of vibrant color. The sand is the canvas, the life is the paint, and the water is a thick varnish, sealing the bold, resplendent creatures with a bubbly, subtle cover.

"Woah!" Luke yells from my side. "I thought the forest was amazing, and I mean no hate to you, either, but this is the best." He touches his hand to the water, softly cutting through its tension and swirling the colors of the sea's light with his touch.

"Look up there." I point to a bright figure in the distance.

Nearing the source of the light, we find a pink whale with blue specks. The cobalt covers the pink flesh like a mask, leaving fuchsia circles and ovals in its wake.

"That is so cool!" Luke looks into the water with excitement, practically kicking his feet as the creature approaches. "It looks kind of like an orca!"

"No clue what that is, or really what this is. I think I learned about it in school a while ago... its species name starts with a Q or something." I reply, shrugging off my lack of knowledge.

"So cool!" Luke says as we pass the unnamed creature.

It dips into the water, its light slowly fading into the backdrop of bright blue plants.

As one miraculous chapter closes, our salvation appears on the horizon.

"That's it! That is the island we are stopping at!" I didn't realize so much time had already passed; the island was supposed to be hours out from the shoreline. The mesmerizing waters, extraordinary animals, and the sheer thrill of running away must have distracted me from time itself.

"Okay, I put all the money I have saved on one card. It really isn't much, but it should help us for a little while."

Luke looks at me with concern. "Does your mom have access to it? I'm scared she'll see our location."

"Damn, give me some credit. No, she does not. I made sure of that. She'll probably find us somehow, but my charges won't be it." I reassure him, knowing that not only is this stressful, but that he wasn't given any chance to prepare.

We approach the island, which houses a small dock, the Inn, and a resort. As appealing as the sandy shores of the resort may be, we don't have time to enjoy this stop.

The Inn itself is tall, with enough floors to house twice as many people as my apartment building. The entryway is ornate, with a large tan arch traced in gold and dotted with bright blue bulbs. With an even more luxurious lobby, harlequin gold and white flooring, tall pillars, and a spiral staircase lead to the in-house restaurant.

"Can you put up our bikes while I pay for a room?" I grab a bag from my bike and, when he agrees, let Luke take it.

Making my way into the building, a smiling woman at the front desk greets me. "Hello, sir. How may I help you?"

I motion to Luke, who is struggling to hook up our bikes to the chargers. "Could we get a room for the night?"

"Just tonight?"

I nod in affirmation and slide her my card. With a chime and a green flash, it's accepted. As if its confirmation was Luke's sign, he approached, and we wasted no time heading to the fourteenth floor.

"Here it is." Luke gestures to a slate blue door. "Room 1418."

"Let's see what we've got." Opening the door, two medium-sized beds come into view, and I sigh. "I love you and all, but I can't say I'm upset about getting my own bed..."

I turn to look at Luke, but he's already gone. "I agree!" His muffled voice creeps out from between him and his mattress, which he has already belly-flopped onto.

"That's good, but don't get too comfortable." He slowly sits up at my utterance, his exhaustion showing, and I continue, "We still have something we need to do." Feeling around in my bag, I pull out bleach, hair dye, and toner.

"What is that?" Luke asks, his eyes widening in concern.

"Hair dye! We need to do *something* to change our appearance. I mean, that's escape 101."

He studies the bottles in my hands. "So we are swapping hair colors? Because that's what it looks like."

"Oh, give me a break. I had like four hours to prepare after I stopped having a mental breakdown. Also, you're buff, so you won't look like me, even with black hair."

"I'm flattered, so I'll do it." He gets up and follows me to the bathroom, snatching the bleach. "I do you, you do me?"

"That sounds so bad, but yeah."

I start getting out some gloves and a poncho, which is more for the floor than him, and lather his pale hair with the black gel. Given its short length, it doesn't take long, and his head is covered in just a few minutes. He lets it sit for a bit, then washes it out in the bath, making sure to clean any traces left in the tub.

His hair is wet, but it looks different enough for now.

Starting on mine, he takes his time as he lathers my head in bleach, then toner. After it processes for a bit, I wash it all out and let it dry. His hair looks great, but it is a little jarring considering I'm so used to seeing him blonde. Its pitch-black hue looks odd but cute, with his freckles.

My hair, however, is a different story.

"This is orange," I complain, tugging at a couple strands.

"I did everything you told me to!" he argues, folding his arms over his chest.

"Well, next time don't listen to me. It's fine, let's just sleep."

After I clean the mess in the bathroom, I fall onto my bed. The mattress is a little hard, but the pillows and blankets are soft. Adjusting to its differences from my one at home, I'm about to fall asleep when Luke's voice reaches over the void between us.

"So, do we need to change our names too?" he asks softly. "I mean, I think 'Luke Dinyre and Lunion Moire On The Run' is a pretty revealing headline."

"Bold of you to assume your name would be first," I tease. "But yeah, probably."

"I think you should go with Randall."

"*Randall?* Are you fucking kidding me?"

"Damn, okay! My bad." He laughs, and I can't help but find myself smiling. "Maybe your name can be Dylan or something."

"I'll consider it," I say sarcastically. "You can be Leo, I don't know."

His mockingly sincere answer catches me off guard. "Absolutely, because you chose it."

"Don't use that on me! Fine, I'm Dylan now." I concede.

"Leo and Dylan Randall, what a happy family."

Rolling my eyes, my grin only grows. "Oh, so Randall still snuck its way in, great."

Somehow, I don't hate it. The names may be awful, but the idea of sharing a last name and starting a new life together makes me feel like everything might just work out.

24

LUKE

Lunion's shout wakes me from my slumber. "There are gunshots coming through the window! Get up!"

"What?" My eyes snap open, working to adjust to the room's bright fluorescents. "Are you okay?"

Lunion stands before me, fully dressed and not the least bit panicked. "Yeah, but you never know. We definitely have a warrant out for our arrest. Stay alert."

"You... are insane." I look at him for a second, then turn back over, hoping to go back to sleep.

"Woah, not that fast." He shakes me awake, pulling me out of bed. "We do need to get up if we want to make it on time."

I practically trip over my feet as he throws me into the bathroom. "Okay, okay!" I yell as he slams the door for me. "Damn." I gather the toiletries offered by the hotel, which, luckily, appear to be reputable brands, and take a shower.

Gathering the toiletries offered by the hotel, which appear to be from somewhat reputable brands, I take a shower. As I rake my fingers through my newly dyed hair, it quickly becomes apparent that shampoo isn't the best, but it will suffice. The same could be said for everything else, too, but at least the conditioner smells good.

To appease Lunion, I hurry up, brush my teeth, and throw on some clothes he packed for me. "Okay, we can go now."

"Okay, they serve breakfast downstairs," he says calmly.

"What? We aren't just going to leave?"

Glancing down at the ground, his confession comes as a near whisper. "I don't want to listen to you complain about being hungry, and we have like thirty minutes before we *really* need to leave."

I gasp. "You lied! I could've slept longer."

"Not really. Besides, would you really pass up eating just to sleep a few minutes longer?" He cranes his head in confusion.

"Whatever, let's go."

I follow him to the elevator, which takes us to the second floor. The dining hall is filled with a large range of clients. From businessmen to groups of girls who are clearly on beach trips, each table is a mark of diverse experience.

"What do you want?" I ask, watching as he squints at the buffet before us.

"Honestly, nothing looks very good. I'm just gonna go find us a table. I'll wave you down when you're done." He slinks behind me, browsing over the swath of options, hunting for a seat for the two of us.

I grab a tray and load it with pastries, cereal, and juice. Once satisfied, I turn to find Lunion seated at a table for two in the far left corner, his right arm high in the air to signal me to him.

Approaching, I glance down at the items I selected. "Okay, so I got you some cereal and juice, please eat it."

"Why? I mean, I said nothing looked good."

"I don't want to hear you complaining about being hungry

on the trip." I retort, using his own words against him to coax him into eating.

"Okay, good one." He takes a spoon and starts on the cereal. To my surprise, he eats most of it, leaving only the soaked pieces and milk at the bottom.

After about fifteen minutes, we are ready to head out. I follow him down the spiral staircase, which spits us out into the lobby. Taking my keycard with his, he turns and approaches the front desk while I head out to our bikes.

From a distance, I hear the concierge ask, "I never got a name, what should I put this transaction under?"

"Oh, Dylan Randall," Lunion says with a sigh.

"Okay, Mr. Randall, you have a great day!" Taking the cards, she offers him a smile, to which he returns before joining me.

"That was painful."

I smirk, a light chuckle escaping me. "Sorry for your turmoil, *Dylan*."

"The first name is not the issue..." He jokes back, taking his bike slowly from its charger.

I follow suit, quick to straddle my bike and ride with him from the hotel to the boardwalk. The sea glitters under the morning sun, its waters calm and inhabitants inconspicuous against the light.

"How much longer do we have?" I question, wary of the answer.

"Like eight hours of travel," Lunion states matter-of-factly.

"I thought you said we have to travel for like a day and a half?"

"Oh, that included the night at the hotel."

Without another word, he moves forward, and I follow him to the water's edge. Tipping my bike in, I watch as the waves lap against it before I speed away from the shore as soon as my bike bounces back up.

While the sea at night is undeniably a better sight, the scenery around the resort island is nothing to scoff at. Behind the hotel, a towering cliff side juts out, its rocky facing covered with vines. Ziplines cover the mountain range, ending at the docks. Hover bikes and large boats alike swarm the surrounding sea. For leisure or business, the waterborne vehicles dot the sea, inviting commerce and creating a community of tourists.

I point at the steep cliff, "We should've started there!"

"With all of these people around? Hell no," Lunion laughs as he passes me, using his hand to throw some water my way.

"Oh! So that's how you want to play?"

Dipping down, I gather a palmful of my own. Determined to get my revenge, I chase him across the water, exceeding his speed slightly. Once the gap is closed, I get right behind him and drop the water on his now burnt-gold hair. Not finished, I cut in front of him and slap the sea. It splashes up as I trail away with him close behind.

"Wait!" I yell over my shoulder with a laugh. "I don't know where I'm going."

He approaches, his drenched hair covering his eyes. "Thanks," he pauses for a second to run his hand through his hair, trying to regain his vision, "this way."

I follow him again as we pass the rest of the crowd. Not wanting to draw too much attention, I refrain from messing with him anymore. I can tell he doesn't mind, but I don't want to lose him in the mix because I dropped a gallon of water on his head and sped away. That would be unfortunate.

After the island vanishes, so does the intrigue. The ocean became a blank slate of deprivation. I had abandoned any sense of fun, and so had nature. I couldn't see the life below the water's surface, and there were no stunning cliffsides to gawk at either.

Every now and then, a harlequin formation of birds would pass us by, but I was more concerned they would shit on me, so my excitement at their arrival was minimal.

It feels like it's been eight hours, so I ask the taboo question to beat all taboo questions. "Lunion?"

"Yeah?"

"Are we there yet?"

"Are you kidding me?"

"Sorry," I reply, letting out a light chuckle.

"But it has been around four hours, so we should stop for a second." He slows, and we hover above the deep blue water. "Park in front of me," he instructs.

Once I do as he asks, he rifles around in my basket for a moment, digging out two charger packs. "Okay, I'll put one on your bike, and you put one on mine."

Finding the charging port on my bike, he easily slides the pack into place. Not having the same luck, I fumble to slide on the pack even after easily locating the port. "Sorry."

"It's fine. We have time." He doesn't sound fully convinced, and it appears as if he has this entire thing on a tight schedule, so I increase my focus. Once I get it in place, we continue our trek toward the town.

The rest of the trip is similarly boring, but takes an immediate turn for the better as a city comes into view. Large spiral buildings jut out of a large, elevated mass of land. Each one ends in a spike, sealing its shape, reminiscent of a shell. Below this city, a peninsula sprawls out in a similar spiral shape.

Littered across the peninsula is a town, made of old-fashioned shacks made of wood, grasses, and rusted metals. To my surprise, the wood is much like that of Earth's wood, with light brown detailing. It's only the dead grass and plant stems that line the roofs that are different. Pale, sunbleached blues and reds mix into a light, slightly browned purple.

We dock at the end of the peninsula's swirl, its tip covered in dock space. We ride up a ramp to the side and dismount from our bikes almost immediately.

The wooden dock *feels* historic. The chipped paint and uneven planks reveal a storied past of trade, immigration, and discovery. A gateway to the other inhabitants of Nalia, its position on the ocean is a perfect welcome to other solans, and now, humans.

Large ships occupy various stretches of the dock, each wooden leg inviting all classes of sailors. From luxurious boats to small bikes, the docking station is home to everyone and anyone.

Lunion leads us to the village itself, which stretches beyond the peninsula. The land beside the cliff is lined with a tight row of houses, all in various colors but with the same general structure: log walls, planked porches, and faintly colored roofs.

"We need to go over there." Lunion points to a building at the start of the spiral. "I did some research, and there is a realtor here who can help us as soon as possible."

I follow him to the building he pointed out, a two-story log-style structure with a wooden sign that reads *"LURNALA REALTY: RATED #1 IN THE AREA."*

"Well, that's promising." My nervousness comes out as dry sarcasm.

We walk up to the already open door, and we are instantly greeted by a stout woman. She abandons her desk post with excitement. "Hello! How may I help you two?"

"We would like to rent a house here in Lurnala!" Lunion matches her enthusiasm.

"Aren't you two a little young?" she asks, but her tone remains positive.

"We both recently turned twenty, and we are trying to start our life together." He takes my hand in his own and smiles at the woman.

Her bottom lip juts out with a happy pout. "Aww. Well, who am I to deny a happy couple? I've done it before, actually, but you two seem fine. What are you looking for?"

"Oh, just something small for the two of us. One bed, one bath, a kitchen," Lunion responds with shocking ease.

"Great, I think I have just what you're looking for, Mr.?" She fishes for the last name.

"Randall," I speak up.

"Both of you?" She asks with astonishment.

Lying through my teeth, I can only hope she believes me. "Yep! Couldn't wait to marry him, even if it is a little early."

"Apologies, I have to ask some invasive questions, but that's wonderful. Which is why this town is a great option for the two of you! You two do understand that it is pretty simple to stay here, right? No documentation or anything like that, but you have to help out and work for someone in the village." The weight on my shoulders dissipates with her explanation.

"Yes! We would love to see a house as soon as possible. We plan to start searching for work tomorrow, but we have nowhere to stay tonight unless we start renting," Lunion offers with a weak grin.

"Well, you two seem to have everything planned out, so I'm going to show you the house I have available. If you two like it, you can start renting today. But, if you don't find employment by the end of the week, I'll have to consider breaking your lease," she warns, but as soon as her caution ends, excitement fuels her timbre once again. "This way!"

We follow her to the patch of houses next to the cliff, passing by many happy residents. It's like they were paid to be perfect neighbors, but they all seem genuinely jovial.

In the heart of the neighborhood, we stop at a small house. She guides us through it, which is basically one big room with a bathroom. Across from the bedroom, hidden by a wooden folding screen, is the kitchen—a simple collection of appliances, some cabinets, and hanging lights

"So, what do you think?" Lunion grabs my arm.

"It's great, how much?" I ask her, slipping out of Lunion's grasp to wrap my arm around his back.

"Five hundred credits per month," the agent replies, fawning over us.

"Sounds great! Do you take card?" Lunion asks, pulling his out with anticipation.

"Absolutely." Her eyes light up as she takes it, sliding it through a portable reader. Once accepted, she roots around in her pocket and pulls out two metal keys. "Here you are, enjoy the house you two!" She kisses Lunion on the cheek before her departure, which is a little weird, but we did just buy a house, so he seems to remain quite unfazed by the touch.

Once she is gone, Lunion speaks. "So we really need jobs. Like bad. I have enough for another month, but that doesn't help with food or anything at all."

"We'll be fine. We are starting a new life together. Let's enjoy it." I laugh, and for the first time, I kiss him.

25

LUNION

I wake up in Luke's arms. For the first time, we are truly together. No petty differences, no one coming between us. It's perfect.

Or it would be if we weren't on the run from two governments.

However, looking at him, his mouth slightly open, chest rising slowly, I can't help but bask in the traces of joy in our situation.

"Hey, Luke." I rustle his arm as I sit up.

"Mhm?" he grumbles, not opening his eyes.

"We probably need to start getting ready soon."

With one tug, he pulls me back into his embrace. "Really?"

Trying to fight the urge to stay there, I move out of his arms. "Unfortunately. We kinda need jobs."

"Okay, fine." He sits up, stretching his arms, one of which accidentally hits me in the head. "Sorry!"

I laugh it off as I slip from the bed and head to the bathroom. The shower is small, but large enough to fit inside. "Do you want to shower first?" I ask from the bathroom door. No need to yell, the house isn't nearly large enough for that.

Luke steps around the frame. "No, you go ahead." Kissing me once, he slips into the kitchen.

I take a shower, enjoying the soaps and hair products we got from the city last night. The water is cold, the lighting from the window is pleasant, and so far, this new life is amazing.

I make quick work of rinsing off and brushing my teeth. Snatching a towel, I wrap it around my waist to head out of the bathroom, not wanting to hog what little space we have.

Luke stops buttering a slice of bread when I exit the bathroom, and his jaw drops for a second. "I thought we weren't allowed to be shirtless."

"I don't care," I say, grabbing a piece of toast from him. "The shower is all yours."

Enjoying my light breakfast, I keep my eyes trained on him before he vanishes around the corner. Shortly after, I hear the water kick back on, and wait a handful of minutes before I start getting dressed.

The proximity of the city to the village is exquisite. With a brisk stroll, we can get anything we may need. That, of course, means we need to find some more money.

Luke finishes his shower quickly and comes out of the bathroom in shorts and a tank top. "See, some of us adhere to the dress code."

"Oh, shut up!" I laugh before addressing what we both know needs to happen. "We should probably get going, right?"

"I suppose, Mr. Randall."

"I forgot about that..."

"How dare you! That was my last name you took at the altar!" He acts genuinely offended.

"Wow. Broadway is calling with that performance," I retort.

His brows raise, a wave of sincerity washing over his expression. "Wait, do you really think so?"

"Let's go." I try to hide my smile as we step onto our porch.

The village is beautiful in the morning light. Rooftops reflect the sunlight softly, highlighting the colors washed away by the same sun. The streets aren't busy, so it's easy to take in the village's vastness.

Over the peaks of the other houses, you can see down to the peninsula, which is bustling with newcomers and those departing for a commute, vacation, or just back home.

We hurry down to the dock, hoping to find some work there.

A man stands next to a case of fishing rods, and a sign that reads: *NOW HIRING: FISHERMEN. RODS INCLUDED, RATES VARY.*"

Greeting the fisherman, I dip my chin respectfully. "Hello, sir! I see you are hiring."

"That is correct! Are you two interested in becoming fishermen?" he asks, smiling.

"We're looking around for jobs. We just got to the village, actually," Luke says.

The man considers it. "Okay, tell you what. You two can try it out for the day, and I'll even pay you for what you catch. If you don't feel attached to it, you can go find another job."

"Really?" I ask, stunned by his leniency.

"Sure! But I should probably tell you about the rates. I pay ten credits for small fish, twenty for medium-sized, and forty for large. What counts as each size is a little subjective, length *and* width, you know? But it's a pretty easy job."

"That sounds great!" My response is genuine. "What is your name, sir?"

"You can call me Mr. Traxis. How about you two?"

"I'm Dylan," I offer before gesturing to Luke. "And this is Leo."

"Well, let's see what you've got, Dylan and Leo." Traxis grabs two rods from his stash and hands one to each of us. "You can fish pretty much anywhere you wish, just stay out of the way of boats. Come back to me around lunch, and we'll see how you're doing. If you have any issues, you can find me around here. Good luck!"

In addition to the rods, we are also handed coolers that are very large and difficult to carry.

"I'll take the coolers, if you want." Luke extends his hand.

"Oh, thanks!"

We swap his rod for my cooler and walk to the edge of the beach. It's quiet, with only a few beachgoers and practically zero boats. Far out, there is a small dock, which appears empty of any fishermen or sailors.

"How about we go over there?" I point at the dock.

Luke shrugs before turning back to me. "Seems like bad luck that literally no one is there, but sure!"

We pass a couple writing in the sand: M + S. They circle it with a heart and lie down.

"That should be us, but the horror known as employment is taking our fun away." Luke cries, sniffling with fake tears.

"If we get some good fish, we can save up enough to have fun. But for now, you're out of luck, Leo." I reply, hoping to get him focused on the task at hand.

He chuckles, playfully hitting my leg with the cooler. "I hate that you're always right. It's so annoying."

We reach the dock and cast our rods into the dark water. There aren't any tugs for a while, so we just stand there awkwardly trying to find conversation topics.

Luke breaks the silence first. "So, how do you like the house?"

"It's really cute," I reply, my mind elsewhere.

"Yeah, I agree. I wish the bathroom were a little larger, but that's really my only complaint."

"Yeah-" My mundane response is cut short by a tug on my line. "Woah!"

With surprising ease, I start reeling in my line. Soon, my catch is dangling before me. Small and about half a foot long, the fish is a little chubby but extremely cute. Knowing we need the money, I sigh, tossing it into the cooler.

"Well, that's probably like ten credits. Just four hundred and ninety more for next month's rent."

"That actually isn't that bad! But we do need to get some big ones so we can do fun stuff." Luke replies, staring at his line bobbing up and down in the water.

An hour goes by, and I've got five fish: two medium and three small. Luke, however, has caught absolutely nothing. No fish, no plants, no lost shoes. Nothing.

"Maybe this one isn't the job for me..." Luke says quietly, dipping his head down in disappointment.

"Maybe you need to be a little more patient. I keep seeing you pull back your line and throw it somewhere else," I reply, trying to offer advice.

"Yeah, maybe. But I think I'll check out some other options tomorrow."

"Sure, whatever works best for you." Allowing the waves to consume our conversation, I rest my head on his shoulder.

As time goes on, I catch less and less.

The second hour yields three small fish, the third shows two of varying size.

Now, on the fourth hour, I can only hope to catch a fish large enough to increase the profits of the day.

As I begin to zone out, I feel a sharp tug on my line. This is unlike the last time I felt a sudden uptick in pressure, whatever this is, it is strong. I try to reel it in, but start getting pulled to the edge of the dock. "Lu- Leo!"

"Oh shit!" He drops his rod and grabs me. "Give me the rod."

Taking it from me, he proceeds to reel in the fish with ease.

"Wow. That was humbling." I mutter, looking at the fish in his hands that is several feet long and pretty wide.

"You just need to workout, I can help. But at least we have a large one!" He grins.

Watching Luke shovel the fish into his cooler, I can't help but admire him. "Thanks, it's almost lunch, we should go find Mr. Traxis."

The couple's initials have been washed away by the time we pass the shoreline, but the two of them are still there, enjoying each other's company.

"Mr. Traxis! We have our status report for you!" I yell across the dock.

"Wonderful! What have you got?" he asks, squinting as we make our way to him.

"I *think* we have one large, seven small, and three medium!" I smile.

"Let's have a look!" He opens our coolers. "That is definitely a large, good catch! Yep, I see the smalls, I think only one of those is medium, but I'll give it to you for your first day."

"Really? Thank you so much!" I reply, stunned by his kindness.

"Of course, here you go." He hands us physical credits totalling one hundred seventy. "I do want to know, how was it catching that big one? I usually have problems, that's why I'm hiring people now."

"Oh, it took a while to show up, and it took both of us to get it out of the water, but he got it pretty easily." I point at Luke.

"Good job, Leo! But, I don't know how productive it is to have two of you working together for one fish. I'd find a solution to that if I were you two." He winks and takes our fish away.

"Don't worry, we will get you bulked up in no time." Luke punches my shoulder playfully.

"Oh, yippee," I say dryly. I've never been interested in being buff, but if it's what it takes for this job, I guess I'll figure it out.

"So... should we go eat?" Luke asks, holding his stomach.

"Absolutely."

We wander around the village looking at the various shops, restaurants, and leisure areas. I feel a tug on my collar, and I lift slightly off the ground. "Look!" Luke points to a shop I had passed.

"Could you put me down?" I ask.

"Oops. Yeah, but look!"

"I heard you the first time. Give me a second." I chuckle. "Oh, are you talking about the noodle restaurant?"

"Duh." He leads us inside and sits us at a bar-style table. "We'll have two bowls of noodles with quaxie broth." He slides the worker ten credits.

"Wow, that was cheap... should we be concerned?"

"Doubt it, cheap stuff is the best stuff. Don't forget that we are broke." He replies.

"True."

After a few minutes, the worker returns with piping hot bowls of noodles. Luke takes the first bite, and he almost shoots out of his chair in glee. "It's amazing. Tastes just like chicken ramen on Earth."

"Okay then." I take a bite, and while I don't know about that chicken ramen business, it is definitely amazing.

After we finish our meals, we return to the dock. "Hey, Mr. Traxis," I call out, trying to get the fisherman's attention.

"Hey, kids! What can I do for you?" He smiles, putting out an elbow to rest on a support pillar above the dock floor.

"I want the job," I say confidently.

"And I do not, but I will see you every day when I walk him over here," Luke adds just as energetically, throwing playful finger guns at the fisherman.

"That's great! I mean, not that you won't be here, Leo. But Dylan, great choice!" Traxis replies.

With eagerness, I ask, "So, do I need to sign anything? Also, what are my hours?"

Thinking over it before he responds, his words come with ease, "Well, no, and they're loose? I do expect you to work every weekday, but when you do is kind of up to you. As long as you bring me fifty credits worth of fish before sunset, I'm good."

"That's great! Thank you so much, I will do my best." I shake his hand, then give Luke a hug.

"Wonderful news, you have a great day, Mr. Traxis. And Dylan, I saw a shop selling weights during our walk, so you know what that means..." Luke grins.

From senator's child to buff fisherman, let my transformation into the poorly named Dylan Randall begin.

26

LUKE

I didn't think Nalia could get better. Well, I definitely thought that when I was in jail, but not before.

But here I am, waking up with Lunion in my arms while living a simple life in a beachside village.

"Hey, Lunion." I mess with his hair to wake him up.

"What?" His eyes flutter open. "No way you got up before me…"

"You had a big day yesterday, don't feel bad."

"I guess so. What are your plans for today?" He scoots closer, resting his head on my shoulder.

"Employment." I laugh.

"Well, duh." He reciprocates my amusement and gets up, stretching his arms dramatically. "I'm going to take a shower."

"Not so fast!" I put up fake finger guns, an embarrassing habit I seem to have acquired. "You need to lift some weights, then you can take a shower!" I keep my fingers pointed at him as I circle the room and make my way to the weights.

"Do I have to? Like, can't I brush my teeth at least?" he groans, dragging his feet over to me.

"Do you want to be homeless? Do you want to fight for food on the side of the road as luxury cars pass us by, their drivers sticking their noses up at our misfortune?"

"What the fuck kind of monologue is this? I doubt that would happen even if we couldn't pay a months' rent."

"You're right, that fishing guy is pretty nice and would let you stay with him. Still, I'm supposed to motivate you." I lower my hands. "Now, we will start with these."

I hand him some ten-pound dumbbells, and grab the thirties for myself, the heaviest we got.

"So," I begin, "You'll want to keep your palms facing up, then bring the weight up slowly."

He nods, holds the weight as instructed, then lifts it above his head like a flare gun.

Cocking a brow, I blink once. "What are you doing?"

"Bringing it up slowly." He responds flatly.

"Okay, so no. I guess I should've shown you." I raise my dumbbells to my waist, then curl them using my elbows.

"Oh! I've seen that online!" He exclaims.

My tone comes off a bit harsher than I would like: "Then why didn't you do it?"

"Okay, give me a break. Those videos are distracting."

"Sorry." I show him a couple more times, then let him continue on his own as I make breakfast. After a few sets, I finally pipe up, "That should be enough for today."

With a triumphant grin, he looks at me. "Yay! That wasn't too bad, actually."

"Well it was ten pounds..." I mumble.

"What was that?" he questions with a maniacal smile.

"Breakfast should be ready for you when you're out of the shower!" I reply, an equally joking smile on my face.

"Great!" He recedes to the bedroom and takes some clothes from our pile.

We haven't had a chance, nor the money, to do any furniture shopping. To be fair, the house came mostly furnished, but the bedroom is a little lackluster. With just the bed and a tall lamp, it isn't exactly the pinnacle of luxury.

I make us some pancakes, just like that night in his kitchen, and set our tiny, two person table. It's enough, though, because it is perfect for us.

"That looks great!" Lunion says as he steps out of the bathroom. This time, however, he actually put on his clothes in the bathroom.

"Thanks. I hope I didn't mess it up."

"I'm sure they're perfect." He takes a seat across from me, nodding as he eats to validate his statement.

I finish my breakfast quickly, take a shower, and meet Lunion on the porch.

"Ready for work?" I ask, watching as he gets up from the top step of the porch.

"Actually, yes! I hope I can get us a lot more today." His smile is contagious.

"Great. Ready, set, go!" I take off at full speed, jumping off the porch and hurrying to the dock.

"What the hell?" Lunion yells as he follows suit, running a good twenty feet behind me.

"You didn't think I would let you forget cardio, did you?" My shout fills the gap, and I narrowly avoid a couple with interlocked hands, their roadblock displaying my athleticism.

Lunion chases me through the maze of houses, shops, and villagers until I make an abrupt stop at the fisherman's post. He almost crashes into a pallet, but I stop him with both arms before he is able to.

"Hey, Mr. Traxis! I brought Dylan for you," I say, slightly out of breath.

"I see that... Dylan, are you okay?" Traxis looks at Lunion, who is doubled over, nearly hyperventilating, and shaking aggressively.

"Yeah." Lunion throws a thumbs-up at Traxis and leans on me for support. "I'm not a runner."

"I can see that..." Mr. Traxis laughs. "At least you shouldn't be doing too much running with this job."

"Okay, Dylan. Have a good day, I'll see you tonight." I give him a kiss goodbye and start walking away, knowing I'll end up staying there just to be with him and end up fishing for the rest of my life if I don't leave now.

I'm not sure where to go, so I find the realty office.

"Oh, hello, Mr. Randall! How can I help you today?" The agent asks.

Nerves flood my system with my realization. "Hey, Ms... I'm so sorry, I cannot remember your name."

"Well, that would be because you two never asked it." She lets out a laugh that sounds genuine enough to calm me down. "You two seemed so eager to get a house together, so I don't blame you. You can call me Ms. Lias."

"Thank you so much, Ms. Lias." Her understanding helps me gain a crumb of confidence. "I was wondering if you could help me find a job. Dylan is working as a fisherman, but we realized I'm not cut out for that." I bow my head shyly at this admittance, but Ms. Lias lights up.

"Absolutely! Anything I can do to help my new clients settle in, I will do it!" She thinks for a moment. "I heard the lumber yard was looking for more lumberjacks. Oh, and I know most stores around here are hiring. But if you want to put those muscles to use, I'd suggest the lumberyard." She grins uncomfortably, probably realizing her comment was a bit much.

"Thanks, I'll figure out where to go from here. You've done more than enough to help out!" My grin is much less awkward, and I turn after extending my gratitude to leave the building.

I had seen what appeared to be a lumberyard on our run earlier, so I head there first. It was just past the edge of our neighborhood, in the shadow of the city above.

As I approach my destination, it becomes clearer that I am in the right place. The thump of trees falling, the whizz of machines cutting wood into usable pieces, and the hum of chainsaws all greet me.

"Hello?" None of the workers answer. "Hello!" I yell louder, getting some heads to turn.

A man with a dark blue hard hat walks up to me. "Hey, you might want to step back; it can be dangerous around here."

"Oh, no!" I say, eliciting an eyebrow raise from him. "I mean, I was hoping to find a job."

To that, his face turns from angry confusion to pure ecstasy. "Really?"

"Yep, I'm new here, and I need a job."

"Great!" he yells back, making me flinch. "So the rate is fifteen credits per hour, and you can work eight hours a day. You are here a little late, so you should probably just do the training and a few hours of work," he explains.

"Got it. How do I begin?"

"Follow me and watch out for your colleagues." He motions to the five other workers operating power tools or large vehicles.

He leads me to a small shack to the side of the site. Inside, he hands me gloves, a hard hat, and a vest. On the right wall, there are axes and saws.

"Take your pick." He waves over the gamut of tree-cutting tools.

"Okay…" I grab a mechanical saw and hold it at a safe distance from my body.

"Follow me." Leading me to the forest, he points at a tall, slender tree. It has a slim trunk, small branches, and is topped by a dusting of amethyst leaves. "Cut it down."

I nod and turn on the saw. It seems to operate similarly to those on Earth, so I have no issue getting it to run. I approach the base of the tree and touch the saw to its scratchy bark. Given the tree's small circumference, I get it down in a minute.

I get back as it falls, and I watch it cascade down to an empty stretch of grass.

Cutting the power to the tool, I turn to the worker. "What now?"

"I'll get this taken away, but you need to take care of that stump." He tosses me a shovel, then signals a truck over to take away the rest of the tree.

Using all of my strength to dig below the stump, luck does not greet me as I pull up.

Another worker notices my struggle and offers a hand. "Hey, I'm Patsi, do you need help?"

"That would be great," I huff, wiping the sweat from my brow before I add, "Leo."

She begins to dig around the stump, loosening the dirt and revealing the roots. "Here you go."

Passing off the shovel, I take it from her, and she watches as I lift the stump out of the ground. "Thanks," I say through gritted teeth. It takes a lot of strength, but I rip the stump out and set it aside.

"Okay, good job! You need to replant now." She grabs two items from her vest pocket. "Place this sapling in the hole you left, then sprinkle this powder over it. It's a new invention, but it works wonders. We have trees fully sprouting in less than a *week* now."

"Wow! That's insane!" My enthusiasm seems to catch her

off guard. "Sorry, that is just really cool." She takes away the stump, and I plant the sapling.

Imagine what we could do on Earth with this technology. *This* is what we should be getting from Nalia, not oil. Inventions like these are worth the expenditure, the contracts, the interference. Not just a few barrels of oil, but an infinite solution to our forestry issues.

I continue working for a few hours and finish just as the sun sets, with a total of seven trees removed and replanted.

"Would you like to be paid weekly or daily? Assuming you're staying on, that is." The worker I originally spoke with asks.

"Daily is good. I am working with my husband to get settled, so any bit helps," I admit.

"Perfect. Leo, thank you for your work today." I don't remember giving him my name, but Patsi probably did. He hands me seventy credits. "Twenty-five for training, forty-five for the hourly rate."

"Thank you so much, Mr...." *I really need to get better at asking people for their names. I look like a fool.*

"Mr. Rede." He shakes my hand and sends me home after I promise to carry his greetings to Dylan.

I RETURN HOME A SWEATY MESS, BUT I AM STILL greeted by a smiling Lunion. "Hey! How was your first day running a marathon?" He looks me up and down, trying to subtly point out the dripping clothes.

"It went well. I am a lumberjack now, apparently." I take

off my vest and sweat-soaked shirt and put them on the back of a chair.

"Well, it's a good use of all of that." He motions to my body.

"Funny, our realtor basically said the same thing." I laugh, walking closer to him. Placing an arm around him, I plant a kiss on his forehead.

"You're going to taint me with your sweat," he grumbles, still not leaving my embrace.

"You'll survive." I tease before my eyes sweep over the kitchen. "Oh, crap, what do you want for dinner? I completely forgot."

"Oh, I made us some steak thingy. There was a recipe at the store, so I thought I would try it out." He touches my arm in reassurance as he peels away to check a pot of food.

We sit down to eat, and the meal is gone almost immediately. "That was amazing! How did you afford all the spices?" I ask, shocked.

"It was actually only a few, but I caught three large fish today!" he says enthusiastically. "I'm putting fifty credits a day into a jar over there," he points to the countertop, "that way we will have our five hundred in ten days, and we don't have to worry about rent."

"Let's make it nine." I get up and place fifty of my seventy credits in the jar.

The job is tiring, and getting money is stressful, but I would do this for the rest of my life if it means being with him.

27

LUNION

In the two weeks I've been weightlifting, there has been little physical evidence of my effort, but plenty professionally. I'm pulling those big ass fish out of the water with ease now, a feat I once thought impossible.

My luck, too, is outstanding.

There hasn't been a day throughout my time as a fisherman that I haven't at least doubled the necessary quota, and it's showing.

In two weeks, Luke and I will have saved enough money for two months' rent, and we will have plenty left to live on. While he does pretty well with his hourly job, I am the real breadwinner of this relationship.

One day, I even earned three hundred credits from fishing alone. Part of me feels like Mr. Traxis is using his fishing business as a money laundering scheme, but I don't care. As long as I'm getting enough money to support us, I'm happy.

Still, we haven't upgraded our appliances, nor have we gotten a real dresser. Tucked in the bathroom closet are the laundry machines that came with the house, but they need some help, too.

We have learned to do our sleepwear in the morning and work clothes at night. If we don't do smaller loads, I swear the washer is going to explode soon.

The kitchen is actually holding up quite well, which is likely because as soon as we pooled our income and had some extra, we've been eating out constantly.

What's more embarrassing than taking out the trash is that the noodle shop owner knows our names. Every time we walk in, Mr. Sola gets up from behind the counter, lets out a cheer, and then says, "My star couple! Table for the Randalls?"

It's nice to be appreciated, but it does elicit some strange looks from the other customers.

Mr. Traxis granted me the day off thanks to my exceptional numbers. I'm one of his two employees, or freelancers, I'm not sure what a better title is for what I'm doing.

The other is Tia, a cheerful girl, maybe a year younger than me. She claimed she wanted some extra money to pay for dates, shopping, and more. Given her lifetime love for fishing, she raced down to the docks when she realized how expensive life can be.

She's still in school, though, so I only see her at the end of my days, but she's fortunate. Even though she usually only has an hour or two to work, she can reel in one hundred credits' worth of fish in no time.

Thanks to my break, I got to sleep in. I could feel Luke leave this morning, and I remember him kissing my forehead before he slept out for work. It's been a couple of hours since then, so I force myself out of bed.

On a kitchen cabinet door, a note from Luke awaits my attention. It reads, "Have a great day. I love you so much, Dylunion." Next to the combination of my two names is a smiley face, with one eye slightly larger than the other.

"That's cute," I say to no one, and take down the note. Flipping it over, I write one of my own: "Meet me by the docks after work!" I sign it affectionately as Dylunion, and draw a heart next to my signature.

I plan to use my day off to plan the perfect date night.

Mr. Traxis had told me earlier in the week that I could use his small boat for whatever, as long as I told him first. Last night, I requested it for today, which confused him.

"You're going to work on your day off?" He exclaimed.

I had to explain that, no, I am not that motivated to do my job. I am, however, motivated by Luke, and I want to use the boat as a restaurant table.

I collect some of my excess credits and begin a trek into the big city. Every time I enter the major urban center of Lurnala, I am on edge.

So many people could recognize me, and it doesn't help that my roots are growing out.

Still, I have to make sure I make the most of this date. I can tell that his job is much harder than mine, and he rarely gets breaks. He says he enjoys it, but I can't tell if he is lying just to please me. Given his love for nature, I find it hard to believe he enjoys destroying trees. But the way he talked about their new nutrient mix with such delight and curiosity was promising.

I follow the path behind the neighborhood that leads up to a city elevator. Lurnala itself is split into the traditional village and the main city, with the latter rising about one hundred feet above the village, which is why the lift exists.

I GET ON WITH THREE GIRLS, ALL DRESSED IN THE

latest fashion. One has a messenger bag engulfed in plush keychains, which honestly makes me jealous.

As I step onto the platform, I hear the one with the bag snicker. "Hey, do you need help with your roots?"

"Girl, don't start... but yeah, I know it's a mess. I was gonna touch them up today." My tone comes off just as condescending as hers, even though I know she is right.

"I recommend this brand." Her voice warms up slightly as she pulls out her tablet and shows me a picture of the product.

"Thank you!" Gesturing toward the expensive material and key chains, I offer, "I love your bag, by the way."

"Ahh! Thank you! No one ever compliments this mess." Her snarkiness is gone, and we are both friendly by the end of the elevator ride.

"Well, I'll see you around!" I wave as the trio exits the platform.

Now, I have a new first stop. The beauty store is only a few feet away, so I walk over. *Alluring Cosmetics,* as it is called, is a large store occupying the first two floors of a large, white building.

The first floor is dedicated to makeup and skin care, and the second to hair and nail care. I buy the exact product she showed me, which is actually a bundle of bleach *and* toner, and return to the busy street.

It takes me a moment to orient myself, but I find that Lurnala is much like Lelarea, except there are no hover bikes or other vehicles in the air.

Here, the buildings are similarly structured: tall, generally slender stalks with stores stacked atop each other. What is different is the pedestrian element. Each store is accessible via swirling staircases or, if you're tired, interior elevators. The staircases themselves create an illusion that the entire building is surrounded by a pale helix, and it maintains its shape until a shell-like point at its peak.

The streets are busy but clean, the people are determined yet kind, and the air is tight yet comforting.

The city is alluring, just like the cosmetic shop, but its pull is too dangerous to fall for. I need to find the ingredients and candles, then get out.

My goal was to make the noodles that Luke is so fond of from scratch. I'd tried to hone my cooking skills with the few at-home meals we have had, and I have a sliver of confidence that I can do this.

I only have a couple of hours before Luke is home, so I line up all the ingredients and begin cooking. The noodles boil on a portion of the stove while I cook the quaxie. I tried to season the meat similarly to the shop's, using a blend of spices based on memory.

In about an hour and a half, I have the chicken in a container, and I'm racing to the dock.

The boat is waiting for me in the water. Traxis did as promised and set it aside, ready for me to use.

I slide into the boat, which is terrifying because I've never been in one. Luckily, it is still tethered to the dock, so I don't have to worry about drifting away.

I start placing the candles I brought strategically around the boat, and jump as soon as a noise sounds above me.

"Ahem." Luke coughs sarcastically to get my attention. "Hello."

"Hi, get in!" I yell back, grabbing at his legs from the low boat.

"Don't rush me!" He kicks at my arms, then begins to ease down into the small vessel. "What is all of this?" The smile on his lips earns one from me.

"Dinner date, surprise!" I throw up weak jazz hands.

"It's amazing, but a warning about the dress code would have been nice." He chuckles as he points at the suit I'm wearing. On the way out of the city, I found it at a discount shop and thought it would be somewhat humorous to wear tonight.

"Sorry about that." While I am dressed far more formal, he wears a tank top and shorts. "But your outfit is very classy," I laugh.

"Oh, yeah, one second." He pulls a pen out of his pocket and draws a tie on his tank top. "There we go."

"You are so dumb." Rolling my eyes playfully, I grab the container of noodles. "I hope this is right." As I place the container between us, I hand him a fork.

He studies the meal for a moment, then takes a bite, trying his best not to slurp up the noodles barbarically. "Oh, my god. This is amazing, good job!" Settling his hand on my knee, he brushes his thumb across it a handful of times. "Thank you, Lu- I mean Dylan."

"Anytime, Leo." I return his cheesy grin. "Oh! I have a project for us when we get home."

"That's eerie."

"You get to bleach my hair again, congratulations!"

"Oh... yay!" He mutters with fake enthusiasm. "I wasn't too great the first time around..."

"It'll be fine," I reassure him. "As long as my roots are gone, I'm good."

"What about mine?" His question confuses me because I hadn't noticed the quarter inch of blonde showing at his scalp.

"Oh... We can do that another day." I take a piece of his hair with two fingers and twirl it. "Not much showing."

"What's with these?" He changes the topic.

"Oh, I was trying to light those before you got here." My gaze falls on the unlit candles scattered across the boat.

"Do you want to light them?" He asks, holding up the lighter I got out.

I consider it for a moment. "No, I think this is nice."

We sit there together for hours, just watching the life below glow. Or, in my case, watching him. Even when we put away our dinner, and I was in his arms, I couldn't stop looking at him. The way my own body illuminated his was incredibly fascinating. Each muscle, each hair on his arms, each scar with stories I had never heard, each detail of him was amplified by my presence.

He had called me the moon, and he was the sun.

But at night, it seems to be different. In the light of day, it's his personality that becomes the bright star, bringing me figurative light, like a sun to a moon. But here, under the night sky, I am the bright star that physically illuminates his moon.

In that way, I presume that we are one and the same.

He is the sun to my moon, but I am the sun to *his* moon. He brings me light, and I bring him some as well. We both carry the privilege of completing one another when one cannot shine.

We work as a unit, a couple, a natural force drawn together by logic. Every day, even in the shortest bits of conversation, the slightest of glances, and the momentary touches of the skin, we constantly eclipse each other.

We are meant to be, to be as one, to be separate, and to amplify each other. If I have to run forever, just to keep that, I will.

28

LUKE

A month of labor, and it's finally paying off. Not only does the crew respect me now, but so does Mr. Rede. He respects me so much that he is giving me a day off.

"Hey." I brush Lunion's bangs, now platinum blonde, from his face. "Are you awake?"

"No," he groans, flipping over to burrow into the pillows.

"Got it." He may have started working out, but I still have the upper hand. I flip him to his side and press myself against him. Closing my eyes softly, I try to go back to sleep.

After a few minutes, Lunion gives up. "Okay, nevermind. I can't sleep."

"That's too bad." I roll on my back and start to sit up. "Are you excited for today?" Mr. Traxis had granted Lunion another day off, so we were free to do anything we wished, but together this time.

"Oh, yeah. What are we doing again?" he asks, trying to shake off the last traces of slumber from his eyes.

"Nothing specific, just spending a day in the city."

"Okay." He rolls back over, taking all the bedding with him.

"Hey!" I grab him as he attempts to cocoon himself. "I thought you were getting up."

"Do I have to?"

Groaning, I run a hand down my face. "I suppose not *yet.* I'm going to take a shower, and when I'm done, you'd better be up." I shake him one last time and head to the bathroom.

Now that I share a house with Lunion, I have to be careful. His penchant for cold water is a dangerous habit, and he took the last shower.

I turn the water to hot and step in.

As I exit the comfortably scalding shower, I notice that I forgot my clothes outside. Throwing a towel around my waist, I step back into the bedroom.

"We need to get a real dresser while we are out. It's been an entire month." I say, but Lunion doesn't reply. Gazing over to the bed, I admire his peaceful expression, eyes closed and breath heavy. "Wow, even a strip show won't wake you up. I really have failed."

I grab some clothes and put them on immediately. Though I don't mind if he sees me, I know he is too knocked out to get the chance.

Due to Lunion's increasing interest in cooking, the kitchen has become a mess of random experiments, as well as their consequences. So, while I wait for him to wake up, I decide to tidy up the space.

AFTER ABOUT AN HOUR OF WAITING, LUNION IS dressed and ready to head into the city. He has more experience with the hustle and bustle of Lurnala, so I let him take the lead.

Past the village and surprisingly close to the lumberyard, we get on an elevator and shoot up into the city. The city itself is as impressive as it is from below, with its spires intimidatingly beautiful, its streets stunningly clean, and its inhabitants passively hasty.

It's as if New York City were clean, or if Tokyo were on another planet.

"We need to go there!" Lunion points to a vintage clothing store on the third floor of one of the buildings across the street.

"Okay, are we taking the stairs?" I ask, somewhat concerned because he still seems tired.

He nods in affirmation and leads me to the spiral staircase.

Once inside, I can tell that "vintage" is a loose term for intentionally tattered and acid-washed clothing. Despite the deception, the prices aren't that bad.

With Lunion consistently bringing in large numbers every day, and with my hourly pay, we have plenty of money now.

Somehow, despite running away from luxury, we have made our own.

I make my way over to a rack lined with baggy denim pants. Most are cargo pants, which is fine by me. I find some in my size, and hurry over to Lunion.

"Can I get these?" My tone comes out far too desperate for my liking.

"Sure... I found this for you, too." He holds up a white tank top with a yellow patchwork star in the center. "A reminder of what you've lost."

"Huh?"

"Your hair color," he laughs, throwing the top into my arms.

"It's nice, thanks! We need to find you an outfit now." I grab him by the hand and run him around the store, trying to find black pants. "Here you go."

"Do you think I'm emo?" He asks, confused by their color.

"No, this is a reminder of what you've lost," I reply, a stupid grin forming on my face.

He doesn't respond, just takes the pants and bolts to the checkout, likely to avoid more "emo" clothing picks.

He calls for me after he's done checking out. "Hey, Leo, get over here!"

"Yeah?"

"Do you want to change into this outfit here?"

"Do you want me to?"

"Yes. I need to see the vision come together."

I take the shopping bag to a dressing room and put the ensemble together.

"It's amazing!" he claims, his eyes lingering far too long on my arms.

"Sure..." I joke, handing him the bag with my old clothes and his pants.

We leave the store and head back down the stairs. As we reenter the street, I get separated from Lunion.

I can see a group of girls looking at me, then one of them approaches. She has short brown hair and a messenger bag filled with stuffed-animal keychains.

"Excuse me," she utters quietly.

"Yes?" I keep my reply short, my eyes scanning the crowd for Lunion.

"Could I, maybe, potentially, hypothetically, have your number?"

"I'm sorry, but I'm taken. And I hate to ask you this, but could you help me find him? He has platinum blonde hair, and he's wearing a dark green shirt."

I feel horrible, but the more eyes, the better.

"Oh, yeah. I'm sorry. We can help out, though." She calls her friends over. "He has a man... and we need to help him find him." Her tone gets progressively angrier as she explains the situation.

"How nice..." A girl with space buns retorts.

"Is that him?" The bag girl points.

"Yes, thank you so much!" I shake her hand graciously and yell for him, waving in his direction. "Dylan!"

"Hey!" Lunion races over to us.

"*You're* his boyfriend?" The girl's jaw drops.

"Yeah! He's great. Nice to see you again!" Lunion replies cheerfully.

My brows furrow in confusion. "You two know each other?"

"Yeah, we met on the elevator a couple of weeks ago." Lunion answers.

"I see your roots are much better now." The girl adds with new warmth in her voice.

"Yeah!" Lunion laughs. "I got the exact stuff you recommended."

"Well, it looks amazing. At least *you* get him." She motions back to me.

"I agree, he's also pretty amazing," Lunion says, turning to link his arm in mine. We wave off the girls as they head into another clothing store. "So, what was that about?"

"She asked me for my number," I reply honestly.

"Well, I'm glad you didn't give it to her; she is pretty cute."

"Oh, did you want to give her your number instead?"

"Nah, I'm good." He kisses me on the cheek and leads me further down the street.

There, I stop in my tracks. On the bottom floor of one of

the buildings is a glowing light of salvation: *LURE IT IN FURNITURE.*

"We have to go." I practically pick up Lunion as I speed into the store.

"What? Okay…" He tries to resist, then relents as he realizes there is no point in struggling.

"We need a dresser. That pile is getting out of hand." I declare, pointing to a section labeled *"Bedroom Furniture."*

"Your pick." He puts his hands up in submission and follows me.

"This one. Definitely this one." I point to a light-pink dresser with white trim.

Lunion almost collapses in laughter. "This one? Are you serious?"

I look at him with a deadpan expression. "Well, yes."

"That girl never had a chance with you, you're so fucking gay! Oh, my god!" He's wheezing and leaning on me for support by now.

"Okay, screw you. You didn't even know that word for the first ten years of your life."

"We can get it. I'm just kidding." He tries to silence his amusement and switch to a more serious tone, but fails.

Ignoring him, I take a slip from the tag and bring it to the counter. "Can we have one of these, please?"

"Sure, do you want it delivered, or would you like to take it home today?" The clerk asks.

I look to Lunion for advice.

He catches my gaze and continues without missing a beat, "Will it be in a box?"

"Yes, you will have to assemble it if you take it today."

"Perfect." He nods. "When can we get the box?"

"It should be ready for pick up in a couple of hours. Can I get a last name?"

"Randall." We say in unison, garnering a soft chuckle from Lunion.

We sign off on and pay for the dresser, then head back out to the city.

"Well, we have a little while. Do you want to get anything to eat?" Lunion asks.

"I'll let you take a guess," I reply, knowing that out of the two of us, I will always be the one who wants food.

I take charge this time, making sure Lunion is safely secured with our arms linked. Losing him in a crowd is terrifying, especially when two different governments are definitely hunting us.

I find a noodle shop, as he probably expected me to, and grab us a table.

He sets down the bag of clothes but doesn't sit. "Can you get me the same thing you do? I really want to check out this store next door."

I'm a little uneasy about letting him go alone, but I concede. It's only next door, so if I get worried, I can pop over to check on him. "Sure," I grab his wrist, "please be safe."

"Of course." He smiles and walks away, leaving me to order our food.

I get the same noodles we normally order, and Lunion is back before the bowls are even out.

"I got you one, too!" He exclaims as he takes two small boxes from his bag. The box features what appears to be a plush frog keychain.

I flip it over to see that there are various options we could get, each with a different bow color: pink, blue, green, purple, red, or yellow.

"I want the yellow one." Lunion proclaims, slamming a finger down to show it to me.

"Well, I want the pink one, no shocker," I reply calmly.

We both open our boxes; however, I get yellow, and he gets pink.

Stunned by the odds of us getting the opposite colors, but each other's colors nonetheless, I turn to him. "Do we want to trade?"

"No, actually. I think it's cute that we got the wrong ones. I'll keep it." Lunion says with a smile, to which I return.

The noodles come out almost immediately after we unbox our keychains, and we finish the bowls at a similar pace.

AFTER A COOKING STORE, ANOTHER HOME STORE, and more toy stores, our dresser is ready for pickup. The cashier takes one look at us and slides a box our way.

Spending a month's rent on the dresser was the easy part, but now we have to get it home somehow. The box is too large and heavy to carry for long, so we opt to push it through the crowd.

Lunion, unpromptedly, acts as a crossing guard. He yells at people in the way and gives me directions that I already know.

"Love, is this productive?" I try to be calm, but this is a stressful situation.

"Ooo! New term of endearment unlocked? Also, I don't know. We can swap, if you want."

"Please." He takes over, doing surprisingly well at pushing the box without complaining.

Once we reach the elevator, the trip becomes one hundred times easier. We get on once it's empty, and because of the box, no one wants to join us on the platform. When we exit the lift, there is hardly any foot traffic around the village.

The sun is down, and the streetlamps that line the village pathways pierce the night sky. We get to the house, and Lunion lets me carry the box inside.

Before we can even close the door, an unfamiliar voice cuts through the darkness.

"Hello, Lunion."

29

LUNION

I cannot believe my eyes.

Or ears.

Or really any of my five senses.

I feel like they have all betrayed me, because why the hell is Veronica standing over my stove, attempting to heat up some leftovers?

"Hello? What the fuck are you doing here?" I yell, flipping on the light as I put an arm in front of Luke defensively.

"Lunion, who is this?" Luke asks with a hint of fear. "How does she know your name?"

"It's Veronica, my mom's assistant," I reply, not taking my eyes off of her.

Veronica frowns. "You can drop the defensive act, Lunion. I'm on your side here."

"What?" I shake my head. "I don't believe you. Why would you seek me out if you were on our side? You would have just left us in peace."

"I'll explain all of that. Can we just sit down, please?" she begs, her hands shaking slightly.

Luke walks over to the bed and sits on its edge while I pull up our two chairs to form a triangle.

Clenching my jaw as I settle into my seat, I meet her gaze with a hint of coldness. "Sorry, we don't have a lot of furniture. Didn't expect to entertain any guests..."

"It's all good. Nice little house you have here, isn't it?"

"Okay, can you please just start talking? I can't keep waiting to find out if I need to run or not." I practically hiss, moving my chair closer to Luke.

"Well, the short answer is yes, you do," she begins, "but not from me."

"That's eerie and nondescript as hell," Luke mumbles, his hand making its way to my own as he talks.

Veronica takes a deep breath. "They've basically figured out where you are. They don't know the house yet, but that won't last long."

"Well, then, how did you find us?" I pose.

"I went door to door, and you two left yours unlocked. I thought it was a dead end until I saw this." She pulls out one of the notes Luke had left me.

I had kept them all in a drawer, and each one was dedicated to Dylunion, a stupid nickname that I never thought would be dangerous.

"Oh." Luke swallows, tears forming in his eyes.

Veronica nods, but sympathy lingers in her gaze. "This kind of confirmed it, so I've been waiting here since."

"So what? Why are you here then?" My question comes out more as a plea than an attempt to defend Luke.

"They said that once they found you, you two would never see sunlight again. I don't know if that means life in an underground prison or death." The tremble in her voice lingers as she continues, "Either way, I knew I needed to find you first. I don't agree with anything they are doing, please believe me."

"Who are you referring to when you say 'they'?" I ask, hoping it's not my mom.

"The humans," She turns to Luke. "*Your* father."

"That tracks." He says quietly, still shaken by everything.

"What about my mom?" My timbre cracks, practically fracturing as I contemplate the possibility.

"She is trying to accommodate what they want, but she is getting to her limit. I can tell that if you called her, she would do anything she could to help you." Veronica reassures me.

"I believe her." Luke squeezes my hand to offer reassurance. "Your mom signed that deal for *you*. If you aren't alive, then she has no reason to be doing anything."

"Yep." Veronica nods.

"Well, what do we do now?" I whisper, wiping away tears I didn't even realize were flowing.

"I'm so sorry," she pauses, "you two will have to run again."

I remain silent, and just as soon as I get up from my seat, I fall into Luke's arms. I start bawling, and it doesn't stop.

I knew we would have to leave as soon as I saw her in my kitchen, but I didn't process what that meant.

That means abandoning this perfect life we've made together. This life where we share a house, a bed, and our meals.

This life where we function like the happiest married couple to ever exist.

This life where we are one unit, one small, safe unit.

But I guess this life could never have been, and it was foolish to stay here.

To stay in this house, to build a life, to get a job, was nothing but an Icarus adjacent dream.

"Why?" I say over, and over, and over again. Luke tries to comfort me, but I think he is more destroyed than I am.

He was the first to fall, the first to love, the first to want all of this. And because of his dad, it is all getting taken away.

"So, if you found us, how long do you think we have until *they* get us?" Luke pushes out between sobs.

Veronica herself is a mess. "A few days, maybe? I'd leave tonight, if possible."

"Great," I whimper, sitting up to rest my head on Luke's shoulder. Bringing my knees to my chest, I wrap my arms around them and stare blankly at the wall.

"What are you gonna say?" I ask Veronica.

"I'm on leave right now. They don't know where I am, and if they're tracking me, they'll think I'm here on vacation. If they figure out I'm here for you, I don't really give a shit. I'll just say you never showed up, or they can jail me, I don't care."

Luke brushes a tear from my cheek before turning back to her. "Thank you, really. It hurts now, but I know leaving is for the best."

"You should take this." Veronica uncaps a pen and writes something down on the note she had shown earlier. "It's a private line to call your mom. If you stop along the way to your next location, give it a call. But only right before you are about to leave," she warns, passing it to me. "I think she will be sympathetic, but just in case, make sure you are ready to run."

"Thank you." I fold the paper into a couple of squares, squeezing it as a form of comfort.

"Of course, and if I can do anything to help you tonight, let me know. I think I'll stay here in Lurnala for a little while. The city has some pretty good hotels, from what I've heard." Veronica smiles, trying to stay optimistic.

After the conversation, Veronica stays for a little while longer while we pack. We haven't used our bikes since we got to the village, but we kept them charged—thankfully. Gathering

our most important possessions, some clothes, and our battery
packs, we lead our bikes out to the porch and try to prepare to
abandon our picturesque life.

30

LUKE

Lunion is refusing to move from the porch.

"We need to go," I whisper, trying not to sound harsh.

"I know," he sighs, remaining in the same spot. "I just don't want to."

I squeeze his shoulder tightly, trying to relieve his stress. I'm heartbroken to be leaving, too, but I have to act strong for him. If I show how upset I am, this whole thing will probably fall apart.

It's my fault we are out here, anyway.

"Do we have to?" he asks, more than just a hint of desperation in his voice.

"Yeah, I think we do."

"She said we have a few days."

"Do you really want to risk staying longer?" I ask, my tears returning. It hurts to leave, but it hurts even more to think about what might happen if we stay.

"No, yes? I don't know." He takes a deep breath. "Can we at least wait until we can say goodbye to Mr. Traxis?"

I mull it over. The negatives outweigh the positives because telling someone we are leaving only increases the risk of delaying our absence. But the upside is that the person I love gets a hint of closure, and that alone outweighs any negatives.

"We can," I declare, trying to hold his hand.

"Really?" His eyes widen in surprise.

"Yes, really." I kiss him on the forehead and turn to reenter the house.

Veronica immediately sits up, concern lacing her expression as we walk inside. "What are you two doing?"

"You said we have a few days," Lunion answers quietly.

"You're not thinking of staying, are you?" she questions, her eyes bulging with disbelief.

I speak before Lunion has the chance, "Just until the morning, so we can say goodbye."

"That sounds like a horrible idea..." Veronica's voice trails off as she notices Lunion walking towards her. He is sniffling, his arms wide and expectant for a hug. "I can't convince you otherwise, can I?"

I shake my head at her and let Lunion find some comfort in this strange woman from his past.

After a few minutes, Veronica leaves. She tells me she is staying at the Chellina Inn in Lurnala and asks me to come see her in the morning, if possible. I reply with an empty promise, saying we will try our best, but I know we won't be able to even go near the city safely.

We make sure to get our extra batteries and bikes back on their chargers, then crash on our bed. We will need to be rested for whatever comes next.

THE MORNING LIGHT PIERCES THROUGH OUR window for the last time. It illuminates the kitchen where we shared more meals than I can count. It highlights the folds of the blankets on our bed, and reflects off the box for the dresser we will never get to put together.

I was looking forward to that. Being able to build something together. The fun of searching for pieces, drilling parts together, and hoping we aren't sitting on the screws we needed. But now, even the idea of that is all gone.

I make sure everything is ready while Lunion gets a few more minutes of sleep. He deserves so much more than this, and he could've had it if he never met me.

The bikes are fully charged, and the baskets are mostly full, carrying rolled-up clothes, some food, and now the full battery packs.

"Luke?" I hear Lunion's voice from a castle of blankets.

"Yes?" I step away from the bikes.

"Come back to bed." His voice is somber, his head is turned away, and his entire body is covered in bedding.

"I can't, we need to head out soon," I breathe.

He doesn't respond; he just forces himself out of the bed and inches slowly over to me. As he has been doing since we got the news, he falls into my arms helplessly. It's like he's lost the will to go on, the hope to keep running, the value of his own life.

"I'm so sorry," is all I can get out.

"You're okay. *I* chose to break you out. *I* chose to run. This is all my fault." He isn't crying, and I fear it's because he can't, not anymore.

"That's the dumbest thing I've ever heard." I embrace him, but try to bring him back to a standing position.

"I'm going to change, then I guess we leave." He moves sluggishly across the room, grabs some clothes, and shuts the bathroom door behind him after he slips inside.

While he gets ready, I do my best to cook something for him to eat. He's done a good job of getting groceries, so I find ingredients for pancakes almost immediately. It's a bittersweet reminder of that first night we actually connected and of how I ruined the life we could have had.

"Hey, I made pancakes," I say as Lunion exits the bathroom.

He looks at me, his eyes devoid of any trace of life. "I can't eat right now."

I dip my chin in understanding, making quick work to fix myself a plate. After I finish eating my breakfast, I grab some sodas for the road.

"Drink this at least, please." I hand him one of the cans and hop on my bike.

"Okay," He says dryly, his hands fumbling to grab it.

"Get off of your bike," I instruct, watching as his tired body slowly spills off of the vehicle.

He doesn't put up a fight, just does as I say. I sit him on the back of my own bike and link the two together. I hold his hands to my waist and drive out towards the dock.

Not many people are out this morning, only a few eager sailors and older couples out for walks. Fortunately, Mr. Traxis is out by his little outpost.

"Hey!" I try to get his attention while still holding onto Lunion's hands.

"Oh, it's you two! Lovely to see..." His voice trails when he sees Lunion practically asleep against my back.

"Yeah... I'll let you two catch up." I carefully get off, supporting Lunion's weight, and walk him over to Mr. Traxis. I can't tell if he is actually *that* tired, or if the sadness of leaving is just destroying his functions one by one.

"Hey, Mr. Traxis," Lunion whispers weakly.

"Hey, son. What's going on?" Traxis keeps a strong illusion, but I don't miss the fear that flashes through his irises.

"We have to leave town. Family matters," Lunion replies, his tears returning.

Mr. Traxis frowns for a split second, then tries to cover it with a feeble smile. "Well, you were definitely my favorite worker. All good things must come to an end, I suppose." His eyes become glassy, but he blinks away any tears that are forming. "Please, take this." He hands Lunion a small bag.

"What is this?" Lunion asks.

"A little bonus. Don't think too much of it." Traxis winks then hugs Lunion tightly. "Well, I wouldn't want to keep the two of you for too long. Visit me, if you can."

"For sure," Lunion promises. It's empty, but maybe saying it will give him some hope.

"Bye." I wave shortly to Traxis and give him a polite nod, then I pile Lunion back onto the bike and ride off. I can feel Lunion's head move from my shoulder, and in my rearview mirror, I can see that he is staring at Traxis, at the ocean, at the village.

We follow the path next to the village and past the city. It leads upwards to a hillside that continues to grow gradually until it plateaus.

"Lunion?" I grip his hands tightly. "What is this?"

The hill comes to an end, and in the space beyond it, small islands are floating.

He sighs. "Oh."

"I'm gonna need more than that."

"We don't have these near Lelarea, but I've heard of them. The engineers who designed these bikes set up these courses in the countryside to test their products. It's supposed to show the height and safety capabilities, or something like that." He perks up a little bit, shifting slightly. "Wait, let me off."

"Oh, sure." I stop the bike and let go of his hands.

"I've wanted to try these out since I saw an ad about them." Lunion slowly regains the color and life in his face as he hops onto his own bike. "Let's go!"

"Are you sure you're okay-" As I ask, he speeds away from me and to the islands.

I follow, lagging behind more than I would like. I watch as he drives off the hill and into the air. He gains a bit of height and drops onto the first island.

If he falls, it's on me.

"Luke?" He calls from the second island.

"Yeah?"

"Did you lock the baskets?"

"Yeah, I think so? Why?" He answers my question by flipping from one island to the next, and luckily, I did, in fact, do as he asked. His bike spins a short arc and comes down onto the succeeding island with amazing delicacy.

I finally take my own leap from the hill and follow him across the islands. They continue for longer than I thought they would. At least thirty islands lay before me, each varying in size.

The hover bikes can only float high above an open land source for a few seconds, and that's what makes this course so terrifying. This isn't like the city, where magnetic fields can keep you aloft longer. One gap too long, one moment of hesitation, and you're falling down at least fifty feet.

Not that much damage would happen, but if you lose your grip on the way down, that would be the end.

Luckily, Lunion is happily jumping from island to island with no issue; his speed is even increasing as he goes.

"Woah!" I scream as I attempt to do a flip just like Lunion. Somehow, I don't land after the first spin, and I do two. To my surprise, I have enough time to stick the landing after my second flip, and even start going faster.

It's not enough to catch up with Lunion, but it's still exciting.

Before I know it, we've run out of islands. The last one comes unexpectedly fast, and I barely have time to switch modes and glide down to the grass below.

"Look!" Lunion yells once I join him on the ground. He points to a sign, which reveals the location of a nearby railroad. "We need to head to that."

"Why?" I ask, still concerned about him. "Are you sure you're okay?"

"Kind of, I don't know. But I am better now, at least better than earlier. I was so focused on what we were going to lose that I didn't consider what we would gain. Yeah, we will be running forever, but there is so much more to see, to do, to try."

"Wow, that is a surprisingly positive change in perspective," I say, offering him a small round of applause.

"Thanks. I'm sorry, it's been a lot, but those islands reminded me that I can still enjoy *something*." His eyes widen in regret. "Something in addition to you, of course."

"Thank you. Anyway, why do you want to go to the... railroad?"

"I think it's a good way to get us to another city. I remember learning about this system in history class, specifically that it's a large hover train that follows a magnetic charging platform."

"Wait, so the train runs on electricity and is constantly charged? That is insane!" *I love the technology here, my god.*

"The best part is that the platform extends hundreds of miles, and there are plenty of stops to get to a myriad of villages. Small and large alike," Lunion recounts with excitement.

"Okay, so what's your plan when we get there? Slide into a random train car with our bikes? Is that even allowed?" I ask, more worried about being judged for having our bikes on a train than about the regulations.

"I'm so glad you asked." A smirk appears on his face. "We are going to ride the rails with our bikes!"

31

LUNION

This was perfect. Just the thrill I needed to get out of that awful headspace. And the best part is, if I fall off the tracks, I don't give a shit.

If I fall, I'm letting go of my bike, because I truly have no fucks left to give about my life. This planet is small, which means they'll catch up to us at some point. And when they do, will there be any point in even believing in a life? No.

"Lunion? What the hell is wrong with you?" Luke asks, laughter escaping between his words.

"Hey, you fell in love with me, now you get to deal with it." I stick out my tongue tauntingly and race towards the tracks. I didn't know that hover bikes could kick up dirt, but as I spin, a trace of dust leaves the ground and flies towards Luke.

Based on the sign, the train tracks aren't *too* far away. A few treelines, several empty fields, and a noticeable shift in the sun's position far? Maybe.

But that isn't too bad when you have nothing else to look forward to than the destination itself.

The first train station appears on the horizon, and luckily, a train is leaving its port just as we approach.

"Are we really doing this?" Luke groans from behind me.

"Duh."

Once we get to the station, I go around it and onto the tracks.

The beginning is boring. A tunnel blocks out all natural light, and the track is narrow. However, once we exit the tunnel, everything changes.

Another track runs parallel to ours, so Luke can ride side by side with me. Better yet, the surrounding environment is like something out of a movie. Tall copper bridges connect the mountains, and up ahead, a bolster slices the tracks in two.

This bridge support, which I would expect to be mundane, is far from it. From the middle, a waterfall flows down to the river below. Tracing the entire bridge, not just the leg, purple vines twist ornately along its edges connect them by shooting up. Within this net of vines, flowers blossom potently.

Every inch of the exterior bridge pieces is veiled in overgrowth, but it doesn't seem sloppy; it seems planned.

"Have I mentioned how beautiful it is here?" Luke yells over from his track, now forced apart from mine by the bridge.

"I don't think so!" I lie, knowing that he has called both this planet and me beautiful.

"Smartass!" he shouts, and even though he is too far to make out clearly, I know there is a dumb, cute smile curling on his lips.

While I knew how the architects of this railroad plotted, I have no idea about any of the other feats of creation in the area.

I feel as if the bridge was meant to blend with nature, its copper tone merely soil that cultivates the life of the surrounding flowers, which accent its beauty. But maybe that's just some dumb form of hope seeping into my heart.

We finally pass under it, watching the vines swing above as we retreat to a normal path. Luke and I are close once again, and he doesn't have to scream.

"That was amazing. It was like it was built for nature," he says.

My brows raise in surprise, then fall. "Yeah." Of course, he would have drawn the same conclusion as me. How could I be shocked?

We ride the rails for a few more minutes, and the coexistence of nature and technology continues to thrive. Birds fly in formation above us, frogs croak below, and butterflies dance in the air between us.

"Oh, look." I point at a town in the distance.

"You don't sound too thrilled." Luke comments, and he's right, I'm not. This little distraction on the tracks has been too good, and now I have to return to real life.

I have no intention of making this new town my next temporary home. It's too close to Lurnala. However, even with dread settling in my gut, I will use this opportunity to call my mom.

The thought of hearing what she has to say, knowing it will be negative no matter what, twists my stomach. She could be on our side, and I know what is happening back in Lelarea will still be horrific. Or, it could be horrible there, *and* she hates us, too. Win-win.

We find a ledge that seems jumpable enough, and we leave the tracks. Luckily, we are in the air for just short enough to save us from falling, and we land.

"Well, let's hope the people are nice there." Luke stares straight ahead into the village before us. It's still pretty far, but I can make out the basic details of the town.

In the front, I can see a tall, rectangular building. It has two smaller structures attached to its base, and large windows in each.

Luke tries to conceal a laugh.

"What?" I ask, smiling out of confusion.

"You don't think that building there is a little... phallic?" He grimaces.

"Oh." I take another look at it, and he's right. "Ew."

"Don't you like men?"

"Yeah, just... as a professional city planner, this really hurts my soul." I am not, nor do I ever plan to be, a city planner, but it's fun to make shit up.

"Oh, absolutely." He silently applauds my creativity

Around the dick-shaped building, several smaller, similarly rectangular buildings line the streets. As I complete my scan, I cannot find a single curve in the infrastructure of this town. Not a bridge, well, or lamppost in sight. What I do see, however, are small, blocky poles that emit light and line the streets.

Just short of the entrance to the town, we find a lot and lock up our hover bikes. To my dismay, there is a five-credit charge per bike parked. "Great." I feel around my pockets, then remember I locked them in one of the bikes. "Do you have any credits?"

"Oh, yeah! I got some from Traxis. I don't know if you were actually awake for that." Luke responds with a fading smile.

"I remember something about that," I mumble.

"Okay, let me check." He digs in his pocket and reveals a small drawstring bag. "Holy shit!"

"What?" The question comes out with far more fear than intrigue. "Is it a bomb?"

"He gave us two thousand credits!"

I'm silent, but my eyes, which are almost flying from their sockets, reveal everything.

"Well, thank you, Mr. Traxis..." Luke takes out a few credits and feeds them into the machine.

Approaching the village is intimidating. The streets are empty, except for a few people out walking their pets or tending to personal farms.

"Excuse me!" I chase after an older man, but he doesn't hear me. "Never mind." I slink back to Luke, who is trying to play with someone's dog.

"Why is it pink? And why does it only have three teeth?" he asks through a gritted smile.

I place a hand on his shoulder to appear pleasant. "The teeth are a Nalian thing, don't ask. The color is their doing." I smile at the couple who let Luke pet their dog, trying to be kind. "What brand of dye did you use?"

"I think it's called Fantabulous Fuschia by Freetyme Hair!" the woman states cheerfully.

"Lovely, you two have a wonderful day." I pull Luke from the small dog. "That is the brand I used for my bleach and toner."

"Oh, wow. If you get neutered, let me know. I can drive you to your appointment."

"I am not getting a vasectomy," I say without laughing as we continue down the street, struggling to find more residents.

"Damn, we should've asked them if they knew about any way to get calls through," Luke grumbles, slouching down like a defeated cartoon character.

"They look nice, let's ask them." I subtly point to two men sitting on the steps of what I assume to be their home.

"Hello!" Luke waves at the pair, gesturing between them. "I love the sweaters!" Thankfully, he leaves out their twinned haircuts.

Given Luke's sunny disposition, luckily, they assume he is being sincere. "Thank you!" the one on the left says.

"I was wondering if you knew how we could call someone? We aren't from around here, and our tablets stopped working a while ago," Luke lies. We, or I, left the tablets back in Lelarea. I couldn't risk them tracking us, but I guess that doesn't matter now.

"Oh, absolutely!" The one on the right beams. "If you go straight, then take the second right, you'll find a call box to use."

"Thank you!" Luke shakes their hands, and we continue down the path.

Sure enough, there is a large rectangle sitting to the side of the road where the man said it would be.

Before I can stop him, Luke grabs a man walking by. "Excuse me, why is everything rectangular here?"

"It's the most efficient shape when you consider surface area to volume ratio, duh." The man replies, then walks away.

"Efficient for what?" Luke calls after him. "For what?" The wavering terror in his timbre is kind of cute.

"I'm 100% sure that is 1000% wrong." I say, recalling learning about a sphere being the best.

"Where the fuck are we?" Luke asks, grabbing my hands fearfully.

"I don't know, let's make this call and get out of here." I open the box and slide in.

"Can I come in?" he asks, his bottom lip quivering.

"Uh, I guess?" I answer, wondering if he genuinely wants to see my mom or if he is just concerned to be alone in this town.

"Yay!" He hops in, squeezing into the corner of the slender box. My shoulder is pressed against his chest, and I have barely any room to put in the twenty credits it requires to make a call.

"Oh shit. I don't have the number." I remember leaving it in my pants from yesterday.

I feel Luke shift behind me, pulling a slip of paper from his pocket and handing it to me. "Well, luckily, I am perfect."

"How did you get that?"

"I have my ways."

"When?"

"Before I went to sleep last night."

"So you were just... playing in my laundry?"

"Obviously, it's my favorite sport." He shrugs.

I know he's joking, but I'm surprised he can read me so well. That he could just know he'd need to hold on to that paper for me, and that he rescues me from my failures without flaw every single time.

"Okay, let's put it in." I tap the transparent keyboard: 10072025.

The box illuminates, and the keyboard disappears. Bright white lights sputter on the walls of the box, and the entire room turns into a giant screen. A blue loading symbol spins on the wall in front of us. After a few seconds, the wheel drops, turns into a liquid, and joins the rest of the screen.

In an instant, the room transforms into my kitchen. The view is from a little higher up, obviously on the table.

Eye level with us, however, is my mom.

"Lu-" she yells, then glances around the space hesitantly. She holds up a finger to the camera, grabs whatever device she's getting the call on, and runs to her room.

The door slams, and I hear the lock click into place as she leans against it in relief. She shuts the blinds in the room, then sits down at her desk.

For several moments, she just stares at us. Fixing her hair, she takes a deep breath and finally says, "Hello, Lunion."

Staring into the camera with intent, her pupils widen and

her breathing increases. It's obvious she is genuinely happy to see me.

After a couple of awkward beats, she speaks again. "Oh, hey Luke, you're here too. Nice hair."

32

LUKE

"Hello, Mom," Lunion says, his timbre wavering.

"Uh, hi!" I add, waving at her nervously. Her gaze darts between us. "How are you two doing?"

I feel Lunion grab my hand and squeeze it hard. "Do you really even care?"

"What?" she asks, her eyes filling with concern instead of the evident love they just held.

"Do you really care? Because if you're just going to have us killed, you can drop the bullshit and tell me how you really feel." Lunion's voice catches on every single word, and it's hard to watch him force the question.

Ms. Moire stares at him for a few moments, and a tear rolls down her cheek. "Starchild."

"Don't start with any sentimental crap until I know if it's authentic. After Veronica showed up at my house, I don't trust any of you." Shaking, Lunion tightens his grip on me with each passing second.

"Lunion, I truly do care. But how am I going to prove it? I can tell you how *I* feel, which is that I've spent every single night weeping in my room, waiting for my only child to come home. Or how for every second I'm around Luke's father, I am filled with anger, fear, and disgust. All I want is for you to come home safely, and for you two to live like normal kids. Lunion, I can't prove anything, but I would do anything, pay any price, to see you again, in the flesh." Sorrow slips down her face in a steady stream.

Lunion turns to me and cries into my shoulder. I can feel his tears seep through my shirt and onto my skin, the tension of the room only amplifying their prevalence. Each drop feels like a dagger slicing through my skin and into my heart. Hearing his harsh, whimpered inhales makes me weep in tandem, and I wrap my arms around him to silence his sobs.

"I love you, I'm so sorry," Lunion gets out. "I want to come home. I want all of this to go away. Why can't it go away?" He turns back to the screen, only to see the mess his mother has become.

"I know, but it can't. It just can't. You had to do what you did, and maybe that's just part of you growing up." She tries to dry her damp cheeks with an embroidered cloth. "I just don't think I was ready for you to actually *grow*."

With our combined sobs, it feels like we are all together, like this box stitched itself into her room, and we are huddled around her desk in one big crying session.

Lunion cries because he is tired.

His mom cries because she misses her son.

I cry because I know my dad would never say these words. These beautiful, kind words.

Ms. Moire sits up in her chair and tries to shake off her sorrow. "So, when you ask if I really care about how you're doing, trust me that I want nothing more than to know that you are safe, happy, and the Lunion I knew before I lost him."

While she somehow stops crying, Lunion can't, and he

nestles his way past my arms and into my chest, his face against my torso for support.

"I'm glad you called, because it's so bad here." She takes a deep breath, like she is scared to clarify what she means. "He's taken out the woodlands, as he promised. There are a few trees left, but most of the area is either plowed down or scheduled to be."

Lunion's eyes flash quickly from sadness to fury, and he spins away from me. "What? So you really did sign that deal."

"I... yes. But I thought he would stop at the forest, and I was willing to give it up to keep you safe." She looks down in shame.

"Excuse me?" Lunion looks at me, his eyes wide in disbelief. "What do you mean you *thought* he would stop at the forest?"

"I..." she starts, trying to select her next words carefully.

"Spit it out!" He yells, his entire body erupting with noticeable anxiety.

Placing her hand on her temple, she begins rubbing generous circles to help with the stress. "They, or *he*, has decided to look into rezoning Maula's neighborhood."

Lunion goes silent, and I try to hold his hand, but I can't stop his body from going limp. He slides down and collapses to the floor. There isn't much room in the box, so he's sitting on his knees, resting his head on my leg.

"I'm sorry?" I speak up, trying to keep her talking. "How? Why?"

"I don't know, he said something about eminent domain. How our laws had similar rules about land acquisition, and if we just proposed a bill to change it not to be preservation-exclusive, it could happen. He's threatened me, he's threatened my colleagues, and he's bribed other senators."

"Mom?" Lunion tries to lift himself from the ground. "That's where we used to live."

"I know," she sighs.

"Are you really going to let him ruin our past, too? He already has our present and future. You can't just…" His breath hitches, and he starts weeping again. He's almost run out of tears, so each one looks more and more out of place. Like a raindrop in a drought, each line of sorrow he sheds holds more pain than the last.

"So, he's going to install what? Oil drills on all of this land?" I ask, knowing how money-motivated he is and that he'll stop at nothing to bring himself a profit.

"That's all I've been told. If he has any other plans, I don't know them."

"How could you let this happen?" Lunion asks angrily.

Her tone wavers, a plea for understanding replacing its usual sharpness. "I didn't really get a choice, Lunion."

"You say you care about me, that you did it for me, but if you cared, you would know that I wanted none of this. Why did you do it?" Even as he expresses his frustrations, I can't tell if Lunion is truly angry or just terrified.

"Mr. Dinyre pointed out that once my term ends, this cushy life is over. I'd do anything to keep you secure, Lunion. This was the first time that security had been offered to me."

"I would have been fine back in our old neighborhood. I don't give a shit about the fancy life."

She frowns sorrowfully. "I know that now, but I'm trapped. I wish I could do something, but I can't."

"When are the drills going in?" I ask, still trying to get as much intel as possible.

"Installation is set to begin today through tomorrow morning."

"Well-" I start, but she puts up a finger to silence me. She looks at her door, then the transmission flickers out. The room dissolves back into black, and the door handle illuminates in stark contrast.

I open it, and Lunion falls into my arms.

"What are we going to do?" Lunion asks, his eyes void of emotion, but still red and puffy.

I look into his dying gaze, and I know I need to find *something*. I can't just let his hometown, nor the rest of his planet, get ruined. If I stand by and let my father ruin the forests I fell in love with, I'm not any better.

Even worse, as soon as he begins corrupting this planet, the boy I love only hurts more. I have to do something, and it has to be equally as insane as what he is doing.

"I have some sort of plan?"

"What?" He looks up weakly.

"One second." I motion for him to follow me, and I lead him away from the crowd that has formed around us.

On the outskirts, I find a long, rectangular bench.

"Sit here." I point at it and wait until he obliges before I continue, "It might sound a little insane."

Groaning, he rubs his eyes. "Nothing can shock me today. I've heard enough."

"Okay... What if we destroy the drills before they even use them?" I propose, not thinking he'll be too excited by my batty idea.

"Yes."

"That was fast." I laugh, my brows raising.

"They are being built tomorrow morning. If we drive nonstop, we can get there a day late." He pauses, giving the idea a little more attention. "Even if they start drilling, it's best to take them out before they do *too* much, right?"

"Yeah, I guess so." Honestly, I'm taken aback that he is so ready to take on my sloppy plan.

"Okay, do you know what these drills might look like?"

"Yeah, maybe? He was always trying to show me the ones he was so enamored by. He called them beautiful feats of capitalistic fervor, or something stupid." I cringe at my recollection.

"Can you draw it?" He points to the paper with his mom's private number.

"Oh, yeah, let me find a pen." I know I brought at least one with me; I just need to get it from my bike. Running back to the parking area, I unlock the basket, and grab a writing utensil.

Lunion is waiting for me when I return to the bench. "I didn't get kidnapped." He flashes a weak thumbs-up.

"Yay," I huff, glad that my unease about the town didn't prove to be of true concern. "Anyway." I sit on the ground before the bench and set the paper on it. I draw the drill from memory, recalling its large arm supported by a metal lattice base. "See here, this is the thing that lowers the drill. If we can take that out, we can at least halt their progress."

"How strong is that?" He points to the middle of the arm.

"I don't think it's very thick, so it can't be too strong?"

"How about that?" He points to the base.

"No clue, same thing though. Not super thick, but it is all probably pretty heavy."

"It's a risk we will just have to take." Lunion nods. "Thanks for sketching it all out. I think I have an idea. Can I see that pen?"

Lunion grabs it from my hand before I can respond and joins me on the ground. He starts sketching, but he is so close to the paper that I can't see anything.

"Here." He slides the paper towards me. Now, two stick figures ride what I assume are hover bikes, and they are holding... lassos?

"What exactly am I looking at?" I try to be respectful, but a laugh escapes.

"That's us. You're the slightly wider one."

"Oh, wow!"

"We'll ride our bikes to the drills and attach these ropes to the hitches on the back."

"What is at the end of the rope?" I point to the shiny metal loop that gives them their lasso-like shape.

"Hooks. Like a grappling hook from The Legend of Zelda. That game is a great invention by your kind, by the way."

"Thanks..?"

"We will use our fishing skills to wrap the hooks around the drills, then we will drive away. Once far enough away, the drills should come crashing down, or at least some part should come off."

"What if the rope snaps?" I pose first before uncertainty consumes my thoughts. "Also, how are we getting grappling hooks? Oh, yeah, and what do you mean by *our* fishing skills?"

"Great point! We can get chains instead. We will find something to form into hooks, and we can attach it to the chains!" He says, his voice growing in excitement.

I decide to drop where my concern lies—the fishing thing—because I'm just happy to see him excited again.

"Okay, it's kind of feeling like an arts and crafts hour, but I will try my best," I reassure him, squeezing his shoulder with a fearful smile on my face.

"Terrific! Let's begin searching for our materials. We don't have a lot of time, so chop-chop!"

33

LUNION

My fighting spirit is back, if I ever had one to begin with.

No, I'm really just angry. I'm not revitalized, I'm not motivated by hope. I'm just pissed.

And any hint of excitement is toned down by the sea of complexities flooding over me. My heart wishes I could go back to before the humans arrived, or at least before the President did.

However, it also knows, and I also know, that means I would have never met Luke. I want to say he's the diamond in the rough, and he truly is the only thing keeping me alive, but it's still so hard to find light in this.

"Let's hop to it!" I fake some enthusiasm and skip towards our bikes. Forgetting how far away that parking lot is, I'm surprised Luke was able to go back and forth so quickly.

Luke drags behind me, still skeptical of the plan he proposed. I know it sounds stupid, but I don't care anymore.

There are really only two outcomes of this little experiment.

One: we take down some oil drills and buy some time for my mom and the other senators.

Two: we get caught, fail miserably, and get jailed or killed, or both.

Honestly, I'm fine with either.

Luke calls out after me, "Why are we heading to our bikes?"

"While I was super depressed, I did get a glance around this town. There is absolutely nowhere to do the shopping we have planned," I explain. "We have to find a real city."

"Yay…"

"I'll let you get noodles if there is a shop."

"Yay!" His tone shifts, and he starts skipping next to me.

The bikes are just as we left them, but I notice one issue. This lot doesn't have any chargers. We'll have to spend some extra time in the next city to keep them alive.

Hopping on, I wait for Luke to get situated before we pull out of the parking lot.

"So, where are we going?" Luke asks after a couple of minutes of silence.

"Uhh, good question."

He looks at me, jaw dropping. "You don't know where we are going?"

"Sorry?" I shrug. "Let's just head south, back towards Lelarea. We at least know it's there, but hopefully we can find a different city."

That seems to be enough of an answer for Luke. We leave the hauntingly rectangular city behind and latch onto a dirt path through some plains.

It's oddly empty here.

Trees are sparse, but the flowers are rich. Each of the few blue hills are perfectly round, and the environment feels undisturbed. The only time the flowers or grass blades part is when our bikes hover above, applying slight, benign pressure to their soft stems.

"Look." Luke points to absolutely nothing.

"What?" I ask, brows pinching with concern.

"Oh, nevermind." He grimaces. "I thought that flower was a building."

"Are you..?" I was going to say stupid, but that's a little harsh. "Oh, wow."

"Ignore me," he groans, sliding down on the seat of his bike dramatically.

The wilderness continues just like that for a while: beautifully bleak, disappointingly drab, and perplexingly peaceful. Each bend presents a new stretch of unmarked land, each contortion of foliage tricking us into seeing some illusion of manmade oasis.

I can't even call Luke dumb, because from far away, the out of place trees look like buildings. After a while, the plains feel like a blooming desert. Each minute, another town-sized portion of blue seems to load in, like we're in a video game.

Finally, one of these chunks loads in with an actual city on its horizon. The city is similar to Lurnala, with tall buildings but no air traffic.

This means we can get off our bikes, charge them, and walk around without any issues.

As we approach, I am able to get a better look at the buildings. Just like in Lurnala, each one is wrapped in a staircase. Instead of them going up into spires, these lead into hooks. Like a scythe or a tentacle, each structure pierces the sky and hooks clouds like a fishing lure.

I can smell the sea. With its salty breeze climbing into my nose, I know this is also a port city.

All of the factors point to this being tied to Lurnala in some way. Maybe the same planners and architects worked on it, or we are all similar enough to share ideas without any connection. Hell, the similarities between some places on Earth and Nalia point to that possibility too.

We reach the city, and there is an open space ready for bikes. Luckily, each locking area also has a charger, so we elect to leave them behind before exploring. We lock up our bikes and head into the city.

It's pretty much the same as Lurnala, with only a few differences. These differences are tiny nuances, such as more spaced-out buildings separated by only a few feet.

"It's really pretty here!" Luke exclaims, staring up into the sky.

"Yep," I concur, but I'm confused about what has caught his attention.

But then, I see it. Between the buildings that line the street is a giant net. Nestled in it, flowers bloom bountifully. They cover it completely, and you can barely tell that there is any space between the rope pieces. Some even hang down like vines, tickling the space between the road and the sky with childlike mischief.

"Oh, yeah, you're right," I say in awe as I search the rest of the city.

Every building is lined with baskets, each filled with flowers. Here, more exotic flowers bloom. I see oranges next to greens, yellows next to reds, along with the usual blues next to bright pinks.

"Is that green?" Luke asks, his eyes widening.

"Yeah? I mean, I never said we didn't have it *at all*."

"Oh, yeah, you said that most of the plants here just absorb green wavelengths. I guess that is different for flowers?" he proposes his hypothesis with uncertainty.

"Yep." I give him a round of applause. "Congratulations."

We walk further into the city, watching as cats pass us by and butterflies hover above the baskets of flowers.

"You have cats?" he questions in surprise.

"Well, yes," I say, motioning at the furry animal rubbing against Luke's leg. It has a bandana on, which is admittedly very cute.

"Okay, I know our planets are similar, but you don't have turtles, so I don't want to hear it. How was I supposed to know you have cats?" Laughing, he bends down to scratch between the cat's ears.

"Well, I gave you a cat stuffed animal when you first got here." I point out.

"Oh." He tries to feign sadness, but the cat is making him too happy, so he just chuckles. "Come with me, Sam." He picks up the cat, which, to my surprise, has no issue being cradled in his arms.

"You're taking it with you? *And* it has a name?" I look at him, my mouth opening in shock.

"Just until we get out of the street, and that's my Earth cat's name, don't hate. Samantha would be honored."

"Wow." As dumb as it is, his idiotic optimism is rubbing off on me.

We cross the street and head into a camping store, hoping it will have what we need. The store is a little jarring, with taxidermied fish hanging from the ceiling. I assume they are supposed to be "flying" around the room, but it is still eerie.

"That gives me an idea…" Luke disappears to the back of the store. He doesn't return for a couple of minutes, but when he does, I am pleasantly surprised. He is holding six large fishing hooks.

"I think we have the same idea here," I say, staring at the perfect grappling pieces. "I had no idea hooks this size even existed. What are these for? Small sharks?"

"No clue, but they aren't too expensive either." He hands me three of the hooks. "For six, it's just three hundredcredits."

"Nice!" I find a small handheld basket and put our hooks inside. It's a little awkward because the basket has holes, but it will have to do.

I can see a sign that reads *"CHAIN"* dangling above the back right corner of the store, and I had that way.

The wall is covered in different links. From thick to thin, metal to plastic, and short to long, they have it all in a grid-style layout. You can cross-reference the system to find the combination you want. So, because I want a long, thick chain, I go down to the middle of the left side and pick out the perfect one.

"Did you get it?" Luke asks, his eyes wandering to my hands.

"Yep, long and thick, that should work, right?"

"Just how I like it."

"I'm sorry?"

"That works!" He takes my basket from me and heads to the register to pay. We use up most of Traxis' gift, but we should still have enough for lunch.

"Well, that didn't take long," I mumble in slight disappointment.

"Yeah, we have a while to wait for our bikes, right?" Luke asks eagerly.

"Mhm."

"Great! You have a promise to live up to." He drags me over to a noodle shop that I assume he found long before we ever went into the camping store.

"Perfect!" he screams excitedly, pointing at the noodles he loves. "They have everything here; it's amazing."

"Yeah, cats, chains, noodles... Everyone's dream," I say sarcastically.

We order and find a seat, but this isn't anything like our old shop. We don't know the owner personally, we don't get announced as we enter, and we have no home to go back to once we are done here.

Once we sit down, Luke's demeanor shifts, and he grabs my hand. "Lunion?"

"Yeah?"

His eyes meet mine. "Are you sure you want to do this?"

"Eat noodles? Yeah, I'm okay with it." I joke.

"Don't act dumb."

"Harsh. But yeah, I want to do this."

"It's such a stupid idea, though. We could get hurt." Concern flashes across his features.

"Still, Luke, we have to do it." I try to reassure him, but it just comes off as eerie.

"It's just-"

"Luke, I only have three things left to lose: my life, my planet, and you. If I'm losing any, I want us both to be there for it. So, when you ask if I'm sure I want to do this, the answer will always be yes. I'm putting my planet first, and I'm doing it with you, so it will make me happy."

"Okay, if you say so." He nips at his bottom lip but relaxes in his chair. "It's just... if we get captured, I don't think they'll be too keen on keeping us alive. Especially me."

"It's okay, we'll just try not to get caught," I say with a weak smile. It's a meritless statement, because we really have no idea how this will turn out, but I'm trying to reassure him.

The waiter comes out with our noodles, and Luke's sunny self returns.

We took a window seat, which I originally thought nothing of, but now, we have a visitor. "Oh, hello, Sam." I hold out my hand to pet the cat. "Luke, look."

"Hey, queen!" He pets the cat with a beaming grin that I can't help but return.

I study her bandana, which has the noodle shop's logo and address. "Did you find this place from the cat?"

"Yes, I'm surprised you didn't see it earlier."

"Aw, she's back! How was your scouting?" The waiter picks up Sam and carries her around to a cat tower by the entrance.

Luke winks at me. "She was like a sign from the cat gods."

"You're so dumb." I laugh. "Is that sanitary?"

"Oh, definitely not. Especially with the workers touching her too... Maybe we shouldn't finish these bowls." He grimaces and pushes his bowl forward.

"Well, we should start working on our hooks. Do you have any experience with arts and crafts?"

34

LUKE

"Where are we even going to move this stuff to? It's not like we have a workbench in this city. Or, really anywhere." I point out the flaws in our plan.

"We can just use the parking lot," Lunion answers as if it were the obvious choice. "I'll need help lugging all of this back, though." He slides the bag full of chains to me and gets up from his seat.

"Oh, I guess my training sessions weren't good enough?" I joke.

"Yep. You're an awful personal trainer," Lunion sings, leaving me no choice but to take the extra weight with me.

Grabbing the bag, I get up to leave, but a waiter flags me down. "Sir!"

"Yes?" I ask, wondering if my payment didn't go through.

"You were one of our lucky winners! Karen chose you, so you get a free stuffed animal." They hand me a stuffed cat that looks just like this planet's Sam.

"Oh, thank you?" I tuck it under my arm.

"Do you have a moment for a picture?" He waves his hand at a wall of Polaroids, each showing a different customer holding an identical stuffed animal.

"Oh, sure?" I look at Lunion for confirmation, and he holds out a hand to take the chains from me. I mouth "Thanks," and head over to the wall.

"Just stand on the paw prints, look at me, and say meow!" Smiling, the waiter holds up the camera.

"Uh." I try to smile. "Meow?" *God, this has to be some sort of humiliation ritual.*

"Purrfect!" they exclaim. "Would you like a copy?"

"Yes!" Lunion screams. "Please!"

They make quick work of printing off two pictures, one for the wall and one for me. "Have a furtastic day!"

Once we are far enough from the restaurant, I whisper to Lunion, "I'm never picking a restaurant *ever* again."

"Can I see your picture?" he pleads.

"Fine." I don't even look at it and just hand it over.

"Oh, my God." His jaw drops. "Luke..."

"My smile cannot be that bad." I protest.

"It's not that; it's what is around your smile." His own smile is widening by the second.

"What?" I snatch the picture from him. Around my mouth, there are whiskers. Three per side, to be exact. Atop my head are black ears that match my hair. "What the fuck?"

"I think it's amazing. I'm making sure we get copies of this, you know that, right?" Lunion takes it back and slides it into his pocket with a sigh before I can rip it up. "If only we had a video."

"Oh, that's okay, trust me!"

Crossing the street again, we work our way back to the parking lot, passing even more cats on our route.

"You can't trick me again, you hellhounds!" I run away from them, leaving Lunion further in the city.

He calls after me, forcing his way out of the crowd. "Thanks for leaving me with the 'hellhounds!' You do know that cats can't be hounds, right?"

"I don't have time for your corrections; my public image is ruined," I shudder dramatically.

"Well, we generally don't have time, like, at all. So, let's get to work, kitty!" Lunion seems happy, but I draw the line at certain nicknames.

"I'm going to jump you." My eye twitches as I glare at him.

"Threatening, but that is a cat-like thing to do..." He smiles, then tries to do a basketball fake-out, I think.

"Anyway..." I try to change the subject. "Let's see what we've got. Well, I know what we've got, but you know what I mean..."

"Yep! Chains, hooks, less money than before." Lunion empties the bags he forgot he was carrying once he saw me meowing for my photo-op.

"Okay, so how are we attaching these hooks?" I ask, looking at the meager selection before me.

"To what? Each other or the chain?"

"Well, both, I guess."

"Do you have any experience with weapon-making?" He cringes, likely because he knows the answer will be no.

"I'll act like you never asked that. I was in props for a theatre thing once?"

"Did you do anything with metal?"

"No." I think about it. During that camp, I watched as an older technician used a metalworking tool to melt metal between other pieces and join them together. "I might have an idea? I don't know if it works around here, though."

"Well, go ahead and try." Lunion looks defeated already.

"Be right back!" I run into the city and dash into a hardware store. To my surprise, there are short metal sticks labeled "soft" in one of the first aisles I check. On the other end, a heating tool is also available.

The only problem is that it's a few credits out of our budget. That is, until I notice the sign that says their entire store is 30% off.

"Hello, sir. Did you find everything you were looking for today?" The cashier has an odd, curly mustache that pierces the sides of his nose.

"Yes, actually. It was super easy to find!" I praise the store, but he seems to take it personally.

"Spectacular! If you would fill out the survey on our website and use my name in your review, that would be great." He shakes my hand as he hands me my bag. "Have a wonderful day."

"You too..." I smile weakly and head out of the building. As I approach Lunion in the parking lot, I realize how absurd our situation is.

Looking from the outside and seeing a pile of oddly sharp objects in the middle of a random parking lot is very humbling. As if the cat incident wasn't embarrassing enough, this didn't help.

"What the hell was that?" Lunion asks from his post on the ground.

"Sorry, but I had an idea."

"Yeah, you mentioned that."

"Anyway, can you unplug one of the bikes?"

"Sure?" He disconnects mine.

"Thanks." I take the tool out of its box and plug it into the outlet.

I wait a few moments, then check its heat against one of the metal rods.

"Can you hold these two hooks together like this?" I demonstrate the outward position they need to be in before handing them to Lunion.

I take one of the sticks and press it into the tangency line between the hooks. I use the tool to melt the metal, sealing the hooks together.

I add another and repeat the process, sealing all three points of the boundary. I do this twice, once for my hook and again for Lunion's.

"Okay, smartie pants. Good job!" Lunion cheers for my idea, which seems to be working.

"Now, we need to try to attach the chain." I take one and slide the end piece over the hook, then straighten it over the center of the triad. I melt more metal where the pieces touch and in the gap between the chain and the hooks, creating a sort of hill of metal.

"Cool," Lunion says, his mouth slightly ajar.

"It's a little messy, but it might work?" I don't want to be too cocky, but this seems good. Again, I repeat the process on the other set, and we are ready to go.

"Not that I don't trust your abilities, because I do, but I think we should test their strength," Lunion admits guiltily.

"Oh, yeah, you're right. And trust me, don't feel bad. I have my doubts too," I reassure him. "So, how do you propose we test them out?"

"Maybe we can test them on the trees out in the plains? Obviously, we wouldn't take any of them down, just to check the strength of the metal."

"Sounds like a plan." I hop on my bike, wait for Lunion to unplug his own, and we head back into the open fields.

As we get closer to the city's edge, Lunion points at a tree. "There!"

"Got it!" I throw the grappling hook at one of the branches, but I miss. "Oops."

"I'll try!" Lunion yells from the other side of it. He does a cartoonish swing of his chain in the air, but when he throws it, it actually latches onto a branch. "Yay!"

He drives away, and I watch as the branch bends with pressure. The hooks do not break off, so I yell at Lunion. "You can stop!"

The branch relaxes as Lunion comes back and snaps back into place when he removes the hook. "Great! So, I guess that answers our questions." He drives around the tree to join me.

"Yeah, I guess." I sigh, "Even if mine doesn't stay intact, you're the only one who will be able to hit anything anyway."

"Eh, I have faith in you." He smirks, then races away.

"Where are you going?" I yell.

"Time is of the essence! We need to get to Lelarea!"

Chasing after him, we quickly reach the water. It's still light out, so the sea life isn't very noticeable.

The waters are calm for the first few hours of the trip, but that takes a turn. The waves start to act restlessly, making us glide higher and higher each second. They lift us, and I have to admit it's kind of fun. It feels like we are surfing, but we never get under their curls, so we are safe from getting wet.

We dance like this for a while, taking the waves calmly as they appear. Each hill marks another tiny but thrilling challenge. It's not a test of our physical strength, but of our character.

Whether we can keep up with nature in a fun way is the true hurdle here. If we can, even under the most dire context, stay light-hearted when it matters. Because, honestly, if we didn't approach these raging tides with glee, we would be met with terror.

Lunion even seems happy to traipse across the fluid hills,

letting out a "Woo!" every time he succeeds in crossing a big one.

As the sun sets, the sea life begins to glow.

The tides must have been washing up some kelp to the water's surface, because every wave is spotty with blurry blue light. Different patches of softly piercing illumination mark this water as a mosaic, the light barely scratching the surface of each wave and lighting our way as we pass over.

I get so distracted by the beauty below and ahead that I don't consider what is creeping behind.

Before I know it, a large flash of pink light, maybe twenty feet in length, shoots from the water between Lunion and me. The pressure it exerts sends us flying apart like similarly charged magnets.

"Woah!" I scream as I'm thrown to the left. "Lunion?" I yell into the night.

No response.

I zip in the direction it sent him and begin searching for him. "Lunion?"

An immense amount of concern floods my senses. Sure, there is some light coming from below the water, but it's not enough to see anything, anyone.

That's when I remember... Lunion glows too.

I start searching the water for not just a bike, but one with a glowing boy on it. A boy who glows like the moon and stars above, but who can't control these tides like the moon itself. Instead of a boy on a bike, I see Lunion trying to stay afloat on his own.

"Luke?" He yells, his voice gurgling with the water as he slips beneath it.

"I'm here!" Grabbing his hand before he vanishes entirely, I haul him onto the back of my bike. "I've got you." He's dripping wet and shivering, and the worst part is I can't tell if it's from the cold or the fear coursing through his veins. "Let's find your bike."

We hunt where I found Lunion, and luckily, his bike is not far.

Lunion gets off mine hesitantly, hitches his own to the back of it, and climbs on to join me again.

"I just want to stay with you." He's still trembling, but now he's gripping my stomach for dear life with his head on my shoulder.

"Always."

35

LUNION

My heart is racing, my body is shaking, and the worst part is, my hair is wet. That was fucking awful, but at least Luke was there to save me.

I cling to his body like it's the last support rung on a ladder that I'm scared to get down from. "Thanks again," I whisper into his ear, which is easy given that my head is crushing into his shoulder.

"I-" He never finishes what he tries to say, but I assume he is just stunned from the moment.

We continue riding the now calming waves for another hour until we finally reach the island with the Inn. Instead of entering, we elect to stay on the seashore, letting our bikes charge at a nearby lot.

The only lights, aside from those underwater, are the lamps lining the boardwalk. We approach one adjacent to our bikes and sit down. I don't let go of Luke, I just lie there in his arms, grasping his hands tightly.

Looking up at him, a tear almost falls right into my eye. "Are you okay?"

"Now, yeah. That was horrifying, Lunion. I thought I'd lose you, and not in one of those poetic ways either. You wouldn't pass away in my arms as I weep over you. I thought you would just disappear underwater, and I'd never see you again." He sniffles, "I never want to not see you."

I try to sit up, but my body is still weak from fighting the waves. Attempting to hug him regardless, I wrap my arms around his waist and press my head to his chest.

"Lunion, do you think that was a sign?" he asks with a shaky breath.

"How do you mean?"

"Like, what if that was a warning that we shouldn't go to the drills. Like something bad will happen there too."

I tighten my embrace. "No, I don't know why, but we always have shit like that happening. Maybe getting past that obstacle is proof we have to go, that we have to keep fighting."

That was a load of bullshit. To be honest, I am terrified to go to the drills now. Still, I have to prove to myself that I can at least *try* to make a difference.

"I guess. I just don't want to lose you." That seems to be his only fear.

"You won't."

"Hey," Luke shakes me, "I think our bikes are good now, so rise and shine."

I yawn as I get up, but after my nap, I have some more strength. "Thanks for staying awake. I didn't even realize I fell asleep."

"It's all good." He smiles, then crosses the street to fetch our bikes. "Do you want to ride with me again?" His expression tells me that he would prefer it if I did.

"Yeah, sorry."

"No problem." He smiles weakly and gets on his bike. I hop on the back, and we sail back over to Lelarea.

The waters are calm now, and the sun is slowly rising. It's noticeably more peaceful than last night, but I'm still on edge.

I could have died without stopping Mr. Dinyre, and that thought alone is terrifying. Before we heard about the drills, I'd just given up, but then I felt like I was supposed to do something. Supposed to resist and make a change, so almost losing my life meant almost crushing the sliver of hope I'd found.

We head towards the shores of Lelarea for another couple of hours and finally reach the familiar rocky beach. The hill we dove off to reach the water stands tall above the shoreline, and it only makes me want to fight harder.

That's what marked the beginning of our new life, and now that life has been taken from me. I can't let Luke's dad leave unscathed after he butchered perfection.

We approach what's left of the forest, which isn't much. The trees to the left bend fleetingly around a giant construction site like a crescent moon, but the foliage to the right still seems somewhat untouched. We still have time.

Luke drives us into the woods, veering towards the right side to keep out of sight of anyone who may be near. We dive into the trees, snuggling in until we feel safe. Once satisfied with our location, we hop off our bikes and retrieve the chains.

He fastens them to our bikes, hooking each onto the hitches and locking them in place.

"Let's get a better look." Luke motions for me to walk with him to the treeline.

Where trees once were, a dirt field has now found its home.

Tall and slender oil drills, just like Luke showed me, are littering the field. They span from the center to right up to the treeline, making it impossible to pick a first target.

"Do we want to split up?" I ask, studying the expanse of drills before me. Each drill is spaced just right so they all spiral out from the center, leaving each side of the forest lined with drills.

"I can take the other side if you'd like?" he proposes. "So you can escape into the woods if needed."

I think it over because I don't want to put him at risk, but I know he has a better chance if it comes to physical combat than I do.

On the other hand, if he gets caught, there is absolutely no chance of them keeping him alive for long. I don't have time to ponder it, at least not to the extent I would like to, so I make a snap judgment.

"Yeah, that sounds good," I confirm, then head back to my bike. It's hard to comprehend what I am about to do, but I know I need to do it. No matter how naïve, childish, or whatever this plan is, I feel like I *need* to follow through with it.

I take a deep breath, feel the chains of my grappling hook trail my hand, then speed out of the forest. Luke passes me and zips across to the other side of the drilling field.

Okay, first target. I'm in the middle of this field like a sitting duck, and I need to find something to do. I can't see anyone working right now, but I know there are security cameras, and that can change in a second.

I just go for the middle of the spiral, which seems like the obvious option. The drill before me stands at least twice my height, which is intimidating enough without the moving hammer part swinging down.

I get a bit of momentum and throw my grappling hook at

the base of it. It snags the metal beams, and my chain clinks with pressure. I know it's locked, so I pick up speed and rush towards the north edge of the spiral.

Nothing happens.

The drill doesn't budge at all.

Not even a little creak.

I try not to freak out, but it isn't easy. Everything seems pointless now, and I have to go back to rip out my hook. The structure is staying intact, and I can't just break free. If anyone were watching, this would be a humiliation ritual.

"Luke?" I yell from the center, trying to find him.

"Lunion! Any luck?" I hear him call from behind me. I spin around to see his chain in his hands, but zero drills are knocked down behind him.

"No! I think we need to get out of here!" I can feel my eyes glazing over, and I'm trying my best to fight any oncoming tears.

"Okay. Whatever you think is best. I trust you, Lunion." He says, and, on cue, some officers appear on bikes. Each is carrying a blaster and approaching at increasing speed.

"Well, shit." I shudder. What the hell? I knew it was coming, but did they really need guns?

"Um." Luke frowns. "What do we do now?"

"Run?" I spin out of the spiral, gliding by the drills in fear of what's coming. As expected, the guards fire rounds at us. "Rude!" I shriek, part of me unsure why I even try to.

There seems to be only one good way out—heading back to the ocean. We fly off that hill once again, and we abandon Lelarea.

But then what? Getting away from the shots is only a temporary solution to a proliferating problem.

We dodge some bullets, hop across the pond back to Lurnala, and *what else?* There aren't many options I can see.

I rack my brain algorithmically, considering every possible outcome of this equation. We could end up dead by blasters, which is just disappointing.

We could end up running for the rest of our lives, finding fleeting glee in different regions while the planet cries in pain.

Or, we could find a better way to do this.

I was such an ardent supporter of this plan for a reason, and I won't give up now.

I rush to the forest's cover, diving deep into the woods to find some privacy. The trees wrap me in their cool embrace, providing a comfort I had long forgotten.

The safety of being surrounded by life designed just to exist. These trees, vines, and bushes have no intent except to root and grow. They mark their territory peacefully, calmly, and with open arms to any kind of visitor. And I intend to be kind to this forest.

In the few seconds I have to myself, I remember something my mom told me.

"I hate the humans' military." She would always say before discussing a new advancement in weapons technology. "These new blasters can cut clean through metal! How the hell are we supposed to counter that?" She would throw her hands up in frustration and rub her temples.

"Thanks, mom," I say softly before riding back out into the drilling field.

As soon as I break through the treeline, the guards' reactions are immediate, and their shots begin. I guess our attempt to flee was all they needed to void any negotiation plans.

I zip to the middle of the field, taking a brief pause at the center drill, then spinning out, following the spiral.

Their shots miss me, but hit some of the supports on the drills. But not where I need them to.

If the weapons' beams could hit at least one leg of a drill, they could bring it down. *I think.*

Just as I'm about to reach the second ring of drills, my neck shoots with pain. A beam missed me, but its radiated heat did not.

My neck burns with unbelievable potency, and I can feel the skin bubble as I try to speed away. I need to switch up my movement patterns.

I add short jumps and zigzags into my motions as I near the end of the spiral. Once I'm at the last drill, I pause, waiting for their beams to rain down on me. At the last second, just as I see the flare of a fired blaster, I zip into the woods. They all miss me, but two of the blasters wipe away a leg of the drill each.

It's my chance, and I have to take it.

Through the unbearable pain of my searing burn, I throw the hook with all of my might. To my relief, it latches onto the drill's base, and I can carry on with the plan. Without two of its legs, the drill comes crashing down with reassuring ease.

My excitement peaks just as the base is about to smash into the dry ground beneath it, but is quickly squandered. The drill explodes, sending not only me flying but also shooting flames across the sparse grass in the field and straight into the forest.

I look up weakly, my elbows digging painfully into the dirt. The drill was too close to the treeline, and I was too naïve to think my plan was flawless.

I watch helplessly as flames engulf the very forest I had planned to protect. My vow is defiled, and the woods are incinerating before my eyes.

"Lunion! We need to go!" Luke grabs me and throws me onto the back of his bike.

"No, no." I shake my head in disbelief. "No!" I shout, my voice cracking out of anger, fear, and genuine heartbreak. I feel like a wounded animal, but the only thing wounded is Nalia, and it's because of my own foolishness.

"It's okay…" Luke tries to comfort me as I sob.

"No, no, it's not! I'm a plague on this planet! We have to stop it. We have to stop it. We have to stop it." I keep repeating it until I can't speak anymore.

36

LUKE

Lunion is weeping against my shoulder as we abandon the flame-filled forest. He screams and screams without end. Each one contains immense pain and a hopelessness that comes not only from his gut, but from his heart.

They send chills down my spine and tears down my cheeks. I can't stand seeing, hearing, and feeling him like this, but we can't do anything. If we had stayed one minute longer, we would have been dead.

"It's going to be-" I stop myself. Why should I lie to him? It's not going to be okay. Hell, I don't even know what it could be.

Vision blurry with tears and shame, I bring us back to the shoreline. Away from the guns, away from the burning logs, away from any visible danger.

"Luke," he whines, his timbre fracturing as he draws out the vowel.

I get off my bike and sit down on the sand. "Come here."

He obliges and curls into my lap. Wrapping myself around

him, I press him against my chest as I start crying into his light hair.

"I need to leave," he whimpers between sobs so pained I wish I could go deaf.

"Okay, I'll take you anywhere. Wherever you want to go, I'll make sure you get there. And everywhere you desire after that." Slipping my fingers beneath his chin, I pull his gaze to meet mine. "Okay?"

He shakes his head and tries to wipe his tears. "No. I need to *leave*."

"I don't know what you mean, Lunion." The lump in my throat grows. My feigned claim is a lie. I know what he means, but I don't want to hear that I'm right.

"Just let me drown or something. Find a blaster, I don't care," He sobs into my shoulder. "I'm a plague to this planet. Wherever I go, I'm just going to ruin everything. I'll leave a trail of dust and ashes until there is no Nalia left to curse. Just let me die."

I don't respond. I can't. There is nothing I can say that would explain the feelings swirling inside of me.

Regret.

Frustration.

Terror.

Love.

I try to speak up, but a jumble of muffled sounds comes out. "I-"

"Please." He holds my stare, and my chest aches at the vibrant red tainting the whites of his eyes. Lips quivering, tears stain his cheeks as he waits for my answer.

"No," I say simply.

"Please," he insists, punching my chest lightly.

"No, Lunion. Then what am I supposed to do? Do you want me to die too? Because you know I'll do it."

"No! You aren't the problem here! Shut up."

An odd statement, given that I actually am the problem, but I digress.

"Lunion, no. There is no way I'm letting you do that! We will find another way." I scold him, not aggressively, but with enough emotion to show how scared I am.

"Like what?" His eyebrows drop to hood his gaze, whether in fear or anger, I'm not sure. "Wherever we go, they'll find us. There is nowhere safe here. Nowhere."

"So we don't find somewhere here," I whisper.

Shaking his head, he sighs with defeat. "What do you mean?"

"We leave the planet. I mean, there are plenty of countries on Earth we can hide in, or maybe even another hospitable planet out there, just for us."

"That's such a dumb idea."

"Lunion, I'll live on the goddamn moon if it means being with you. Please." I beg him, not for mercy, but for hope.

"How would we even do that?" His tears are clearing up slowly but surely, and he sits up.

"Your mom said she would do anything to help us. Giving us the codes to a small ship should fall under that criteria," I propose.

"Do you really think she would be okay with her son leaving the planet for good?" He frowns.

"If it meant keeping you safe, yes, she would."

Rubbing his temples, Lunion grumbles, "I guess you're right."

"How are we going to get in contact with her, though?"

"We can see if Maula is willing to harbor some fugitives. She at least wouldn't turn us in." Lunion shrugs.

"That sounds good."

"Plus, I need to see if they..." His lip quivers again as he fights off another wave of tears. "If they put it out. The fire, I mean." He shakes off his sorrow, or at least the visual symptoms of his current state, and gets on the back of my bike.

"Let's hope she doesn't try to kill us!" I joke.

"Oh, she is a notorious killer. Always in the news and all. They call her the Dr. Pepper killer, because she leaves a trail of cans behind everybody she slays." Lunion says like he has a flashlight under his chin.

For a brief moment, his humorous response comforts me. It's more than reassuring to see him cracking jokes.

As we near the forest, Lunion was right about one thing: ashes are everywhere. The fire has been put out, but half of the forest is bald, and the other half is littered with dandruff.

"That's good," Lunion sighs, leaning against me as his head rolls to my neck. "But I can't let that happen again."

"It's going to be okay." After taking a breath and talking it through, I'm a little more confident in that phrase.

"Mhm." He doesn't believe it, but I don't blame him. He's been through enough today, and it's my fault. Everything is, really.

I'm the reason we are on the run to begin with; I'm the reason we even thought of tackling the drills. I'm the reason he wishes he were dead.

We near Maula's street, and Lunion suddenly jerks up, obviously on alert. "Stop here." He makes me hide the bike behind a store, then reaches around in my basket for something. "Put this on."

"Where the hell did you find a hooded poncho?"

"The Tracy's in Lurnala, duh?" In striking similarity, Tracy's was essentially the Nalia version of Macy's.

"Thanks, mom." I throw on my pink poncho and follow Lunion down the road. He tries to act stealthily, hiding behind crates when he can and squatting as he runs.

We reach Maula's doorstep, but Lunion takes a detour. He winds around the house and ends up in her backyard. Which is an odd choice, given it really isn't a yard.

The only difference from being on this side is that the door is brown instead of blue, and the small grass strip is slightly less vibrant.

"Maula?" He knocks louder than he says her name.

In an instant, the door swings open, and Maula slaps a hand to her mouth, muffling what I assume would be, "Lunion?"

She motions for us to hurry inside, then shuts the door quickly once we are.

"What the hell?" she yells, throwing her hands up in confusion. "Where have you two been? Other than on the news, I mean."

"Sorry about that..." I scratch my head.

"Oh, *you*. Did you really stab your father five times?" She takes a step back from me.

"Well, no. I *did* flip a knife that *he* was holding back onto him, but I never stabbed him."

"You should've." Lunion mumbles.

"What was that?" I ask jokingly.

"Hell, he's right! I'm about to go homeless thanks to that man!" Maula shouts again.

"Where are your parents?" I ask, considering how they might react to our sudden reappearance.

"Oh, don't worry about them. Thanks to your father, they are taking up extra shifts to *maybe* be able to move before we get crushed. They won't be back until 5:00 a.m. at the earliest."

I stay silent. There is nothing to say to that; it's kind of my fault, but it also isn't. It's complicated, and I don't want an argument.

"Well!" Lunion claps his hands together and sways back and forth. "Let's get to business, shall we?"

"Oh, yeah." I cough. "Maula, do you have a tablet we could use?"

"Yeah, I'm not *that* poor. Why?"

"Lunion will fill you in, but could I use it?" I smile awkwardly.

"Fine." She reaches into a drawer and hands me one.

"Thank you so much. I'll be right back." Slinking through the back door, I head straight to the treeline. I don't want any potential signals to jeopardize Maula.

I dial the number we were given earlier and wait for Ms. Moire to pick up.

"Hello?" She says, squinting. "Who is this?" I guess it is a little dark.

I turn on the flash.

"Oh, hi." She checks around her. "It's safe to talk."

"Hi-"

She cuts me off with urgency. "Where is Lunion?"

"He is safe, but that is what I wanted to talk to you about..."

Her eyes grow wide in frustration. "You let him go to the drills, didn't you?"

"Yes, ma'am." I face the tablet's camera away from me.

"No, show your face and look at me while you tell me what's wrong with my boy," she snaps.

"Sorry, ma'am." I take a deep breath. "He is okay. He was burnt, though, not terribly."

"A burn?" she yells at me through the screen, and for a second, I think she's about to reach through and strangle me.

"Mhm. But he is okay, physically speaking."

"Well, I would assume that an oil rig explosion would shake him a little bit, too."

"Shaken is a word for it…"

"What is wrong with him? You'd better tell me the truth."

"He is incredibly hurt by what happened, mentally, I mean. He was the one to pull down that drill. He thought he was going to save Nalia, but when he saw the fire…" I trail off.

"Oh…" Her breath fractures.

"He started asking me these crazy things. I was so scared. He wanted me to let him die, or kill him myself. I don't really know."

"If he dies, I'm killing you." She gets up from her seat and smashes her hands down onto her desk.

Sighing, I hold her stare. "Trust me, we are on the same page with that one."

"Well, is he still trying to..?"

"I don't think so? I redirected his attention."

"What does that mean? Stop avoiding the issues and just talk to me!" Her anger is understandable considering how much Lunion's safety means to her.

"Well, that is where you come in." That gets her eyebrows to raise even higher. "We need the codes to a spacecraft of some kind. The only way to get him not to leave this world in death was to convince him we could literally just leave. Get on a ship and go."

Her brow furrows, but it isn't in anger; it's in understanding. "I can't believe this, but you are right. We have discovered plenty of habitable planets, and I could get you there." She thinks for a moment. "Are you sure this is what he wants?"

"I don't know, honestly. It's the only option I've got if I want him alive, though. So I am going to see it through."

"Good call, because if you didn't, I'd kill you." She finally takes a deep, unsteady breath. "I just have one request."

"What?" I ask with bated breath.

"I see you have that uncomfortably fashionable poncho on,

so I assume it's some kind of disguise?" She strains to see exactly what I am wearing.

"Yeah…" I roll my eyes.

"I want you to take me to Lunion."

"What?"

"Yes, you heard that right. Please take me to wherever he is. If my son is leaving this planet, I want to see him before he does." She makes a good point; there is a very slim possibility that it will ever be safe for him to return.

"You have every right to do so, but how do I get you without getting caught?"

"Well, you have some sort of disguise already. I'm not asking you to come to the apartment, just… go to the edge of the woods. I can go for a walk and end up over there. Then, you take me to my son. While I wait for you, I'll start running diagnostics to find an available ship, and once we are all together, I'll give you the codes."

"Okay, sounds like a plan."

A very, very risky plan, but a plan nonetheless.

37

LUNION

"So... Are you going to tell me what the hell is going on?" Maula's voice rings through the room. She should've joined theatre, because her projection skills are insane.

"Well, I'll get there."

"Hurry up, please." She adds on the polite end after a pause, obviously trying to calm down.

"We are going to leave. Like, leave Nalia."

"Excuse me?" she gasps, her hands shaking. Grabbing her right wrist, she tries to stop it, but the tremors persist.

"Yeah, we are getting info on a ship we can use from my mom, that's why Luke needed your tablet," I explain, a little ashamed of us.

"Oh, that's wonderful. My best friend is leaving for good, *and* I might have officers at my doorstep soon." She grabs her face aggressively.

"I'm so sorry."

"Well, sometimes sorry doesn't cut it, Lunion. You left me

alone for over a month with zero explanation. For what?" The anger in her voice shifts slightly, and it's then that I notice she's crying.

"I-"

"And now, once I finally get to see you again, you're leaving the planet. Are you insane?"

"Um-"

"Lunion, I'll support you no matter what, and you know that. So why didn't you ask me for help earlier? I would've gone with you if I had to."

"I didn't want to put you in danger!" I shout, my voice fracturing with a sob.

She just shakes her head in disappointment. "I guess it's too late now. We don't need to fight about it." Sighing, she sways over to the kitchen. "Do you want to help me make dinner?"

"Huh?"

"I have to make dinner. You can help me, or you can watch. It's up to you." She starts to get out pots and pans, then fills a bowl with warm water.

"Okay, how can I help?" I follow behind her, watching as she puts frozen meat into the bowl.

"Set a timer for forty minutes, and by then these should be defrosted." She throws me a kitchen timer. I spin the top until it reaches forty, then set it next to the bowl.

"Done."

"Okay, here." She tosses an apron at me. "You can help get the sauce ready." Maula reaches into a cabinet, pulls out a variety of spices, and sets them on the counter.

"So, how am I preparing it?" She opens her fridge and pulls out dairy products, specifically a container of butter, which she places in my hands.

"Measure out two Mecilimiters of butter. Then add them to that saucepan." She uses her shoulder to point at the one waiting by the stove. "Actually, here is the recipe." A large cookbook is placed before me, and Maula points to the section for the sauce. "I know it by heart, so just follow along here."

"Got it." I roll my sleeves back and section out the butter. Once I have it in the pan, I check the recipe. Needing to measure out some smaller amounts of each spice, I grab the measuring spoons and add in each one as the butter melts on the stove.

Next, I have to add some heavy whipping cream. I pour in a small amount, then stir slowly.

"Wow. Since when did you cook?" Maula praises my mediocre cooking skills with a hint of condescension.

"Since I... Well, since I lived in a house without anyone to help out." I didn't want to talk about fleeing to another region, but that was the truth. I knew how to cook box mixes and heat food before Lurnala, but I really learned how to *cook* once I had to support us.

"Oh. I guess that makes sense." She frowns slightly and spins back to focus on the noodles she is preparing.

For the rest of the forty minutes, we work in silence. There is an unsaid understanding as we dance about the kitchen, dodging pans and grabbing spices, playfully getting out of each other's way. The understanding was simple: I love you, I'm sorry.

Nothing had to be said, but both knew that, as soon as we began talking again, everything would go back to normal. No arguments, no anger, just joy.

Because, for so long, that is what our friendship was. As escape, salvation from a world of uncertainty. When we were together, all the pain could dissolve in the solvent of our joy, even if for only a couple of hours.

The timer goes off, and I grab the meat from the bowl.

"How are we cooking this?" I ask.

"Searing it here." She takes the meat from me. "By the way, it's quaxie meat. I hope that's okay."

"I didn't know I was getting any, but yeah, that's great." I watch as she pulls a mat out from one of her drawers.

"Here." She hands me a meat tenderizer. "Do you know what to do?"

"Surprisingly, yes, I do." I laugh, take the hammer, and start on the meat.

We slide all of the quaxie into an oiled pan and set the heat to medium-high. The two of us take turns timing and watching each piece cook, and soon, all of it is seared through.

"Okay, the noodles should be done, too." Maula gets out a spatula to check them, finding that they are soft enough to eat.

I'm tasked with cutting the meat into smaller pieces while Maula strains the water from the noodles.

Once we are both done, we reconvene and mix everything. First, I slide in the pieces of quaxie, which are about the size of my thumb. Then, we pour in the sauce I prepared and fold the noodles into it.

After a few minutes of turning the spatula rhythmically, we are done. We portion out two bowls' worth of the pasta and put the rest in the fridge. "My parents can heat it when they get home," Maula says.

We take ours and sit on her couch.

"So, do you want to watch anything?" Maula asks quietly, probably just trying to break the silence.

"Sure, do you have any recommendations?" I try to keep the conversation going.

"I've been watching this new show; it's called Bad Dye Job." She looks at my hair and chuckles. "Anyway... Let me think of a real show."

As predicted, we are right back at it. If anyone is going to take stabs at my poorly dyed hair, I'm glad it's her.

"Wait, I think I have one." She turns on her TV and begins opening streaming services. Once in Orlix, one of the more popular services, she enters a string of letters into the search bar.

Before I know it, I'm watching a show called "Waves of Love," which follows couples that live in a beachside mansion. Apparently, the objective is not to get cheated on, and whichever couple stays faithful gets a ton of credits.

"The premise of this is absolutely evil, oh my god," I mutter with terror.

Sarcasm drips from her voice, "Yes, that's what makes it entertaining."

"My biggest fears are, in order: going bald, getting cheated on, and being in debt." I recount the list I made one night when I was bored.

"Wow, that's interesting... But we all know Luke would never cheat on you." She rolls her eyes playfully.

"Yeah, I hope so. I mean, he did reject some girl in Lurnala that tried to ask him out," I chuckle thinking about that interaction, and can't help but wonder how that girl is doing.

"How did that go?" She looks thoroughly amused.

"I have no clue. I got lost." I try to stop laughing. "But he made her help him find me."

Maula grabs my arm and starts cackling, about to fall off the couch. "Why would he do that?" She catches her breath. "That is evil."

We continue cracking jokes throughout the entire episode. We watch as couples break up in written notes, leave the mansion early to go home with someone else, and break up with their original partners while crying.

It's anyone's game, and honestly, it is entertaining.

The episode keeps us entertained until it ends, and until there is a knock on the door.

"Lunion?" I hear Luke's voice call from the door.

"Come in!" Maula says, scrambling to get up to actually let him in.

"Lunion!" That is all the warning I get before my mom rushes past Luke and hugs me tightly, her tears dropping onto my shoulder as she embraces me.

"Mom? What are you doing here?" I'm not sure how to feel. She could be here to rat us out, or maybe she just wants to see me before I leave. Either way, I'm not enthused. I didn't want to have to face her and tell her what we plan to do.

This is going to hurt.

"Luke filled me in. I had to see you before you leave. I understand why you have to, and that's why I am not going to try and stop you." She doesn't let go of me, just keeps her arms wrapped tightly around me.

"How have you been?" I ask, trying to shift the focus off myself.

"Fine. I mean, not really. But you know everything; I'm just happy I get to see you." She kisses my forehead and takes a seat, dragging me with her. "How are you doing, Lunion?"

"I'm okay," I lie. She doesn't need to know that I would rather shoot myself than stay here. Or that I think my weak body is a vessel meant to destroy the planet I love.

She doesn't need to know how I feel. She just needs to be happy before I leave.

She turns to look at Luke, her eyebrows dropping with defeat. "I don't believe you, Lunion, the things I've heard-"

"You told her?" I glare at Luke.

"Told her what?" Maula asks, cutting into the conversation.

"Nothing. Just forget it." I get up and go to stand near Maula. "Mom?"

"Yes?" she questions with the shake of her head.

"What are you going to do about Maula's neighborhood being uprooted?" She's not going to be happy now, so I need to get answers at least.

"I'm trying, I really am. It's harder than you think," she sighs, pleading with me for some ounce of understanding.

"I know that, but I wish you could do something. At least for her." I squeeze my eyes tight together to avoid crying.

"I mean, I was thinking about that, actually." She gets up from the couch and approaches Maula. "If you would like, you could come live with me. I can work on getting your parents a place, too, but I have an empty room now." An uncontrollable, quivering frown appears on her face as she says it.

"Sorry about that..." I interject.

"Really?" Maula asks.

"Yes, of course. Anything." My mom hugs her. "Not only is all of this on me, but it would be nice to have some sort of child around the apartment."

"Again..." I trail off into a nonverbal apology.

"No, don't apologize, Lunion. This is all my fault. When I saw how Luke reacted, I should have reacted with the same anger. Maybe without the fighting, but you know what I mean." She lets out a short, defeated laugh.

"I'll miss you." The tears start falling because, for some reason, I've lost any ability to control my emotions—something I used to pride myself in.

"Well, duh!" She tries to make a joke, but she just starts making weird noises instead of laughing. Like she's whining through her laughter, crying through the joke, and carrying her pain past any trace of light she may find in this situation. This decision I'm making is going to ruin her, but at least I'll be alive.

She runs back to me, holding my face and trying to wipe my tears. I'm not sure how she can see through all of the sorrow flowing from her eyes.

She takes a deep breath and levels out her trembling body. "About that ship."

38

LUKE

"Okay, so I was checking our database. It looks like every single one of our ships is off planet," Ms. Moire explains, her confidence unwavering.

"That sounds bad." Lunion scratches his head.

"They are all on a recon mission to check out an asteroid, but it's okay. Kind of." She pulls out a tablet and shows us an image. "Your father," she points at me, "gave me the code to one of your ships. He said it would recognize me as the person controlling it, and there would be no issue. I can go into hiding for a little bit, so people actually think I'm off planet. At least until you are somewhere else."

"That should work, right?" I look to Lunion for approval.

"Yeah, that sounds legitimate. I mean, it's only a couple of days to Earth, you should be able to hide for that long."

"Yep, that is what I was thinking. Okay, so the code." She switches to another screen. "You may want to write this down." Lunion grabs a piece of paper and a pen. "It's 10131092."

"My birthday?" I say, stunned. No way he made the code

my birthday. Maybe he did care about me at some point. *Some point*, but not anymore, obviously.

"Sure, if that is what it is." Ms. Moire shrugs. "Anyway, it will be on dock five. That's what this says anyway. If we want this to work, you two will have to be careful. No one can see you, and you can't make any noise. That means no hover bikes," she warns.

"Got it, what about when the loading ramp opens?" I ask, knowing how loud and sketchy those ramps can be.

"Run in and put in the code as quickly as possible. The control tower will see that it's me, and they should clear the departure." Her confidence seems to grow as she weaves together the plan.

"Okay, I guess we will walk to the dock." I nod, feeling strongly that we can do this.

"Yes. We will," Lunion speaks up. "That way I can say bye to Nalia." He hugs his mom tightly. "Thank you so, so much."

"Anything for you, Starchild." She holds his cheek softly.

"Now don't start with that." He backs up and wipes away his tears with a soft chuckle. "I cannot cry anymore today."

"You're right, let's make this short and sweet," Ms. Moire says, coming to hug me. Lunion and I hug her, and then Maula, only to leave the house with our hands interlocked.

"Okay, off we go," I say, trying to keep him focused on the task. We are too far in to turn back now, and I would do it too, just to see them again. I can't imagine how hard this is for Lunion.

"Look!" He points at a pink frog resting on a fallen tree branch. "Can we take it with us to the dock?"

"I guess, just not on the ship itself." I laugh, surprised by his positive attitude.

"Yay!" He scoops it up and places it on his shoulder. To my

surprise, it sits there as we continue moving, never bothering to hop off.

"Wow, are you a frog whisperer or something?"

"Oh, of course. I have a bachelor's degree in Amphibian Linguistics." Lunion picks up the frog and holds it out before him. "What should we name it?"

"Hmm... maybe Jumper?" I propose.

"So surface level... Amazing."

"Hey, at least he can jump from the surface!" I chuckle weakly, knowing my joke wouldn't land with *any* audience.

We continue down the path until we reach the charred end of the forest. "Can we stop for a second?" he asks, his eyes dark.

"Yeah, of course."

"I'm so sorry," He bends down and touches a tree root. His tears fall onto the burned brush below him, hydrating the dry leaves and making the ashes muddy. I allow him the handful of minutes he needs before he pushes himself up and mutters a soft, "Okay, let's go."

Just past the last of the trees, I can see the dock. The same dock I was locked up in, and the same dock where Lunion rescued me.

"How do we know which is which?" I glance between the myriad ships, all of them identical.

"Maybe if we get closer, there are numbers somewhere?" Lunion suggests, as he sets Jumper free.

We follow his plan, creeping up on the dock and trying to sneak around the ships. We look like seriously untrained ninjas, but no one catches us.

"I don't see anything," Lunion whispers sharply.

"Me either."

We continue to run around the dock, searching for any trace of numbers. We find a pile of boxes and dock behind them to reconvene. "I don't know how to figure out which one is ours," Lunion complains.

"I don't know, let's go back out." I begin to get up, but feel a hand push me down. "Lunion, we don't have time for this. Let me get up," I mutter.

"What?" He asks, then slaps a hand over his mouth.

I turn to see what's going on and see someone looming over us. "Shh!" The guard puts a finger to her mouth. *Her* mouth.

It's her, the kind guard who helped us earlier.

"Where are you trying to go?" she whispers.

"Dock five?" I raise my hands in confusion.

"The one on the far right by the tree." She points with her gun, using it to line up our eyes with the ship. "Be quick, I'll distract." Stepping back, she vanishes.

"Thank you," I mumble. No one but Lunion can hear me, but it needed to be said.

We race to the other end of the dock, then stand in front of the ship. It doesn't send out the ramp. "Come on..." Lunion's foot taps aggressively against the asphalt.

The ramp slowly begins to come down, and I don't even give it time to unfurl fully. Grabbing Lunion's hand, I jump onto the moving metal and run full speed to the main room of the ship.

A voice comes on over the intercom, "Welcome, traveler! What is your code?"

"10131092," I say hopefully.

The ship lights up, and the ramp snaps back to its origin point. "Hello, Ms. Moire. Where are you traveling to today?"

"Earth," Lunion and I say in unison.

39

LUNION

I feel the ship lift off and shoot into Nalia's atmosphere. We're out. We did it.

"We did it!" I yell, running to hug Luke. Grabbing his hair, I kiss him, basking in that moment before slowly pulling away to breathlessly say, "We fucking did it."

"I love you so much," he sighs, looking at me with glimmering eyes. They are as bright as the stars around us, so optimistic and hopeful.

"Well, that's obvious." I joke, smiling as his brows drop. "I'm kidding, I love you too." I kiss him again, this time for longer.

"Again, pretty obvious," he replies smugly. "So, what is our first order of business?"

"I want to sleep, honestly." I laugh. We have had a hell of a day, and I mean that literally.

"I'm going to take a shower, then I'll sleep." He points at his sweat-stained shirt.

"Oh... yeah." I forgot that our day also included another hellish element: exercise.

"Do you want the first shower?" he asks. "Wait. No. I need hot water; you like cold showers. I'm taking the first one." Stripping down to his underwear, he runs to the bathroom.

I take the time that he is in the shower to refamiliarize myself with the ship. The good news is that right beside the cafeteria is a laundry room. We only have these clothes, thanks to ditching our bikes, so we will need to use it religiously until we reach Earth.

I retrace Luke's footsteps, picking up his trail of clothes and discarding my own to throw them in the washer.

"Well, this is a surprise." Luke is rounding the corner, a stupid smile on his face as he sees me shoveling clothes into the washer, only in underwear.

"Don't get used to it," I scold.

Remembering seeing pajama sets on board last time around, and given Luke's incomplete outfit, it is obvious this ship has them too. He is wearing striped pants, slippers, and no shirt.

"Boring." He leans on the doorframe with a soft smile. "The shower is all yours."

"Thanks." I walk awkwardly over to the bathroom.

Making sure the water is cold, but not too cold because some warmth would be relaxing after today, I take a shower. Once finished, I brush my teeth and get ready for bed. The pajama sets are, in fact, real, striped purple, with confusing lacing on the shirt. There are inner strings that attach to others, and even more confusing ones on the outside. I just leave it open and leave the bathroom.

Luke is already in bed waiting for me, and I crawl under the covers to lie on his chest. "Oh? No complaint about me being shirtless?"

"No," I let out a sigh, not a bad one. No, it's a sigh of relief.

"I have too much to look forward to than to carry on with that little bit I had going."

"Bit?" He raises an eyebrow.

"It started serious, but as I fell for you, I thought reverse psychology would work. You know, you'd be shirtless more, or something. I don't know, it was funny to me either way, so I kept it going."

"Wow, this whole time I thought you hated how I look," he jokes, knowing that could never be true.

"Oh yeah, totally. Abs are *so* repulsive."

With my cheek resting against his chest, I can feel his heartbeat. It's like a song, sweet and beautiful. One about our journey to get here, the adventure we have ahead, and the future we are promised together.

There is nothing sexual about it, just something incredibly intimate. An unspoken language of love and hope, all locked inside the pitter-patter of the heart that opened for me.

40

LUKE

I wake to the sound of an alarm blaring.

Last night, I fell asleep to Lunion glowing faintly against my chest. Now, the entire room glows brightly with a fluctuating scarlet light.

"Luke?" Lunion is terrified, grabbing my arm like it's a flotation device. "What is going on?" His eyes are wide, his breathing is rapid, and his fear is almost tangible.

"I don't know, come on." I wrap an arm around his waist and walk us out to the main room.

As we enter, the ship's robotic voice speaks loudly. "Self Destruct Sequence activated. The ship will disassemble in two minutes."

"What?" I shout. "Ship! What is happening?"

"Hello, traveler." The voice rings about the ship. "We have detected two fugitives aboard, so a self-destruct is only protocol."

"What? Fugitives? Give me a fucking break!" Lunion yells between sobs.

"Yes. Lunion Moire and Luke Dinyre. Wanted for

harboring a fugitive and attempted assassination, respectively." The ship recounts.

"What the hell? Stop the sequence!" I scream, starting to cry myself.

"Unfortunately, I cannot do that, Luke Dinyre." That fucking AI. That is the only way it could have figured out it was us. Facial recognition or some shit. Something that goes beyond the ship's base functions. Something only humans could have fucked up so badly.

"Luke, I'm scared." Lunion buries his face in my chest, sobbing silently.

"I know, me too." I hold him, not sure what to say. When I met Lunion, he was the strongest, most opinionated boy I'd ever met.

I don't know what to do when I see him this way. Especially when I feel the same way: *hopeless.*

"It's okay. It's okay. It's okay." I lie over and over again.

"No, it's not. It's not." Lunion falls to the ground, bringing me with him. We sit there silently, staring into each other's eyes as we await our fate. He shakes his head slowly, keeping eye contact. "I love you."

"I love you too, Lunion." I'm about to kiss him as I hear an unlocking sound emanate from all around us—light cracks from between those dreadful hexagons that make up the walls of the ship.

The air grows thinner, and I know there is only one thing I can do. Pulling Lunion close, I grab his shirt strings and tie them around my body before pulling him in for one last kiss. I feel the air growing thinner, and I know there is only one thing I can do.

Our lips collide like reckless asteroids in the emptiness of space. We lift from the ground and, with the air no longer breathable, we begin to freeze over.

My body eclipses his, like the moon does the sun. Though he is *my* sun and my moon, and I am his. No matter what, we'll shine like twin stars.

We were born from the dust and ashes of the stars, and we will return to the night sky. Wrapped together, our bodies will endure eternity, lighting up the sky in a blaze of love.

ACKNOWLEDGMENTS

I have found that as my career becomes more public, and my catalogue grows, that my list of people to thank grows even more. Please bear with me through all of these acknowledgments, as each and every person mentioned deserves that attention.

First, I have to thank the Indie Forge team. I can't believe I am with you all for a second time in less than a year, putting forth a book I am wildly proud of with a publisher that instills me with even greater pride. Sami, I know you had to step back for this one, with the arrival of your little one, but I cherish every behind-the-scenes decision you've made, as well as the multitude of tangible support you've given on this project.

Jazzy, your support for *The Sleepless Knight* meant more to me than I could describe, but your continued support through to *Dust & Ashes* somehow means more. You ensured that I got this book out before graduation, and you worked so, so hard, through so much strife, to make sure that it happened. You also did my amazing paperback art, alongside character and event designs, and just so, so much for me. Your kindness is unbelievable, I love you.

Asher, when I heard that you were interested in editing, I didn't hesitate to say yes. I adore you, your work, and your presence in our community. Signing alongside you with Indie Forge was intimidating, I'll admit. But, ever since, you have been the kindest peer I could have asked for. Your little comments on my drafts, your cheerleading on my posts, your fits of joyful rage when reading this book, it all warms my heart with a heat that rivals the sun (*Dust & Ashes* reference).

I of course could not have made this book what it is without the context in which I began writing it, which includes my academic environment at the time. Mr. Powell, thank you for everything, without your encouragement and, sometimes, kind grading, I would never have had the confidence to write a whole book, and definitely not two. You also taught me about polysyndeton in AP Lang, which came in handy for some scenes in this book. That is, if I used it correctly.

Mrs. Haley, where do I even begin? I'll first say I am sorry, for I know some of the scientific elements in her definitely defied the laws of biology, but I did try to apply concepts I learned in your class to this book. Having your class year-round stimulated the conceptualization of this book, and your support throughout said year saved me from doubt and stress even in the darkest of times. I love you so much.

Now, we move on to the most devastating and time consuming portion of these acknowledgements: the friends and family section.

Oh god, who isn't to thank? Since the publication of *The Sleepless Knight,* the circle around "Jack the Author" has only grown, and so has the support from my friends. It's so hard for me to feel like I deserve any of it, but you all remind me of who I am, and how much I matter. Journey, you already know how much I love you, but I'll say it over and over until my throat is sore. I love you. Penelope, the second you heard that I even had an interest in writing, you became my biggest fan, and honestly, personal assistant. Your work in orches-trating my little release parties has made me cry on several occasions, and your general kindness fills me with indescribable happiness. Lena, Bianca, Kai, Jessie, and so, so many more - I love you, your support means the world, and I will definitely cry to you about it in person soon. You are all stars, and you shine so brightly. You bring light into my life that I would not survive without, and a piece of you, all of you, is found in every strong, kind, or even comedic character I write.

Abby and Noel, my sisters, you never make fun of me for this, no matter how laughable it can be. I love you both so much, and I've avoided writing siblings into my books because I know I could never capture your quirks, kindnesses, and beauties. Maybe someday, we will all end up working on a film adaptation of this together, that would be fun.

I would like to mention that halfway through writing this book, I took a trip to Japan and Korea. The trip, which was made with some odd company, brought many realizations, heartbreaks, and joys that I could not have written the latter half of this book without. Through the trip, I learned that despite logic, and despite effort, my love will always persist, even to my detriment. Thank you to those who brought joy and confusion alike to the Eastern Hemisphere, I love you all.

I don't think this counts as "friends and family" but I would like to shout out the artists on the book's playlist. Many have actually commented or liked posts detailing their involvement, and that support means so much to me. Caroline Kingsbury, thank you for reminding me that this is my book, and that I can do whatever the hell I want with it, including putting two of your songs on the playlist. Kevin Atwater, your copy you requested is waiting whenever you want it.

And of course, thank you to the reader. I was delusional enough to put out my first book, and somehow held onto that delusion long enough that it turned into a little tiny career. If you read the full thing, or skipped to these acknowledgements for some reason - I adore you, I appreciate you, and I could not do this without you.

I wrote this book out of fear, but the moral is not what it seems. It may appear that though we aggrandize ourselves to be as impactful as the sun and moon, we end up as just stars in the face of rebellion, but that isn't true. Together, we can make an impact, and we can change things for the better. Keep reading, keep creating art, keep loving.